Stuck in the Country with You

Also by Zuri Day

Two Rivals, One Bed
A Game of Secrets
The Secret Heir

Visit the Author Profile page at Harlequin.com for more titles.

Stuck

IN THE

Country

WITH

You

ZURI DAY

HARLEQUIN

afterglow BOOKS

Recycling programs
for this product may
not exist in your area.

ISBN-13: 978-1-335-57489-3

Stuck in the Country with You

Harlequin Enterprises ULC
22 Adelaide St. West, 41st Floor
Toronto, Ontario M5H 4E3, Canada
www.Harlequin.com

Printed in U.S.A.

This book is dedicated to my day ones in the mix

To the DayDreamer Divas who assure me "we've got this!"

You're the wind beneath my writer wings,
worth more than words can say

I've set the stage, now turn the page and have a zuri day!

One

The day was wet, cold, cloudy, gray. Genesis dispassion-
ately viewed the rain. As if to generate a bigger reaction, the
downpour increased. She all but gave the sky a side-eye. For
her the rain was perfect. The dreariness fit her mood. Matter
of fact, her world had been cloudy for a while now. When it
came to the proverbial storms of life lately, it hadn't rained
but poured. Lost job due to downsizing. Lost cash due to bad
choices. After becoming unemployed, she'd put everything—
heart, soul, time, money—into a dream that wasn't her own,
but one that was supposed to pay off. Now she'd be lucky
to get back any of the $5,000 from her rainy-day fund she'd
loaned her ex. In her world it was literally and figuratively
monsooning right now.

And the latest? Hearing that one of her favorite people in
the world had died. The onslaught of back-to-back, one-
thing-after-the-other situations threatened to derail the mo-
mentum she'd proudly gained before all hell broke loose.

Present uncertainties had stirred up old, deep insecurities. Childhood-deep. Teenage-deep. Ones she thought long buried, involving self-esteem, confidence and feeling like she mattered and belonged. Said insecurity now presented itself as a low-level panic as she headed to the office of her great-uncle's attorney. Cyrus had two sons with children, which meant Cyrus had grandchildren. Her distant cousins. Plenty next of kin. What could the attorney need to discuss with her? One of her fondest teenage memories on her uncle's farm was riding his tractor. Maybe Uncle Cyrus had willed her that old John Deere.

The image of a younger her in dungarees—Cyrus-speak—traipsing across the land on a farm implement lifted her mood and brought out her first smile of the day. Traces remained as she crossed the hall and went through a door marked Young and Associates. The cheery receptionist, an older, attractive woman with gray hair in a contemporary bob cut, directed her to a nearby hallway.

"They're in the conference room," she said with a hand in that direction. "First door on the right."

They? Genesis thanked the woman, crossed the room and walked to the door. The sound of voices drifted through the door. Cyrus's sons? A room filled with next of kin? The nervous flutters increased but one thing was for sure. Nothing was going to be found out standing in the hallway. She tapped lightly before opening the door.

Three pairs of eyes looked over.

"Hi."

The greeting sounded how she'd felt as a ten-year-old thrown in a room of strangers.

A short, balding man stood and walked toward her with the authority of someone who owned the place.

"Ms. Hunter?"

"Yes."

"Hello, I'm Al Young, Cyrus's attorney and longtime friend. Come join us." He gestured for her to have a seat at the table. "You know Cyrus's sons, Clarence and Cleo."

The men stood, their expressions unreadable. One raised his brow and took a step toward her with an outstretched hand.

"You're Walker's daughter, Genny?"

"Yes." A small smile eked through. "I haven't heard that nickname since graduating high school. I now prefer and go by my full name, Genesis."

"Genesis. Okay."

"You're…Cleo?"

"Clarence."

They all shook hands. She sat. "What happened? I just spoke with Uncle Cyrus two weeks ago. He sounded fine."

"Prostate cancer," Cleo replied. "He didn't want anyone to know."

"My condolences to both of you. And apologies for not being able to tell you apart. Embarrassing since we're cousins."

"No problem. It's been a long time."

It had indeed. Genesis didn't have many memories of Cyrus's sons on his property. During the weekends she visited the Holy Mound countryside, it was their children, namely their daughters, spending time on the farm.

"You look different than I remember," Clarence said.

"Ten years, weight loss and corrective eye surgery," Genesis replied.

"That'll do it."

They shared a chuckle. The tension lessened.

"How are Tiffany and Kayla?"

Cleo responded. "Kayla's fine, busy. She's married and has two children. Her husband's military. They live in Virginia."

"Nobody'll marry Tiffany," Clarence joked. "She loves her job, though. Works for a casino on the Strip. They'll be at the funeral."

"I saw them almost every summer at Uncle Cyrus's house from childhood through my early teens. Good memories. Unfortunately, I haven't seen or spoken with them in forever. It will be great to see them again."

"Your father, Walker, loved the country. Before leaving the South, I know he spent a lot of time on the farm. Is that how you met Daddy?"

The question was a legitimate one, and not asked unkindly. Still, it was like pulling a scab off a wound. Memories of Genesis with her father were hazy, and rare. At the time her mother became pregnant, a baby didn't fit into Walker's plans. Theirs had been a casual hookup while on a brief break from the woman who would become his wife. After their wedding, he'd left the South and, while she knew Cyrus had encouraged him to do otherwise, cut off contact with mother and child. Forgot his firstborn. Genesis's arrival had almost cost him the love of his life. Walker's dad, her paternal grandfather and Cyrus's brother, had died relatively young. She felt that was why Cyrus worked so hard to make her feel special, included, part of the family. For that alone, she would always love him and felt bad that in later years, and with him now gone, she hadn't reached out to him more often.

"I didn't really know Walker," she finally answered. "Cyrus kept in touch with my mom, Lori. Do you know her?"

Cleo shook his head. "I never met your mother. I do remember Dad mentioning her, and you."

Another dash of salt spilled into Genesis's emotional wound. Had her mom met any of Walker's family besides Cyrus? Or was it his shame of her that got passed down to Genesis? Created the maternal emotional distance she'd always felt. Questions about her father were strongly discouraged. Lori didn't like to talk about the past.

Genesis forced her mind back to now. "She'd drop me off on weekends and longer during the summer to hang out with Uncle Cyrus and...his lady friend."

The men shared a look. "Which one?" Clarence asked.

Genesis laughed. The men did, too, including Al Young the attorney, bringing warmth to the cool, still slightly uncomfortable atmosphere permeating the room.

"Daddy loved the women," Cleo offered, with a smile.

Al cleared his throat. "If I may add, the women loved him, too. And as fascinating as we all find Cyrus's colorful love life—" he checked his watch "—we should probably get to the business at hand."

"I'm not sure why I'm here," Genesis softly admitted.

"I have brought you all together to convey Cyrus's wishes as laid out in a will contained in his trust."

Clarence eyed Genesis thoughtfully, with what-does-this-have-to-do-with-her written all over his face. His eyes shifted over to the attorney. "Okay, Al, let's do this."

Cleo leaned forward and steepled his hands. His expression was measured. No verbal response.

Al flipped through a few pages, adjusted his glasses, then, after spouting a page of legalese mumbo jumbo, came to the bequeathing. "'To my son Cleo, I bequeath my stamp and coin collection. The stamp collection might not be worth much but some of those coins might become valuable someday, at least more than the rocks and dead bugs you collected as a child.'"

Genesis watched Cleo's eyes mist over. His smile was bittersweet.

"You did collect some crazy stuff, bro," Clarence reminded him, with a soft poke to his arm.

"Digging in all that dirt as a child is probably what turned me into a city man."

The two men laughed. Clarence added, "Dad didn't get the farmer he hoped for, that's for sure."

The two men bumped fists.

Their attention returned to Al.

"'To my son Clarence, I bequeath my pocket watch. As a boy, I swore you'd be late to your own funeral.'"

Cleo laughed. "That's Daddy. He used to tell you that all the time!"

Clarence nodded. "Sure did."

Genesis listened, appreciating this banter between her cousins. She knew so little about them and wanted to know more. She also couldn't wait to see Tiffany and Kayla. Meanwhile, she started thinking about where she could store a tractor.

Al continued, "'Regarding the property located in the unincorporated section of Holy Mound, Tennessee...'"

Genesis's mind drifted as Al went on about longitudes and latitudes, SW here and NW there.

"'...all such lands along with all outer buildings and properties, and all contents contained within or without, except that which is otherwise stated, shall become the singular property of Genesis Hunter.'"

Genesis's jaw dropped as she slammed back into reality. The air left the room. The warmth from the brothers that moments ago cascaded like a snuggly wool blanket receded like a wave before the tsunami it created crashed into her as raised voices, in stereo.

Clarence: "What the hell?"

Cleo, over Clarence: "Excuse me?"

Clarence, over Cleo: "What do you mean, she gets the farm?"

Al, with hands raised: "Gentlemen, please—"

Cleo: "There's no way Daddy did that."

Clarence: "Let me see the will."

Al, louder: "Clarence. Cleo. Gentlemen, please!"

The cacophony ended as abruptly as it began.

Al placed his elbows on the conference table. "I understand your reaction. I can imagine this news comes as a surprise."

"You got damn right it does," Clarence said, looking ready to huff, puff and blow down the house.

Cleo, easily the calmer, more restrained of the two, simply crossed his arms.

"That you two would be upset is something I reiterated to Cyrus more than once as we went through various revisions."

"Revisions?" Cleo asked. "You mean her stealing what's rightfully ours?" He looked at Genesis. "Just how exactly did you talk our father into this?"

"I had nothing to do with any of this! I'm…shocked!"

"She's right, gentlemen," Al said. "Ms. Hunter is also just now hearing the news. Your father knew the two of you would be upset. However, I can assure you these are his wishes."

"Daddy must have lost his mind," Clarence mumbled.

"Couldn't have been thinking clearly," Cleo agreed.

"I need to see a copy of the will," Clarence demanded.

Al looked from one brother to the other. "That will be up to Genesis. As sole executor of the trust, she is the only one to whom I can issue a copy."

Clarence stood abruptly. "This is bullshit."

"They can see the will," Genesis said, emotion painting the outburst. "I can't believe Uncle Cyrus did this. Y'all can have the farm."

A soft chuckle accompanied Al's tight smile. "Genesis, that is exactly what Cyrus imagined you'd say, which is why there are specific instructions accompanying the deed transfer to your name. We'll go over those details in a moment."

He stood, walked over to a credenza and picked up two boxes, one larger than the other.

"Cleo, the collections." He set down the larger box.

"Clarence, your dad's prized pocket watch. Over our two-decade friendship, if I saw him check that thing once, I saw it a thousand times."

He walked to the office phone and buzzed the receptionist. "Kate, I need copies made of Cyrus Perry's will."

He turned to Cyrus's sons. "Gentlemen, I wish we'd met under more pleasant circumstances. Cyrus was a good man. They don't make 'em like that anymore. As shocked as you may be about his decisions, know that he loved the two of you very much. Spoke of you often. Wished you well. So do I."

He continued standing, an obvious dismissal.

"That's it?" Clarence asked. "I'm supposed to walk out of here with a watch and call it a day?"

"Kate will give each of you a copy of the will on your way out. Take time to read it. Let everything settle. Then feel free to give me a call next week. I'll be happy to answer any questions you might have to the best of my ability."

Clarence looked at Genesis. "I'm not willing to wait until next week. We need to discuss this now."

"We were going to grab a bite in town after this meeting," Cleo added in a nicer tone. "A place called Holy Moly. Maybe you can join us."

Genesis felt she had no choice. "Okay."

Clarence rubbed a frustrated hand over his face. "I apologize for my earlier outburst. This news is completely unexpected, but as family, I'm sure we can work it out."

"I agree," she readily admitted, still in shock.

The group shook hands. The twins left the office. Transferring the property and its contents from Cyrus to Genesis took ten minutes, three pages and two signatures. She left the building in a daze and followed the GPS instructions by rote. If asked details about the short trip, she would have been stumped. She'd basically driven across town without seeing a thing.

Holy Moly was a casual, bustling establishment with blond floors, stark white walls, stainless steel fixtures and live, leafy plants. Genesis shook out and folded her umbrella before stepping into the dining area and looking around. Her eyes drifted across the crowded room and landed on Clarence. She started in his direction. He sat at a booth with two men sitting across from him. She recognized the side of Cleo's face, but who was the other guy? Had they already contacted a lawyer and were preparing to sue? Genesis mentally braced herself and continued to the table. Clarence looked up as she approached and stood.

"Genesis!" he said, smiling, an expression completely opposite of the one she'd last seen as they parted ways. "Come. Sit. There's someone we want you to meet."

He moved to the side. She slid into the booth, careful not to knock over Clarence's water glass with her purse. Once seated, she looked across the table...

And straight into the eyes of a man, a one-night stand it had taken her years to forget.

Two

"Genesis, this is Jaxson King," Clarence explained. "I'm sure you've heard the name. His farm is next to Dad's. When he realized we were Cyrus's sons, he came over to offer condolences."

Jaxson reached his hand across the table, trying to figure out why the face he stared into was familiar. "Nice to meet you...Genesis."

Genesis crossed her arms. "Hi." And then to her cousin: "I don't mean to be rude, but I can't stay long. Can we discuss our business—" she glanced over at Jaxson "—privately?"

What in the hell was her problem? She may not have meant to be rude, but she'd nailed the role. Then again, if she was related to the brothers, she'd just lost a family member. Everyone grieved differently. He prepared to slide out of the booth.

Cleo stopped him. "Wait a minute, Jaxson." He looked at Genesis. "Genesis, this young man may very well need to be part of our discussion. As Clarence said, his farm is next door to Daddy's place. They sometimes worked together. When Daddy became ill, and since he's passed, Jaxson has continued to take care of the property."

Jaxson looked at Genesis, who gazed out the window. Again, he felt a pang of familiarity and began flipping through a mental contacts list, trying to make a connection. If there was one, it wasn't recent. Since returning to Holy Mound, he'd been very selective. And discreet.

"Jaxson has presented a solution that Clarence and I think will work best for everyone. An option that's fair, quick, and allows us all to…move ahead with our lives the way…" He paused and cleared his throat. "The way Daddy would have wanted."

Genesis pulled her eyes from the window and looked at Cleo.

"He's offered to buy the farm," Cleo said.

"Fair market price or above," Clarence added.

Jaxson sat back and observed the confusing exchange. He'd assumed she was a relative, but it sounded as though hers was a legal position. Was she an attorney, maybe the executor of Cyrus's will? He wanted clarification but remained silent. One thing that decades of playing football had taught him was that better moves were made when one took time to read the field.

"Both Cleo and I have businesses back home, and families. A quick transaction is what's needed here."

"You've already acknowledged our rightful ownership," Cleo said. "Except for a minor technicality."

"I—" Genesis caught herself and clamped her mouth shut. After a calming breath, she looked at Cleo. "This is a family matter, and not a conversation we should be having right now."

"Why not?"

Jaxson watched Clarence's cool begin to slip away faster than a running back shaking the corner.

"Why not?" he again demanded, with barely held restraint.

"Because Uncle Cyrus is not yet buried. And the farm is not for sale."

Whoa! The chill that sister delivered was like a blast from the Arctic. Jaxson almost shivered. Instead, he stood.

"I apologize for causing any upsets. It wasn't my intention."

"You've done nothing wrong," Clarence said. He looked at Genesis before standing as well. "Jax, I'd like a word with you, if you don't mind."

He did mind.

"Now is not a good time." Jaxson pulled out a card. "Here's my number. Let's speak after the funeral. Cleo. Genesis. Again, I'm sorry for your loss."

Jaxson didn't wait to hear a response. He knew what a proverbial bullet coming toward him looked like and was glad he'd dodged it. Whatever was happening between Cyrus's sons and that Genesis lady was none of his business. The last place he wanted to be was in the middle of drama. He'd had enough of that to last two lifetimes. It was why he'd traded in the bright lights of a big city for the peace of a small town.

The only thing he missed about Phoenix was his daughter. In a perfect world, she'd be in Holy Mound.

Four years ago, when Jaxson traded the fast life for slow living, Cyrus had become like family. The old man was funny and wise, with the kind of practical common sense that these days wasn't that common. Reminded him of his grandfather, who'd also been friends with Cyrus before he passed. Which brought his thoughts back to Genesis. Who she was to Cyrus wasn't his business either. Still, inquiring minds wanted to know.

Jaxson nodded and exchanged waves with a few familiar faces, but instead of heading toward the bar and the burger he'd come for, he walked out the door. Seconds later he stepped into his favorite new toy, a shiny black Dodge Ram pickup with all the bells and whistles. He pulled out his phone, opened a browser and began to type. G-e-n-e...

The phone vibrated.

Blake Shelton. Jaxson's friend turned business partner, often teased for sharing a famous name. He briefly considered ignoring the call. Couldn't. Blake was in Memphis working on a flip. Jaxson had laid the laminated flooring yesterday. He hoped Blake hadn't run into problems with the granite countertops.

"What's up, man?"

"The crew canceled."

"No way."

"Yep. They were supposed to be here ten minutes ago. Called just now to say they couldn't get here for another hour. I told them not to bother."

"Why'd you do that?"

"It's not the first time they've pulled this stunt. But it was their last."

"Meanwhile, another mortgage payment is due in a couple weeks. We were hoping to avoid paying that."

"I know. How quickly can you get here, and who can you bring to help?"

For the rest of the afternoon, Genesis was forgotten. Jaxson focused on finishing a kitchen and bathroom in the corner-lot bungalow Blake had gotten as a bank foreclosure. That interested buyers were already lined up made finishing the project ASAP a priority. More than eight hours after getting the phone call while parked in front of Holy Moly, a weary yet satisfied Jaxson stopped at a favorite Chinese spot for takeout, then headed back to Holy Mound. Back home he plated a healthy serving of kung pao beef and veggies, tossed a couple of egg rolls and wontons on the plate and zapped it in the microwave. While waiting, he pulled out his phone. Typed **Genesis** in the search bar, then realized he didn't have a last name. He added **Perry**, Cyrus's last name. Got a few hits. Facebook. LinkedIn. A sports recruiting website. None of the matches were in Tennessee. None of them were her.

The microwave dinged. Jaxson retrieved the plate, grabbed a cola from the fridge and walked into the large and comfy living room of the farmhouse his grandfather had owned and loved. When renovating it three years ago, he'd decided to keep Dixon King's country styling and masculine aesthetic. Very different from the flashy lifestyle he'd left behind in Phoenix, but much closer to who he was at his core. He liked it.

He set everything on a wooden TV tray, turned on a sports channel and began eating. Halfway through, he walked back into the kitchen to get his phone. Got back on the hunt for one Ms. Genesis Perry. Or Genesis…somebody. This time, knowing he didn't remember her from Holy Mound, he added the word Memphis behind Perry. Several options came up. None about *her*.

Another combination, just Genesis and Memphis. The algorithm changed. Car dealerships. A jewelry store. An insurance company. Jaxson gave up. He finished his meal, hopped in his truck, did a quick check of Cyrus's farm, fed Cyrus's dog, Nipsey, then came back and fed his dog, Butch. He tried not to think about Genesis. Honestly couldn't figure out why she was still on his mind. Sure, she was attractive. He'd dated hundreds of attractive girls. He figured it was her complete and utter lack of interest that sparked his. If she was a relative of Cyrus's sons, he'd probably see her at the funeral. If not, he'd spent time he couldn't get back thinking about a woman he might never see again.

Three

Hours later, Genesis still felt all kinds of WTF. Friday nights were great to make big money for deliveries, but she didn't turn on the app. How could she concentrate on locations and pickup times? Cyrus had bypassed his sons and left her a whole farm. One he didn't want sold. The twins had copped an attitude about her stance on the issue, especially when they couldn't immediately talk her out of it. She didn't blame them. What her great-uncle had done wasn't right. Clarence was sure Cyrus had been battling dementia and vowed to challenge the will. Cleo agreed but had a plane to catch and suggested they revisit the situation after the funeral. Genesis was relieved. She'd been ready to go since she got to the table. Since she sat down and, as one of her friends loved to say, "got her wig blown back" by a blast from the past.

Seeing Jaxson was like getting cold water thrown in her face. It took everything in her to act unaffected. Last she'd heard, he had a child and lived in Phoenix. Not that she'd followed his career or anything. Okay, maybe a little. Accidentally on purpose. When he went pro, almost everyone in Tennessee had cheered on their homegrown star. Emphasis on *almost*.

Neither Genesis nor her family had wished him well. There were reasons.

Seeing him today after so many years stirred up emotions she hadn't known were still there. It didn't help that he was more handsome than she remembered. And he was her great-uncle's neighbor? *And* taking care of his property? *And* had offered to buy the farm, the one Cyrus didn't want sold? What the heck had she done to incur this type of karma? More importantly, was there any way to reverse it?

Hoping to catch a break on at least one problem, she reached for the phone and dialed her ex's number. Before they'd slipped on a bottle of vodka one night and fallen into bed, she and Lance had been great friends. It was the only reason she'd nearly drained her savings account to support what he'd called "a chance of a lifetime investment," in a blues-and-BBQ spot being opened in Little Rock, two hours away. He'd assured her the loan would be paid back in a month, "no problem." Except there *was* a problem. That conversation had happened two months ago.

She got voicemail. Not surprising. It was Friday night.

"Hey, Lance. What's up? It's Gen. I know you're super busy, but can you give me a call as soon as you get this message? Thanks."

For the rest of the evening, Genesis went through the motions. Tried to act like her life was still normal. It wasn't.

Everything was changing around her. She had no appetite for dinner. Not enough focus to watch a movie. Went to bed. Sleep was fleeting. One good thing came out of the tossing and turning. An idea. It had been six months since Genesis visited Cyrus. The last time she saw him. In the morning, she'd go to the farm.

It was raining when Genesis began the forty-five-minute drive from Memphis to Holy Mound. The weather helped her feel a little better about not turning on the driver app the way she would most Saturday mornings. For delivery drivers, weekends were busy. She tried not to think about the money she'd lose, cash she needed to pay next month's bills. She hadn't slept well, but the decision to visit Cyrus's farm produced an unexpected calm. Stopped her head from spinning, her heart from hurting so much. It felt like the right thing to do.

She tried to view Cyrus's decision objectively, without the combustive emotions. Her great-uncle had thought enough of her to leave something he treasured to her care. In death he'd continued what few others did in life—made her feel special, wanted, a part of something.

She got teary-eyed, wishing she'd spent more of the last months with him. Instead, she'd been back and forth to Little Rock helping her ex Lance try to get what had sounded good on paper to live up to the expectation.

Woulda, shoulda and coulda sneaked in for a visit. She allowed their negative talk for a moment before shutting down regret. Cyrus was gone, and maybe her money. No way to change the past. Focusing on the present and future would take enough energy. The cell phone beeped. She checked the dash. Lance. Thank God. She hoped he had good news.

"Hey, Lance."

"Gen, hey. I hope you're not calling about the money."

Her shoulders slumped. "You know I was. What happened to that rapper becoming a partner?"

"Still working on it," he said with a sigh.

"You know my lease is up next month. Without that money, and in this crazy job market, I might not be able to afford to renew it."

He sighed loudly. "I wish I could help you. I'm struggling, too."

"How was business last night?"

"You don't want to know."

"You're right. I don't need more bad news."

"Why? What happened?"

"Uncle Cyrus died."

A brief silence and then, "Sorry to hear that."

"Yeah, me too."

"He was cool for an old dude."

"He was cool, period."

They continued to chat about Cyrus. It felt good to share pleasant memories with someone who'd known him. Even though Lance had met Cyrus only once in person, when Genesis called to check on her uncle, the two men often spoke.

She chatted with Lance until taking the county road exit that led to the farm. Memories of Cyrus, mostly from her childhood and teenage years, continued to make her want to cry one minute and laugh the next. The continuing rain was a perfect backdrop. She turned off the side road, placed the old key she'd been given into a rusty lock and swung back the privacy gate, then returned to her car and drove through. In a moment, she was the seven-year-old who'd ridden her bike down this road to retrieve the mail. Cyrus made doing that seem like a big responsibility.

"Make sure you don't drop anything. I'm expecting a million-dollar check from a contest I entered."

She drove closer, passed a few cows she hadn't noticed on her visit six months ago. Did they belong to her uncle? Besides Nipsey, her uncle's dog, were there other animals that needed tending? What about the house? The utilities. The expenses. The general upkeep of everything. As the new owner, all of these issues were now her responsibility to handle. She fought against panicking and feeling overwhelmed. She'd never even owned a house or condo, much less a farm with land.

Turning a gentle curve, she came upon a now-empty chicken coop. She'd once shooed away hens from the wired enclosures to gather their precious eggs. Beyond the coop was the tractor she'd thought might be her inheritance. Boy, had she gotten more than she bargained for. Her eyes drifted to the rambling ranch house, where she saw something else. Something unexpected. Something that caused her brow to furrow and eyes to narrow. A shiny Dodge Ram truck was parked askew in her uncle's concrete drive, taking up both spaces.

Who was on her uncle's property? And how did they get past the locked gate?

As she parked on the gravel road and got out of the car,

a tall figure wearing well-fitting jeans—yes, she noticed—
a windbreaker and a baseball cap rounded the corner. *Jax-son*. She began walking toward him, not even bothering to
grab an umbrella.

"What the hell are you doing on this property?"

He adjusted his cap. "Genesis, right? Let's get out of the rain."

Without waiting for an answer, he bounded up the steps
as though he owned them. She begrudgingly followed suit.
It was either that or get drenched.

"I'm glad you're here. We were just—"

"What makes you think you have the right to come on
private property? Because you're Uncle Cy's neighbor or because you're a washed-up pro baller?"

"Washed-up?"

He cocked a brow. Given that it seemed he'd forgotten
her, Genesis mentally berated herself for letting it slip that
she knew who he was. He continued to study her. Genesis
refused to melt under those fiery, almost-onyx orbs or to
process the emotion she saw there. Had she assumed wrong?
Had he finally recognized her?

"I believe 'retired' is more accurate." A confident smile
punctuated the sentence.

She didn't know what made her angrier—his smugness or
seeming lack of memory of the night they'd spent together.
There'd been years and probably hundreds of women since
then. But still.

She crossed her arms, raised herself up to her full height
of five foot five. "What are you doing here?"

"Right now, I'm trying to find Nipsey. I was headed to the shed to get a treat to entice him."

"Now you won't have to. *I'll* find Nipsey."

"Are you sure you want to relieve me of my duties? As Cleo mentioned yesterday, I've helped Cyrus off and on for a while now, especially after he got sick. Unless you've got experience handling land and livestock, you just might want to lose the attitude and accept a brother's assistance."

"I don't need your help."

She totally needed his help. While yesterday's events and conversations were somewhat foggy, she did recall hearing something about him helping her uncle.

"Why are you so angry?"

Because you don't know who I am! "Because I know your true motive for being so helpful." She used air quotes for emphasis. "You want to buy the farm. What I said yesterday holds true today. This property is not for sale."

He didn't offer a rebuttal. Instead, his stare grew more intense. "Do I know you?"

Oh, how well he knew her. Almost every inch of her chocolate skin. Since it was obvious he didn't remember, it was time to let him know. The sooner he realized he was an enemy, the sooner he'd leave her the hell alone.

"As a matter of fact—"

"I found him!"

Genesis looked around as a bundle of energy rounded the house and dashed up the steps. The young boy was dressed for rain from head to toe—a bright yellow rain slicker with matching hat and camouflage-colored boots. She assumed he was Jaxson's son, and imagined a wife was somewhere nearby. The thought sent a slight pang to her heart. She ignored it.

"Come on, Uncle Jax. I found Nipsey. We've got to help him. He's stuck!"

This comment jolted Genesis off her high throne of indignation and placed her squarely in the present moment. That aging German shepherd had been Cyrus's constant companion, whom he'd probably loved more than his two-legged sons.

"Good job, Mario!" Jaxson high-fived the young tyke. "Where is he?"

"Come on. I'll show you!" Mario practically tumbled down the steps, then took off in the direction he'd come.

Without another word, Jaxson turned on his heel and followed him. Genesis pulled up the hood of her jacket and followed Jaxson. They ran behind the house to a hedge of bushes growing next to a worn-down fence. She watched Jaxson kneel beside the dog, who was clearly trapped in a thorny bush. Jaxson began to quietly issue instructions.

"Think you can open the toolbox in the back of the truck?" Mario vigorously nodded. "Good. Get my gloves out of there and the first aid kit. And bring the bottle of water from the console." The boy took off, clearly excited to have clear-cut directions to follow. "And a towel!" Jaxson yelled at the boy's retreating back.

Genesis watched Jaxson reach into his pocket and pull out a knife. He knelt beside the whimpering animal and spoke in a soothing tone.

"Hey, there, Nip." He reached for the dog's paw. He

growled. "Hold on, buddy. I know it's uncomfortable. We're going to get you out, okay?"

He began cutting away the thorny branches. The young boy returned with the requested items. Jaxson cut off part of the towel and wrapped it around the dog's mouth, preventing him from lashing out in pain and biting the hand that was trying to free him.

"Hold his legs," he instructed. The boy did as he was told. In less than five minutes, Jaxson freed Nipsey from his thorny prison, then tended to the dog's scrapes and cuts with medicine from the first aid kit. Finally, once assured the dog was calm, he loosened the towel from around Nipsey's mouth and let him lap water from the young boy's cupped hands. Even for someone she despised, the act was impressive. Had she come upon the dog alone, she wouldn't have known what to do.

"Thank you," she said, once he stood, brushed off his jeans and returned his attention to her. Given their history, she really wanted to say "Eff you," but he had rescued Nipsey, so, though warranted, the invective wouldn't be nice.

"It's no problem. I admired your uncle. He was a good man whom I considered a friend."

"Is that why he asked you to help him?"

"He didn't ask. I offered."

The comment didn't sit well with Genesis. Sounded like an ulterior motive lurked close by.

"A man as proud as Cyrus would never ask outright. I knew with his health challenges he couldn't work like he used to. I was more than happy to lend him a hand and

promised him I'd continue to do so. We looked out for each
other. Neighbors around here are like that."

"I see."

Genesis had the heart to feel embarrassed. And conflicted.
The football star who'd helped ruin her brother's pro chances,
then slept with his sister on a dare, didn't sound like the
man speaking right now. He was still as sexy, though. There
wasn't enough conflict in the world to not recognize that.
There was a maturity about him. An unpretentiousness she
hadn't expected, given his worldly, pro athlete past. Here
in the country, he exuded a shrewd intelligence and seemed
comfortable in his own skin. Skin that she'd once explored
with her hands and vice versa. He was the first one to—

Girl…don't even go there.

She wondered about his reaction if she revealed who she
was. But why even tell him? Why bust open that decade-old
can of worms? Or more like sack of snakes! Someone else
could give her the ins and outs of the property and take care
of the responsibilities Jaxson had done. She'd likely lease the
land, making regular visits unnecessary. There was enough
distance that even as neighbors they wouldn't see each other.
It was a small town. He'd probably learn her identity eventually. Hopefully by then this whole farm situation would be
worked out and make additional conversation unnecessary.

"Do you always keep the front gate locked, even when
you're here?"

He nodded. "A private back road runs between our properties. Little more than a dirt path that either my grandfather

or your uncle created. If you'd like, I can show you where it is and help you navigate it."

"Thanks, but I'll figure it out."

"Hopefully not in that Kia you're driving. These lands have rough spots and hidden hazards. Your vehicle rides low. It could get tricky." He looked up. "Especially in weather like this, where all the rain we're having is creating a muddy mess. More storms are forecasted throughout the weekend."

Nipsey, obviously feeling more like himself, came up and nuzzled her hand. Genesis was thankful for the distraction from Jaxson's perfectly shaped cushy lips making it hard to hear the words coming out of his mouth.

She knelt down. "Hey, Nipsey. Remember me? Good to see you. We'll have to learn how to avoid those thorns and stay out of trouble, right?"

A piece of advice she felt appropriate not only for the canine but for herself as well. She felt the sooner she put distance between her and Jaxson, the better.

She stood and managed to eke out a tight smile. "I appreciate whatever you did for my uncle. This place meant everything to him. He probably needed the help."

"He did. Would have loved for his sons to be more interested or involved, but that was not the case. I was happy to step in. Like I said, it's what neighbors do. That said, if you guys need anything at all, my place is just down the road. Don't hesitate to ask."

Genesis wouldn't be needing anything from Jaxson King. But she figured she could show him better than she could tell him. With a quick wave, she turned and headed toward the house with a battered yet brave and loyal Nipsey trotting beside her. *Good boy!*

She went inside her uncle's home and tried to forget about Jaxson. Memories of both men assailed her. The rooms felt gloomy and claustrophobic. Fresh air was needed even though the rain continued to fall.

Despite Jaxson's warning, she jumped into her Kia and headed down a back road where, if memory served correctly, the cracking concrete of a slaughtering slab from a bygone era had been turned into the perfect surface for mean hopscotch competitions. She turned up the music, humming along as her car jerked along the bumpy trail. She slowed as the slab of concrete came into view, the once-white paint and colorful numbers faded with time. When she reached a fork in the road, she saw that one direction continued around her great-uncle's property line while the other led to the home she assumed belonged to Jaxson. He was the last person she wanted to see. She headed left and sped up, her car doing a slight fishtail in the soggy tracks.

Probably should slow down.

The idea came a second too late. At that exact moment, Genesis heard a loud clank beneath the car before it suddenly swayed to the right. She stopped, put the gear in Reverse and pressed on the gas. The tires spun, clinging to the mud Jaxson had warned her about. She tried several more times to unstick the car, "rocking" it by going from Drive to Reverse, but to no avail. Just as she decided to walk back to the house, a big splat of rain hit the windshield. Genesis shook her head and opened the door. Not only was the car stuck, but it looked like she'd get soaked, too.

She'd just walked through a patch of tall grass when a sound stopped her. The rain, coming down harder now, muffled the sound. One of Cyrus's cows? She continued moving, cautiously looking around her. To her left, nothing. Right, same thing. Determined to make it back to the house unaided, she squared her shoulders and pushed away fear. Before she could move, a snort caused her to look behind her. That was when she saw it. Not a cow. She could handle that. No, this was a big black bull, pawing the earth and looking at her like she'd eyed Jaxson—like she was about to be lunch.

"Oh, shit!"

She took one step, then two, then began to run in a panic. She didn't get far. Tripping over a hard object buried beneath the grass, Genesis's foot twisted. She went down hard. The pain was excruciating, took her breath away. She tried to scream but couldn't. The rain's intensity increased, a full-blown deluge. She thought about Jaxson and how she'd haughtily dismissed any help he'd offered. That neighborly assistance would come in handy right about now. His strong arms could easily pick her up and carry her to safety. She eyed the beast, slowly moving toward her. It stopped, stared back, unblinking. She tried to move. Bad idea. Tried to scream. Too difficult, since it hurt to breathe. Genesis and her hard head had gone off and created a dire situation. And to think Uncle Cyrus had imagined her a farm girl. That, she now knew, was a bunch of bull!

Four

"Uncle Jax."

"Hmm?"

"Why was that lady so mad?"

As he maneuvered his truck down the back road to his place, that lady Mario referenced fully occupied Jaxson's thoughts. They had to have met before. She felt so familiar. He was 99 percent certain she was about to enlighten him with the hows and whys before Mario interrupted.

"Why, Uncle Jax?"

"I don't know, buddy." Jaxson shrugged his shoulders as though it was no big deal, though he'd be lying to himself to say her attitude hadn't throw him off. While no longer the cocky, even arrogant football star who'd ridden the waves of success from high school, through college and into the pros, Jaxson knew he was a good-looking man, one who usually didn't have to work to win over a woman. Not that he cared how Genesis felt about him, or any woman, for that matter.

Four years had helped to heal the wounds of being betrayed and barely avoiding a national scandal, but Jaxson guarded his emotions like he used to guard players carrying the ball.

"Was Mr. Cyrus her grandpa?" Mario asked. Jaxson hadn't been the only who'd noticed and been affected by Genesis's rude behavior.

"That's a good question."

Jaxson thought back to the day before. Her countenance had seemed melancholy when she reached the table, before noticing him brought on a different kind of expression. She could have been the daughter of one of Cyrus's sons, but Jaxson didn't think so. Nipsey knew who she was, so she wasn't a stranger. Something told him this woman's roots grew somewhere in Tennessee.

"Maybe she's sad Mr. Cyrus died."

"You're probably right."

His nephew was silent for a moment, and then, "Hey, I know! Maybe we can buy her some flowers! When Daddy gets them for Mommy it always makes her smile."

Jaxson thought of his rascal of a brother-in-law and could just about imagine the reasons for coming home bearing gifts, and how often. His sister, nieces and nephew seemed happy, so he decided to stay out of their household affairs. Given his own track record, and the problems he had with his daughter Jazz's mom, he was the last person to give relationship advice.

They pulled into the driveway. The rain, light when they'd headed to Cyrus's house, was now a flat-out downpour. His mind immediately went to Genesis. Hopefully she'd use common sense and not try to drive around out here. With all of the rocks, large roots, holes and partially buried tree trunks dotting the landscape, navigating the area as a novice in anything less than a pickup like the one he owned, or an ATV, was an accident waiting to happen. Oh, well. Wasn't his problem. The only thing still niggling him was how they knew each other.

After fixing grilled cheese sandwiches served with large glasses of chocolate milk, he watched Mario settle in front of a large screen in what had been turned into a game room. Then Jaxson retreated to a quieter part of the house. As was habitual with a majority of the population, he pulled out his cell phone and began scrolling his social media sites. He'd just taken his last bite of the sandwich when the phone rang in his hand.

"What's up, Susan?"

Susan was a former classmate who'd chased him in high school. Once back in Holy Mound, he'd allowed her to catch him. He'd known her since they were fourteen and came as close to trusting her as he could anyone. She agreed to his ground rules, and he respected hers. Theirs was a casual, uncomplicated arrangement that worked for both of them.

"I saw your neighbor Hazel at church this morning. She told me about Cyrus. My condolences."

"Thanks, Susan. I appreciate that."

"I know how close everyone is in the valley, and how you support one another."

Jaxson reached for his dishes and walked into the kitchen. "He'll be missed."

"I heard his sons are in town. Somebody saw them at Holy Moly, along with their cousin Genny. You remember her, right?"

A jolt shot through Jaxson's body. Only quick reflexes kept the glass he balanced on top of a plate from falling and shattering on the floor.

Genesis was Genny. *That* Genny? Jaxson's heart rate increased. No way.

"What's her last name?"

"Hunter! Hank Hunter's sister. I know you remember him."

Hank Hunter. A name he'd never forget. The high school all-star running back for the Memphis Mustangs. Ten-year-old memories rushed back to the surface. A crowded, rowdy party. Gorgeous brown eyes staring from across the room. Smiling. Flirting. Dancing, and then…caresses, kisses, making love. It was her. Genesis was Genny! She'd lost weight. Her hairstyle was different. And hadn't she worn glasses? She'd felt familiar. But their encounter had happened so long ago. There'd been hundreds of others since then. Still, that night had been special. He should have recognized her. She damn sure knew him. The attitude. Her anger. Now everything made sense.

"Susan, I've got to let you go. There's something I need to do."

A rumble of thunder drew his attention to the window. Rain pounded the dirt with flashes of lightning zigging and zagging across the sky. He doubted Genesis would still be at Cyrus's place. If she lived in Memphis and had any sense, she was probably halfway home.

Jaxson's cell phone vibrated. His neighbor Granville. He and his wife, Hazel, lived on a small hilltop piece of property overlooking the valley. Folk jokingly called them "Mr. and Mrs. Mayor." Little got past them from their eagle-eye perch. Sometimes that was a blessing. At other times, a curse.

"Morning, Granville. You order up this storm?"

"No, and I sure as hell hoped you weren't the fool down there who tried to drive that back road in it."

This comment got Jaxson's attention. "Is it a white SUV?"

"Sure is. Got stuck, from what I can tell, and tried to force the car forward. Only dug deeper ruts, of course. That's what they get for trespassing, is what I say."

"Shit."

"Do you know 'em?"

"I think so, a woman named Genesis. Ran into her at Cyrus's place when I went to feed the dog."

"Well, she ain't there no more. Looks like she was heading to the pond. You know how easily that area washes out in storms like this. Probably hit a rut, or rock, or worse. Do I need to ready my tractor?"

Jaxson shook his head, already on the porch replacing his well-worn cowboy boots with the rubber fishing boots by the door. He reached for a heavy raincoat and his leather cowboy hat. "My truck can likely pull it out. If not, I'll call you."

"Sounds like a plan."

"Oh, I almost forgot. Miss Hazel can do me a favor if she's home."

"Shoot."

"My nephew Mario is here. Do you think she can watch him while I see what's going on?"

"Only if he'll help her bake some oatmeal chocolate chip cookies."

"I don't think I'll have to twist his arm."

Jaxson pushed away worry as he stopped by the spare bedroom turned game room and peeped in. "Come on, little man. We're going to see the McCormicks."

"I'm playing a game!"

"Okay, but Miss Hazel needs help baking cookies. Are you up to it?"

Mario's frown instantly flipped into a big smile. "Yes!"

Just like Jazz, Jaxson thought. Sweets were the best negotiator. He loved spending time with his nephew, but being around Mario was a constant reminder of how much he missed his daughter.

Soon after getting the call, Jaxson was down the hill and on the back roadway, his heavy, all-terrain tires fighting the deep, muddy ruts and easily winning the battle. Rain pelted the windshield. He flipped the wipers to the highest speed, trying to remain calm while searching for white metal. He drove like a man on a mission, a knight in drenched armor, the fantastic steed replaced by an all-wheel-drive truck. He doubted this chivalrous act would make up for forgetting a woman you'd slept with, but at the moment it was the best he could do.

A half mile from his house and around a bend, he spotted flashing hazard lights. Sprays of mud decorated the once-white Kia's back half where Jaxson imagined Genesis vainly spun the wheels to get free. Even with the recent revelation, he couldn't help the smirk that appeared at the thought of her being rescued by someone she obviously disliked. Pulling down his brim, he got out of the car and carefully made his way to the passenger door. A blast of thunder sounded overhead. He shielded himself from the watery onslaught as bolts of lightning danced across the sky.

'Genesis!" Jaxson pulled on the driver's-side door.

It was locked. He peeked inside. Where was she? He called her name again, rounding the car to check all the doors and confirm the car was empty. This development was totally unexpected. Cockiness gave way to true concern. Where could she have gone?

"Genesis!"

Jaxson swung around and scanned the horizon. The rain fell steadily, thick and unrelenting. He cupped his hands against the elements and walked toward the rut of a road.

"Genesis!"

Instead of Genesis, Nipsey responded. He bounded through a patch of overgrown grass and came straight to Jaxson, barking excitedly.

"Where is she?"

The dog ran back toward the tall grass, still barking. He ran up to Jaxson, then back to the grass—body shaking, tail wagging, barking more furiously—his entire body transmitting the message "Hurry up and come on!"

Jaxson headed toward the grass. "Come on, buddy. Where is she?"

Jaxson caught a glimpse of white fabric just beyond the

patch of overgrown foliage. Genesis. His quickened pace matched his rapidly beating heart.

She was lying on the ground next to a partially hidden tree stump, soaked and muddy, grimacing as she held her right leg.

Jaxson acted without thought. He swooped her up and headed back toward his truck. That was when he saw the bull Granville had affectionately named Randy the Runaway because of how deftly he routinely escaped the fence holding the herd of cattle being raised on Jaxson's land. The bull wasn't far from the Kia. He could imagine her reaction to seeing an eight-hundred-pound animal coming her way, especially if she'd been standing outside of the car. No doubt she took off running and fell.

"Get out of here, Randy!" he hollered in frustration. "Go on! Get!"

The bull turned and lumbered in the opposite direction, his tail swishing without a care in the world.

Genesis spoke through gritted teeth. "Put me down. I can walk."

Jaxson all but snorted. Until now, he hadn't thought there was anyone more stubborn than him.

"Looks like you already tried doing that. Didn't turn out too good for you."

Clutching his reluctant charge, Jaxson walked carefully yet determinedly toward his pickup. Nipsey led the way, then hopped in the truck bed. Jaxson reached the passenger side of his truck, opened the door and eased Genesis into the seat. He fastened her seat belt, then rushed to get in on the driver's side.

Once there, he immediately reached for his phone and dialed the McCormicks' number. Or tried to. When he tapped the number, there was no signal.

Damn.

Even though Cyrus's place was less than a mile from his residence, he remembered how getting service could sometimes be sketchy, especially in storms. He fired up the truck and headed back to his house.

"Where are we going?" Genesis asked, still grimacing from the pain of an ankle severely sprained if not actually broken.

"My house."

"No. Take me back to my uncle's place."

Jaxson glanced over at Ms. Independent. "Is that where you were headed when you tripped and fell?"

No response.

"We're going to my house. As a former athlete, I've had more than a few experiences with injuries and broken bones and have a few items around the house that might help you."

"It's not broken. I'm okay."

"You may be right in believing the ankle is not broken. But from the swelling I see happening already, you are clearly not okay."

"I don't want to go with you," she managed, despite the pain.

"It's either that or go back to your car that's stuck in the mud, wait for the storm to pass, then hope to get a tow and repair service to help you out."

Jaxson mashed the brake, slammed the truck in Park and

turned to her. He took a calming breath, understanding to some degree why she was upset. He hadn't immediately recognized her, and even if he had, they hadn't exactly parted as friends. But surely ten years later she wasn't still blaming him for what had happened to her brother, an unfortunate injury that ended his promising career. That blame was misplaced then. Her attitude was out of bounds now. There was only so much disrespect he would take.

"Your car or my house. Which is it?"

He watched as she tried to keep threatening tears behind tightly squeezed eyelids. The bravado inched its way inside his heart, but he held firm. "Do you want my help or not?"

Her nod was barely perceptible but enough for him to put the truck in Drive and continue to his house. Once there, Nipsey jumped out of the bed and ran through the gate as though traveling home in Jaxson's truck was something he did every day. Jaxson followed just as quickly, jogging around to the passenger door and gingerly lifting Genesis out of the seat. The rain had let up slightly, making it easier to navigate the short walk from his driveway to the wraparound porch and into the house. Jaxson hesitated only briefly before walking down the hall and placing a drenched Genesis on the patchwork quilt that covered his king-size, pillow-top mattress. He immediately checked out her ankle.

In the short ride from her car to his house, which had lasted all of three minutes, it had swollen to twice its size. Genesis's discomfort was easily visible as he helped her into his bed, her supple skin now ashen with the effort it took not to cry. He reached for the home phone next to the bed and tried again to call Hazel, breathed a sigh of relief when he heard the dial tone. After several rings the voicemail came on. Jaxson cursed under his breath.

"Miss Hazel, it's Jax. Can you call back as soon as you get this message? I need your nursing skills. It's urgent. Thanks."

Jaxson turned to find Genesis shivering against the covers and writhing in pain. One look at her ankle and he knew why. The swelling tissue strained against those cute, tight jeans that fit her booty just right. But he shouldn't be thinking about that now, he chided himself even as he pulled on more than a decade of discipline that had made him such a threat on the field and focused solely on an injury that seemed to be growing larger by the second. He knew what he needed to do. He also fully anticipated getting pushback while trying to do it.

"Genesis, um, there's no easy way to say this. We need to get you out of those clothes."

The implications were obvious, but he spoke the truth. Her chagrin was immediate and showed past the pain etched on her face. He usually exhibited more swagger, thought his game with the ladies was tight.

You're not running a seduction game. You're helping someone injured who just might become your neighbor. Watch yourself.

The voice inside his head was spot-on. For the first time in his life, there was a woman in his bed who didn't even like him.

Ain't that a bitch.

"What I'm saying is your jeans are preventing blood flow

to that swelling ankle. And those wet clothes aren't helping. Your body might be going into shock."

"I can do it," Genesis said, panting.

"I tried to reach my neighbor Miss Hazel. She's a retired nurse."

Jaxson reached for the cordless phone on the nightstand and tried again to reach the McCormicks. Both the home phone and their cell phones went to voicemail.

"Still no answer. The storm might have knocked out power on the hill." He sighed, rubbed a calloused hand over his close-cropped hair. "Pain getting worse?"

She sucked in a breath. "No."

"Liar."

Genesis glared as she tried to hide the pain. "I told you I'm fine!"

"Look, I know you don't like me. I figured out why. You're Hank Hunter's sister. Genny." He paused, and said in a softer voice, "I remember that night."

She averted her eyes.

"My mind wasn't on yesteryear when Clarence introduced us. Plus, you've changed. Your..." Knowing how sensitive women were about weight, he continued with care. "...hairstyle is different. And you used to wear glasses, right?"

No answer.

"We don't have to talk about it. Just wanted you to know that I now understand why you've been so resistant and to assure you that I'm only trying to help. I've had a sprain or two in my career, along with a busted kneecap that ended it. I'm not a doctor, or a perv, but someone wanting to keep your leg from getting worse. I want to check your ankle to make sure it's not broken, and I can't do that through those tight jeans. At this point, because of the swelling, I'm afraid cutting them is going to be our only option."

He watched Genesis grimace as she tried to sit up. Despite her stubbornness, he was impressed. Sprained ankles could be some of the most painful injuries one could experience. That she'd held it together this good was a testament to her strength.

"We need to elevate that leg, get some ice on it."

She fell back against the pillow. "Okay."

"Like I said, I've dealt with a lot of these types of injuries. I'm just going to squeeze a little bit and see if I can tell what we're dealing with."

He gingerly touched various areas of her ankle, slowly moved the foot while gauging her reaction.

"Are you sure you're not a doctor?"

"Hardly. Just going from experience." He lifted her ankle and tried to detect anything that looked abnormal beyond the obvious injury, felt along the minor cuts on her shin. He tried and failed to remain impartial. It was a sin for someone acting like a tough cookie to have such soft, inviting skin. The thought flitted by within seconds. He reeled it in and paid keen attention to the task at hand.

"I don't think it's broken," he concluded, reaching for a decorative pillow and placing it under Genesis's ankle. "I'll get ice to hopefully stop the swelling, and some antiseptic spray for those cuts. In the meantime, if you can, try and get out of those wet clothes and under the warm covers. You don't want another illness on top of the injury."

Seeing her dubious expression, he added, "Contrary to what you might believe, I'm not a monster and promise not to attack."

This comment elicited a mere hint of a smile, one he decided looked much better than the frown she'd been serving up almost nonstop. "I'll also try and reach Miss Hazel again to see if she can come down to have a look. Okay?"

Indecision played across her face before she answered. "Thanks."

Barely perceptible. A wisp of a whisper. Yet Jaxson felt as though he'd won the Super Bowl, intercepted a pass and run over a hundred yards for a touchdown with no time left on the clock. Her simple response shouldn't have felt so good. He decided not to overanalyze the moment. There were more important matters that required his attention.

He left the bedroom on a mission to obtain an ice pack, towel, spray and control of an errant libido determined to be attracted to a woman who could barely abide his presence.

Yeah, buddy, good luck with that.

Five

Genesis heaved a relieved sigh. Did Jaxson really think not knowing her was the only problem? That was bad enough, but did he think he'd been forgiven for what happened to Hank? Not to mention that he had no idea of the rift in her family their night together had caused.

Genesis abruptly shifted her foot. An intense pain shot up her leg. She swallowed a scream, held it down by pressing the covers against her mouth and gritting her teeth. Tears pooled. Her ankle throbbed. She hated admitting it, but Jaxson's opinion might be too optimistic. A bone could be broken. He was concerned enough to not take any chances with her walking, to prevent further injury by picking her up. This Jaxson reminded her of the one she'd slept with. The one with gentle hands and tender caresses.

Even now, all these years later, she remembered how carefully, almost reverently, they'd made love. Not only a great lover but thoughtful as well. He'd brought her a washcloth, then further surprised her by initiating a cuddle. She'd been shocked to learn he was still in high school. A whole five years younger than she was. A mature eighteen. His body had felt good then. Looked and felt amazing now. She'd have to be dead to not be affected and a straight-up liar to deny the truth. The guy who had sexed her in the past and cared for her now was totally at odds with the one at the center of the ugly dare rumor and who had intentionally, allegedly, broken Hank's arm.

She lifted her neck and looked out the window. Listened closely. The rain must have stopped. Her mind went back to the accident, replaying what had happened—how one minute she was upright and the next on the ground, writhing in mud with a pain she felt had to be right up there with having a natural childbirth. Okay, maybe she was exaggerating, but it hurt like heck.

She replayed those minutes just after she'd watched Jaxson and the little boy Mario jump in his pickup and drive away in the rain. How she'd bristled against his suggestion—which somehow felt like a command—that she not try driving around the property. How the decision to do so was in direct defiance to this advice. How she'd increased her speed when she saw where he lived. The house that, while eyeing it from a distance, all but beckoned her, tempted her with a promise of something desirous and decadent hidden inside.

Without wanting to, she wondered about how a football star like Jaxson had ended up back on his grandfather's farm in the small town of Holy Mound. Mario was his nephew. Did he have kids? The wife question seemed to have been answered. If a spouse was anywhere close by, she wouldn't be in Jaxson's bed.

Everyone in town probably knew where he lived. Being discovered here would hurt more than her ankle. She couldn't get caught with the enemy, again. News spread fast in a city like Memphis. She could only imagine how much faster it got around in the Holy Mound countryside. The last thing she needed was another rumor involving her lover from a long-ago one-night stand getting to her family. She sat up, eased her body to the edge of the bed and swung her legs over.

Ouch! That. Hurt.

Ignoring the pain standing up caused her, she stood on the uninjured foot, then tentatively touched the floor with the other leg.

Not so bad.

She took a step, more like a hop, before placing her weight on the injured ankle and feeling intense pain shoot from toe to hip.

"Ow!"

The pain sent her to her knees. Quick footsteps echoed from the hallway.

"Genesis! Damn, girl. What are you doing?"

Once again, Jaxson picked her up and placed her back in bed. His face, however, was a storm cloud that rivaled the ones outside. For the first time since he'd appeared roadside, she considered her ungrateful actions. Her feelings were all over the place. Past memories impacted present common sense. Like now, with her behaving like someone with no manners when her mother, while distant, had raised her right.

"The mud," she managed with a nod, acknowledging the wet dirt all over Jaxson's earth-toned patchwork quilt. It was a flimsy excuse for what she was actually trying to do—escape not only the enemy but her clashing emotions—but it was all her pain-riddled mind could conjure up on the spot.

Genesis watched Jaxson's scowl deepen, then disappear with a shake of his head.

"That's the least of your problems." He reached for another pillow and further elevated her leg, and then picked up the ice pack. "You need to let me help lessen the severity of this sprain or risk greater long-term damage. Either that or hop your ass off this bed and back to your car, however you get there. I'm not going to keep begging to help you or be responsible for whatever physical condition results from your being stubborn…" A pause and then he added, "…and stupid," under his breath.

Not low enough. Genesis heard his diss contained in barely veiled annoyance. Spoken without looking at her in a calm voice that belied the fire she felt blazing just beneath the surface. A flame that set her yoni on fire. She ignored the traitorous feelings and refocused on Jaxson, the enemy, and his bad mood. Genesis couldn't blame him for it. To say she'd been an uncooperative patient was an understatement. Driving like a bat out of hell during a rainstorm on unfamiliar terrain might have been stupid, too.

He held a knife that looked like a box cutter just above the jeans hem, which was tightening more every second around her throbbing, swelling ankle.

"Yes or no."

Hell no! she mentally screamed. Outwardly she nodded, then fell back against the pillows that taunted her with his scent, a mix between cologne, soap and 100 percent lean, non-GMO man. With the pain now shooting from her ankle to her thigh bone, nodding was all she could do.

Again, he'd made no eye contact when he spoke, just delivered the question with a calm, steely resolve. Genesis closed her eyes as the words repeated in her mind. She found herself giving more meaning to the simple question, as though the inquiry was about more than her injury. Irrational, she decided. Stupid, as he said.

I must have hit my head harder than I thought. She forced her mind away from the man to the mission at hand. Hard to do, given the long, strong fingers now brushing against her sensitive skin, pulling material away from the injury and cutting it off. She tried not to think about how the jeans he snipped so quickly and expertly were one of her favorite and most comfortable pairs. Not to worry. The cold gel substance he smoothed across the injury, followed by an even colder ice bag, immediately grabbed her attention. She shivered. Whether from the ice or the irony of being turned on by the enemy, she wasn't sure.

"Not to be a broken record, but after I wrap this ankle, you really should get out of those clothes." He walked into the en suite and returned with a wrap made from a different material than the more common ones seen on TV. "This is called a smart wrap. It has a type of thermodynamic action that aids the injury without having to be wound tightly around it."

He sprayed the cuts on her lower leg, then stepped back and reached for the cordless phone on the table. "I'll keep trying to reach Miss Hazel. Once the rain stops, we'll get you to a doctor."

"It feels a little better."

"That's good, but you don't want to take any chances. It's most likely a sprain, but you want to make sure it isn't fractured or broken."

"You sound like an expert."

"I've suffered enough injuries to qualify."

The smile he offered was brief and unexpected. Took away the hint of pain she saw in his eyes. A total turn-on. In spite of knowing she shouldn't, she couldn't help not only imagining it, but *wanting* to be the person to make those luscious lips smile. She shivered, and the wet clothes she wore had little to do with it.

The pleasant expression she admired quickly left, replaced by his normal serious look that regularly alternated with the highly chagrined one. He walked out of the room and returned with a gray sweat suit. Genesis wondered if it belonged to him or was left behind by a random female or, worse, his current girlfriend. None of those choices was something she wanted to wear, which, unless Jaxson was a mind reader, must have shown on her face.

"I bought these for Mario's mother, my sister Ruth, for a workout program that never got started. They might be a little big, but they're clean and dry." He tossed them on the bed. "Looks like the rain has let up a bit," he commented after a look out the window. He tapped the face of his phone and put it up to his ear. "Be right back."

Once Jaxson left the room, Genesis sat up and reached for the warm-ups.

Since their restaurant encounter, the man she'd sworn to hate years ago had been nothing but considerate. From literally plucking her from the mud to tending the injury to providing dry clothes under a dry roof, Jaxson had been a gentleman.

After a quick look at the door—along with the fleeting thought to hop over and lock it—Genesis pulled the muddy, sodden top over her head and tossed it to the floor. Her bra was wet, too, but the thought of Jaxson picking it up off the floor caused her to keep it on. She pulled on the bulky top and was immediately grateful for its dryness and warmth. Taking off the jeans? Not so easy. They were made of a stretchable fabric that was easy to maneuver in and out of under normal circumstances. Trying to lift one's butt off the bed while balancing on one leg wasn't normal. Or easy. At all. She rocked and wiggled the jeans past her ass and pushed them to her knees. But that was as far as she got before a light tap sounded at the door.

"Just a sec!"

Genesis looked around and, after not seeing anything else to cover up with, pulled the quilt from both sides and wrapped it around her partially clad lower half.

"Okay, come in."

Something about inviting Jaxson into his own bedroom felt awkward and thrilling at the same time. He'd changed clothes, too, from the muddy blue jeans and tee emblazoned with his pro ball's team logo to a short-sleeved black pullover and black jeans that enhanced his ebony skin. A five-o'clock shadow brought attention to a set of thick eyebrows and a square jawline. Jaxson was aging extremely well, looked even better close-up than from a distance. Watching him approach as she sat there half-naked caused goose bumps to pop up on her still-damp, bare ass.

His eyes went from her face…to the sweat bottoms…to the scrunched-up quilt around her middle. Genesis tried to convince herself that his darkening eyes was her imagination. His expression held no indication of what he was thinking. Genesis pulled the quilt closer and tried to appear equally unbothered.

The brother had her bothered, no doubt about that!

"Do you need more time to…?" He nodded toward the pants lying on top of the quilt.

"Um, no. I decided that, um, changing the top was enough."

"Do you need assistance getting out of your jeans?"

Genesis shifted, feeling the discomfort of a ball of material bunched around her knees.

"Wait, that didn't sound right. Can I help you take those pants off? Damn, that wasn't much better."

She bit off a smile, swallowed a chuckle and fought off images of Jaxson's hands on her thighs, along with the memory of his body between them. Fortunately, his discomfort helped return X-rated thoughts to PG.

"Keep on digging that hole for yourself."

"Naw, I'd better stop. I'm already waist-deep."

Again, that smile. This time she smiled back. It was hard as hell to hate his fine ass right now.

"I'm okay. This top is warm and so is the quilt. I appreciate it."

He visibly relaxed. "No worries. I reached my neighbor."

"What did she say?"

"Among other things, a long story that involves animals and barns. I'll let her share it when she comes down, she says in about an hour. In the meantime, she suggested I call Dr. Turner."

"Is that her doctor?"

Jaxson shook his head. "She knows about him through her volunteer work at an urgent care near Memphis. He does video appointments and may be able to provide a cursory diagnosis, at least until we can get you to a hospital."

"We? I'm not your responsibility, Jaxson," Genesis said, the guilt of how she genuinely felt about him causing her to look away. "You've been very helpful, a lifesaver. I don't know what I would have done if you hadn't found me. And all this..." She motioned to her foot and around the room. "Thank you."

"Nipsey is who you need to thank. If not for him, with all that tall grass, I might still be looking for you."

"If you hadn't come down that back road, I'd still be there."

"Not with my neighbors on the hill. They don't miss anything that happens down here in the valley. Granville is how I knew you were stuck."

"He saw me?"

"Fortunately. When he said it didn't look like you'd make it out, I jumped in the truck."

"I really do appreciate it."

"As I said before, it's what we neighbors do around these parts." He added a country twang to the last few words.

"You did not just say 'around these parts,'" she deadpanned.

"I did." A twinkle appeared in those alluring dark eyes.

"Sounds like something Uncle Cyrus would say."

"That's probably where I heard it."

They both laughed and in that second something passed between them, something silent and promising, dangerous and alluring, a temporary truce that shifted the room's atmosphere. Jaxson gave her a look that she couldn't decipher, one that sent butterflies fluttering into her heat. She pulled the quilt tighter around her.

If Jaxson noticed, she couldn't tell. "I'm starving," he said, changing the subject and blessedly the temperature in the room. "I'm going to make a sandwich. Would you like one?"

"What kind?"

"What does it matter? Beggars can't be choosers."

"You have a point."

"Unless you're one of those 'plant-based people,'" he said, a near sneer accompanying the air quotes placed around the phrase. "If that's the case, a PB and J is the best I can do."

Genesis didn't try to stop her smile this time. Growing up, PB and Js were an after-school staple.

"Actually, I'd love a peanut butter and jelly sandwich."

"Girl, I was just messing with you. I keep a variety of

freshly sliced meats from the deli in town. I think there's tuna salad, too."

"Okay, here comes a serious question." Genesis paused. "Is the jelly you're offering strawberry or grape?"

"What kind of question is that? Grape, of course. And before you ask, that can come with your choice of smooth *or* crunchy."

"Oh, you've got it like that, huh?"

Jaxson popped an imaginary collar. "I'm nobody's slouch."

"In that case, I'll take crunchy."

"Cool. One PB and J coming up."

Taking advantage of his absence, Genesis pushed the jeans down past her knees for greater movement, then scooted to the middle of the bed so she could pull more of the quilt around her. Again, she looked out the window. What had been a torrential downpour a half hour ago was now a steady drizzle, just as it had been when she first set out on her great expedition to explore the land her uncle had given her. Why couldn't the rain have continued in this way instead of becoming the tsunami that got her stuck in the mud and now sitting half-naked in the middle of Jaxson's bed? The storm had driven her into the home of the worst possible option for safety—the rainy weather outside causing mental and emotional turbulence within. In this moment Genesis wasn't sitting here trying to be the strong Black woman. Right now, got dammit, it was just all. Too. Much.

Before she could get emotional, a light tap interrupted thoughts that served no good purpose. Jaxson entered carrying a bed tray—the finest medical assistant she'd ever seen.

"Dr. Turner can see you," he announced, while setting down the tray with a flourish.

He was careful to position the legs away from where the cover bunched around her. Along with the PB and J on wheat bread, her favorite for this sandwich, was an apple, a glass of orange juice, a bottle of water and a bowl of kettle corn. He'd even added sanitizer wipes to clean her hands before eating, and napkins to wipe away crumbs.

"Miss Hazel insisted on coming down to hear what the doc has to say."

"That's very kind of her."

"She's a kind lady." He eyed the tray. "Everything good? I have chips but they clash with peanut butter. Thought about hot soup because of the rain, but that's not a match either."

Was he always this considerate? This thoughtful? If so, keeping those ten-year-old memories that kept a wall of anger between them was a challenge Genesis wasn't sure she was up to.

"It's fine, Jaxson, really." She used a sanitizer wipe, then reached for a kettle corn kernel and popped it in her mouth. Several more quickly followed. "Um, these are good."

"Best I've tasted," Jaxson said, leaning comfortably against a nearby wall. "They're from Holy Goodness, a bakery and sweets store just down the street and around the corner from Holy Moly."

"Sheesh! A lot of holy going on in this town."

"A lot of sin, too."

He wriggled his eyebrows. She fixed him with a look. He held up his hands.

"My bad."

Genesis shook her head and picked up the sandwich that Jaxson had cut in half.

"How's the ratio?"

She swallowed the bite. "Ratio?"

"Peanut butter to jelly. There's an art, more like a science, to knowing the exact amount of each product to use—forty percent peanut butter to sixty percent jelly. Anybody who does it fifty-fifty is a novice who needs to be retrained."

"I'm not ready to grant you master status, but…you clearly know your way around a jelly jar."

Jaxson's smile revealed a row of teeth that were white and slightly crooked, which Genesis found endearing. Down the hall, a bell dinged.

"My soup is ready," he said, pushing off the wall he leaned on and heading for the door. "Are you sure you don't want some? It's tomato, to go with my roast beef sandwich. I've got plenty."

"I appreciate you asking, but I'm good for now."

After Jaxson left, Genesis dug into the rest of her sandwich. She'd had nothing but coffee since leaving the house and was hungrier than she'd realized. She ate the sandwich, every kernel of the tasty corn and the apple down to the core. She drank the juice and most of the water. Once the focus moved from the food to her foot, she realized it was once again throbbing. She laid her head against the headboard and prayed it wasn't broken.

Jaxson returned wearing a lightweight jacket and a baseball cap. "I have to run an errand, but Miss Hazel is on her way. My nephew Mario is with her. He's a bundle of energy and talks nonstop. I've warned him to mind his manners and respect your privacy, but honestly, I can't make any promises, so…apologies in advance."

When it came to small children, Genesis's experience was limited. Her brother Hank's first child was less than a year old, and she'd only seen her once, when she was about two months old. Most of her friends were like her, single and childless. Life would have to be ideal for her to have a baby. Slim chance since "ideal" and "her life" didn't go together. But since she was basically an interloper in a stranger's home, she didn't actually have a say in the matter. Plus, it wasn't like she'd be there long. As soon as she could think of someone to call and come get her, a friend who didn't know her brother or ask too many questions, and as soon as she could master something similar to walking, she was out.

"I won't be here long enough for him to bug me," she answered, with an assurance she didn't feel. "I'm sure we'll be fine."

"You might want to slow your roll on making the great escape. Doctor's orders will more than likely have you stuck in bed or on a couch like your car in the mud."

The car! That was a whole other situation Genesis had forgotten about. She let out a heavy sigh.

"Don't worry. I've got a hitch on my truck and will pull it out tomorrow. I'll put Mario in the game room so I can sleep in the guest room upstairs."

"I couldn't ask you to do that," Genesis argued.

"It's no problem."

"It's too much."

He shrugged. "Suit yourself. Just being hospitable. Make sure that wherever you are there is someone to help you. My guess is that Dr. Turner is going to want you to stay off that foot."

"Thanks again, for everything."

"You're welcome." He crossed the room. "If you leave, put your keys on the nightstand. The car should be in your uncle's driveway by tomorrow afternoon."

"Sorry for the muddy mess. Let me know the cost to get your quilt cleaned."

"Don't worry about it. Feel better, all right?"

Genesis tried to lie to herself and feel that she was glad he was gone. The truth was that she'd enjoyed his company, their banter, his presence. Thankfully, the silence didn't last long. Miss Hazel was everyone's country grandma, who loudly announced her presence from the hallway and burst through the door with more energy than Mario, working with the efficiency of someone who'd attended to a person or two. She teased Genesis about being in Jaxson's bedroom "half-naked," turned her jeans into cutoff shorts and skillfully eased them down her body and over the ankle. She shortened the sweatpants, too, so they'd slide on easier when Genesis was alone. Dr. Turner's video call was brief. He took one look at her swollen ankle.

"X-ray. ASAP."

He suggested a doctor in Holy Mound with a small practice and limited equipment but the ability to at least confirm whether she was dealing with a break or a sprain. The doctor rarely saw new patients and wasn't open on Saturdays, but since he and Dr. Turner were not only colleagues but friends, he'd made an exception.

Genesis found herself in another pickup truck, this one silver with an extended cab. From the back seat, an animated Mario chattered nonstop about how the heavy rainstorm trapped them in the barn where they'd gone to check on Hazel's goat, and insisted on singing the entire version of the song that entertained them, punctuated with exuberant oinks, moos and quacks.

"Old McCormick had a farm…"

A whole fifteen minutes into the ride, and the song, sleep finally shut him up.

Whew! She could probably babysit someone else's child now and then, but Genesis mentally doubled down on not having babies anytime soon.

Hazel quickly filled the silence. She apologized for not being available for "her Jaxson" and said she'd never again go anywhere without her phone, "even the dat gum barn!"

They reached a clinic the size of a shed. Twenty minutes after arriving, Genesis left the office on crutches wearing an ankle boot. Official diagnosis? Severe sprain. No broken or fractured bones. She was to avoid movement or pressure for at least forty-eight hours, which meant she couldn't walk, much less drive.

More potential money spooling down the DoorDash drain.

"You can drop me off at Uncle Cyrus's," Genesis announced.

Hazel glanced over. "I don't think so."

They returned to Jaxson's house. During the ride back

she'd phoned Brea, a friend and coworker originally from Detroit. As far as she knew, Brea didn't watch sports, was unlikely to know Jaxson and would have no idea about their messy shared past. Brea was more than happy to help her. Too bad she was currently in New Orleans.

"Jax will take care of you," Hazel assured her, with a comforting leg pat as they pulled into his drive. "I know his parents and his grandparents. He had a rascal of a reputation, but his mama didn't raise no fools."

Hazel set her up on the living room couch with a large Cobb salad, chips and soda on the coffee table, a pillow under her boot and the low-dose pain medication the doctor had prescribed her within reaching distance. After assuring Hazel that she'd be fine alone, the neighbor wrote down her number and made sure the TV remote was accessible and Genesis's cell phone was charged up and handy. With a final squeeze of Genesis's shoulder, Hazel reached for Mario's hand and left just as quickly as she'd arrived.

The quiet that ensued felt like the calm after a storm. Genesis knew different. Given whose house she was in, whose couch she lounged on and how that person had occupied her thoughts all day, what she experienced now was simply a lull before the next encounter with a six-foot, two-legged whirlwind named Jaxson.

Six

"Are you sure you don't want to come over? We're supposed to get more rain tonight. We could get it on outside, hot and wet."

Jaxson moaned inwardly at the words dripping from his pickup truck speakers. Not because of what Susan said, but because of the image that immediately sprang up in his mind. Genesis, wet against his chest as she'd clung to him in the downpour. Her body hot to the touch as he cut away the fabric gripping her ankle to try to help ease the pain. The tough-cookie persona with silky soft skin. It was a dead giveaway that beneath all the bravado was a feminine flower with soft juicy petals he'd love to pluck. That was unlikely to happen. Genesis had made it crystal clear that she wasn't feeling him like that.

"Sounds tempting," he dutifully responded to Susan's invitation as he merged onto the interstate that ran from Holy Mound proper to his home in the countryside that locals referred to as "the valley." "I'm going to have to take a rain check, no pun intended."

"I'm sure the pun was quite intended," Susan replied. "And a lame one at that." A pause and then, "What's her name?"

"Who?"

"Come on, Jax. You're talking to Susan, the woman who's known you since middle school and liked you almost as long. Who's the latest attraction?"

It was true. He and Susan had known each other forever. He considered her a true friend and was like an uncle to her children. Throughout the years, between marriages and divorces, breakups and separations, they'd comforted each other, shared intimacies and heartaches, and knew where some of each other's skeletons were buried. She was a woman he trusted not to betray him. Given some of his past experiences, that was a huge trait. He'd always been up-front with her, never played her, never lied. He did sometimes, however, when discretion was called for, omit facts he felt unnecessary.

"His name is Mario."

She tsked.

"My nephew is spending the weekend. Miss Hazel watched him while I met with Blake."

"You two decide to make working together official?"

"Yep, had the attorney set up an LLC. I was already earning a nice side stream by working on some of his house-flipping projects. We're just taking the partnership to the next level."

"I hear that can be a lucrative business. At least that's how they make it appear on YouTube and home-improvement channels."

"Apparently you and half the population believe that. Everybody with a hammer and a hundred dollars is trying to flip a house these days."

They continued chatting comfortably as a light rain returned. Jaxson exited the county road, and soon the two-story farmhouse that had belonged to his grandfather came into view. The lights were on. His body reacted. Hazel said she'd left Genesis ensconced on the sofa and had cleared enough of Mario's toys off the bed for her to lie down if she wanted. She'd also flipped the comforter and changed the sheets, even though he'd assured her that Genesis would not likely want to stay at his house. Hazel often seemed to have a sixth sense about life. Could now be one of those times?

He parked his truck, ended the call and headed up the steps. As he crossed the expansive porch, a feeling of anticipation squeezed his heart. He told himself he was being silly, that maybe he should have accepted Susan's invite after all. It wasn't like him to feel like a horny teenager, but he'd be lying if he said his body didn't react to the thought of Genesis asleep in his house.

After testing the door and finding it unlocked, he quietly crept inside. The living room was dark. A narrow beam of light came from the hallway and another from the kitchen beyond. The hall light cast a shadow over Genesis's face, relaxed and serene, her chest rising and falling in a slow, steady rhythm. Without the frown or sneer that was usually worn when they interacted, he was able to appreciate her natural beauty. Long eyelashes. High cheekbones. Soft-looking, full lips. There was a small scar on the right side of her mouth.

He wondered how she got it. For someone he'd left alone in his home, he knew very little about her. He wanted to know more.

She shifted and winced. He cleared his throat, not wanting her to open her eyes to find him quietly staring.

"Genesis," he called out, his voice soft and low. And a little louder. "Genesis, it's Jax."

Her eyes flew open. She attempted to sit up suddenly and aggravated her ankle. "Ow!"

"Careful. Watch that ankle." He took a step closer. "Sorry about that. Didn't intend to rudely interrupt your sound sleep."

"It's all right." Genesis tried to maneuver to a sitting position.

"Let me help you."

Surprisingly, she didn't object. He reached for a couple of throw pillows and placed them behind her, then doubled the pillow beneath her ankle to heighten its elevation.

"Thanks." She stifled a yawn and amid a half stretch asked, "What time is it?"

"A little before eight. Are you hungry?"

"No, I'm fine. Can you give me a ride back to Uncle Cyrus's house?"

"Are you sure you want to do that, Genny?"

"Genesis. I left Genny back in high school, and reserve Gen for family and close friends."

"You're saying I'm not a friend."

"Right."

"Then Genesis it is. Though I'm definitely not a stranger. We've known each other for a while."

"I don't know you."

"We've got history." He walked to a chair opposite the sofa and sat down. "Do you want to talk about that night?"

He could almost see her thinking before she replied, "What night?"

"You know exactly what night I'm talking about. Don't act like you don't remember."

"I wish I didn't. Your little dare back then made my life a living hell."

"Dare?"

"Oh, so now you're the forgetful one."

"What are you talking about?"

She opened her mouth to respond, closed it and then said, "It doesn't matter. Let the past be the past."

"I have only good memories about that night."

"Negro, please."

"Seriously. I thought about you like every day until I saw you at the mall. Until you told me you were Hank's sister and to go to hell."

"Obviously you don't follow instructions."

Jaxson burst out laughing. "Woman, you're a trip."

Her words were caustic but not the tone. Whatever it was that made her special a decade ago was still there, buried.

"Were you angry at me because of what happened to your brother?"

"What do you think?"

Jaxson shook his head. "It's crazy, that's what I think.

What happened to Hank was an accident, plain and simple. I didn't hear his version until later. Reached out to talk about it, and to ask about you."

Genesis all but snorted.

"You don't believe me? Ask him. He made it clear to leave you alone or there would be consequences."

"Hank said you grabbed his arm when you went for the ball. That's how it got broken."

"That's not true."

"Why would he lie?"

"That's a question you'll have to ask him."

"I'm done talking." She began gathering the leftover food and other personal items on the table. "Can you take me home, or rather, back to Uncle Cyrus's place?"

"I can take you wherever you want to go."

She was angry. That much was obvious. He hadn't meant to upset her, but the truth was the truth. At least now he knew why he was the enemy.

"You live in Memphis, right?"

"Back to Uncle Cyrus's house is fine."

"Okay, but I wouldn't advise you being alone. Having experienced the type of sprain you're dealing with more than once, I can tell you it gets a little worse before it gets better."

"I'm a big girl. I can handle it."

Jaxson eyed Genesis for a long moment. He didn't want her to leave angry. He wished they could keep talking. One thing he remembered about the night they spent together was the easy communication. Like now, in this difficult exchange. They'd argued but no one yelled. Nothing got thrown. He wanted to know more about the dare she mentioned and what he supposedly had to do with it. Another lie, no doubt, but one he wanted resolved. He pulled on the patience he'd learned as a football player to table the discussion. For now.

"Is there anyone you can call to hang out at the farm? I know you think you can handle it, but—"

"I said I've got it!"

Jaxson set his jaw. Even with all he'd learned today, he didn't deserve her misplaced anger. Whatever or whoever she was dealing with, past or present, had nothing to do with him. Plus, she wasn't the only one who'd been through something. He had a few stories, too.

He looked for her crutches. They were leaned against the wall next to the door. He walked over and retrieved them. "Let's go."

Despite his irritation, Jaxson continued to be a gentleman. He helped Genesis off the couch, positioned the crutches beneath her arms and helped her to the door. Once there, he continued to support her as she experienced the pain of navigating steps and getting into his pickup. It would have been much easier for him to carry her as he had earlier that day. He knew she was hurting. More than once he saw the pain on her face. She didn't complain. He didn't force it. Some said pride went before a fall. Sometimes it showed up afterward, too.

He jumped into his truck and fired it up. "I'll bring whatever you left when I pull your car out of the mud." He exited his drive and started down the muddy gravel road.

"Where are your keys?"

She reached for her purse and then slapped her forehead.

"They dropped somewhere in the grass when I fell. I completely forgot about that."

"Don't worry about it. Your car is safe. I guarantee the mayors have kept an eye out."

"The mayors?"

"That's what everyone calls Hazel and Granville, her husband."

"Oh, right."

As soon as they rounded the curve, the bright GMC headlights lit up Genesis's car. Jaxson parked his truck so that the lights faced where he'd found her lying in the mud.

"Be right back."

He got out of the truck and into the bed, opened the toolbox affixed directly behind the cab, pulled out an industrial flashlight and headed for the tall grass. After searching about five minutes, he came back to the cab.

"You didn't find them."

He shook his head. "I'll try again in the morning, after the sun comes up."

"Dammit!"

"Don't worry. Everything will be okay."

"No, it won't. My uncle's house keys are on the ring and the door is locked."

Jaxson put the truck in Drive and continued toward Cyrus's farm.

"Did you hear me? I can't get inside the house."

He shrugged. "You made it clear you don't want to stay at my house. Guess you'll have to sleep on the porch."

That shut her up. She didn't say another word, even after

he'd pulled his truck into Cyrus's driveway. Jaxson only felt a little guilty for purposely working to get a rise out of her.

"Okay, Genesis. Here we are."

She stared straight ahead. He could almost see her mind churning as she chewed her bottom lip.

"Nipsey's probably out there somewhere. He'll keep you safe."

She sighed heavily and looked at him. "I don't want to spend the night out here."

"I can take you back to your car."

"Okay." Said quietly but with resolve.

"There aren't too many wild animals out this time of night. The windows are rolled up, right?"

She turned her head in slow motion. "Wild…animals?"

"Yeah. Bears, deer, coyotes, and of course a stray bull every now and then. But it's cool. You'll be fine."

He put the car in Reverse.

She squeezed the dash with her hand. "Wait!"

He thought about dragging out the ruse, but no. Time to put her out of her misery. He threw the car back in Park.

"Wait here."

He grabbed the flashlight, jogged past the rotting steps and over to a hydrangea bush in dire need of pruning. He reentered the car whistling, with dangling keys.

"Your uncle's spare house key."

"You… Ugh!" She tried to smack him on the arm but with little success. Good thing, too, because amid his hearty laughter it was hard to defend the blows.

"Stop it, Genny! Stop!"

He wrapped her in a bear hug, pinning her arms at her sides. Her squirming did things to his insides, and lower.

"If you don't stop, I'm going to leave you in the dark to make your way up those stairs alone."

She pushed him off her. "I can't believe you did that."

"I couldn't resist."

She took a deep breath, sat back in the seat. Slowly, her lips twitched, barely repressing a smile.

"You are such an asshole."

"Sometimes. I'm sorry."

"Not sorry."

"You have to admit that was pretty funny. You're a true soldier, though, ready to brave the dark alone until I mentioned that bull."

They both laughed openly now.

"What was he doing out there, anyway?"

"I lease some of my land to a breeder. Runaway Randy has figured out a way to be free."

"He's got a name?"

"He earned it."

She sobered. "Are there really bears and other wild animals out here?"

"Black bears are spotted every now and then. It's a rare occurrence. The coyotes appear more frequently."

She shifted and winced with the movement.

"Come on. Let's get you in the house."

A hardheaded Genesis allowed Jaxson to help her out of the pickup, but then insisted on climbing the steps on her own. He unlocked the door and gave her the key.

"You going to be all right?"

"I'll be fine." She stepped over the threshold and turned slightly. "Thank you."

"You're welcome. Granville will help me find the keys and get your car out of the mud. We'll drop it off in the morning."

"I really appreciate it."

She looked ready to close the door. He didn't ask to go inside. Both his ego and manhood had taken a beating. Tomorrow was another day.

Granville was his alarm clock, knocking on his door before 7:00 a.m.

"C'mon, partner!" he yelled through the screen door. "The early bird gets the worm."

"The early bird is going to get shot," Jaxson replied after rolling out of bed and lumbering down the hallway to the screen door. "You're taking a real chance knocking on a brother's door before coffee."

He undid the latch and headed to the kitchen without waiting to see if Granville followed him inside. After his thermos was filled with two cups of joe, he hopped in his neighbor's tried-and-true pickup. It was fitted with a larger hitch than the one on Jaxson's truck, which would make freeing her car from the mud a much easier process. Butch, the dog, jumped in the truck bed.

"Was that one of Cyrus's granddaughters?" Granville asked as they bumped along the gravel-and-dirt road.

"She refers to him as uncle."

"Must be the great-niece he sometimes mentioned."

She's great, all right. Jaxson blew on the steam rising from the thermos opening. Forced his thoughts in another direction. Genesis made it clear that the past was the past. Given how four years later he was finally healing from everything that had happened in Phoenix, it was probably best.

"Walker's kid."

"Walker?" Jaxson asked. "I don't remember that name."

"Walker is Cyrus's nephew. He was born and raised in Memphis but got married and moved away a long time ago."

Granville adjusted the sound of his favorite country station. "Is she good-lookin'?"

"Genesis? Very attractive. Got an attitude, though."

"Aw, heck, son, you don't want nothin' to do with that. Better to have an ugly woman with a heart of gold than a pretty one with no heart at all."

They reached Genesis's Kia. While Granville positioned his truck to hitch up the car, Jaxson searched the grass for the lost keys. Thankfully a beam of sun bounced off Genesis's key chain. Within minutes they had the car pulled from the ruts and rolling behind Granville's ride. They arrived at Genesis's house before seven thirty. Imagining she'd probably be asleep and not wanting to wake her, Jaxson placed the keys under the mat and sent her a text.

Car's in the drive. Keys under mat. You're welcome. ☺

As he walked back to Granville's truck, Nipsey rounded the corner, barking loud enough to wake up the dead. Butch leaped out the truck bed and returned the greeting.

"Nipsey! Butch! Stop all that barking," Granville demanded in a voice that was loud enough to wake them himself.

"Hey, Nip." Jaxson petted the dog that he felt belonged to him as much as Cyrus. Nipsey quietly wagged his tail and enjoyed the mini massage. "That's right. Protect your property like a good watchdog."

He turned to Granville. "We should go before all this noise wakes up Genesis."

Granville pointed at a light inside the house that had just come on. "I think it's too late for that."

Jaxson cursed under his breath, then slowly made his way to Genesis's front porch. He didn't know whether "pretty" or "ugly" would greet him. He was about to find out.

Seven

The night before

Genesis stood with a crutch beneath each arm and surveyed the living room around her. The sound of Jaxson starting his truck and driving away was momentarily distracting. She'd reciprocated his kindness by being a bitch. The pain in her ankle was only partially to blame. The other reason... *Never mind that.* She forced her thoughts away from Jaxson and shifted them to her uncle.

Memories of Cyrus Perry were everywhere. His favorite, well-worn and cracking-leather recliner still boasting handmade throws his last girlfriend had made him. Next to it a tray table with a half-full decanter of brown liquor, a pipe and a pouch of tobacco. Genesis closed her eyes, took a breath and smelled the slightly sweet-smelling aroma still lingering in the air. The ever-present peppermints kept in a boot-shaped glass cookie jar on the large trunk turned coffee table, next to a wooden box of ivory dominoes and a stack of hunting and fishing magazines. Mismatched side tables and other accessories that surrounded a couch covered in a dark brocade fabric, jackets and other clothing items tossed across its back and a general messiness from a seventysomething-year-old man who hadn't placed good housekeeping at the top of his list. She took in a carpet that had seen better days at least a decade or so ago, dingy, smoke-stained walls, and the overall "oldness" of everything.

Could she live out here? In the country? In this house? Difficult if not almost impossible to do, but with a jacked-up foot, no income and little savings, and a condo lease about to expire, she might end up having to do the unthinkable—becoming Jaxson's neighbor.

With a sigh of resignation, Genesis continued to the kitchen/dining combo of the L-shaped ranch house. Here the age of the home and lack of tender loving care showed even more. The once-white appliances were in desperate need of cleaning or, even better, being replaced, as were the cabinets, counters and… Was that actually a linoleum floor? It was so cracked and worn she couldn't tell. A faint buzzing sounded from the overhead fluorescent light. What the heck did that mean? And the plastic that covered it was yellowed and cracked. Amazing how as a child and week-end guest of her uncle she'd observed none of this. With the term "homeowner" came a new set of eyes.

Opening the refrigerator brought on another revelation and made her think about Jaxson for the first time in five minutes. The Cobb salad from earlier was long gone. The fridge was almost empty. A half-empty package of cold cuts, old takeout, a partial pack of soda, a couple of beers and a door filled with condiments was just about it. The freezer offerings weren't much better. A quick search of the cabinets prevented total starvation. She wasn't much of a canned chicken noodles or pork-and-beans type, but they would have to do in this crunch. The medication required she have something in her stomach and the throbbing in her ankle was sending an urgent message to take another pill. It was either canned soup or using money she didn't have to have something delivered.

She thought about her neighbors. Hazel probably had a pantry full of goodies, but Genesis wouldn't think of asking the older woman for more help. She'd spend her last dollar before asking Jaxson for food. She already felt she owed him and that didn't feel good. Neither did entertaining the story he'd told her, that he'd spoken with Hank and asked about her. That Hank had threatened him. Try as she might since being dropped off, the "bad guy" she'd dissed largely due to her family hadn't been far from her mind.

Genesis opened the soup, found a pan and set it on the stove to heat. While waiting, she ignored the fact her ankle probably needed to be elevated and walked down the hall to her great-uncle's room. His house shoes stuck out from under the bed. A wave of sadness washed over her. Growing up, she'd found him to be the one person she could count on to make her feel special. Like she was important and mattered. Unlike home, where her football-star brother Hank and younger jokester Habari were the focus. Cyrus had always made sure that his attention was on her. She already missed him and would always cherish that final phone call. Thinking of that last "I love you" made her think of her cousins. Animosity aside, they'd lost their father. Genesis could only imagine how that felt.

Completely dependent on her crutches, she walked into the kitchen, poured the soup into a bowl and, after facing the unsolvable dilemma of carrying it anywhere, gulped it down at the counter. That done, she made her way to the couch, grabbed the pain pills, propped a pillow under the ankle and flopped back, exhausted. Jaxson was right. She should have stayed at his house. She could have used the help.

Instead of lingering on that revelation, she popped a pill, reached for her phone and dialed the number Clarence had provided. He answered on the second ring.

"Hi, Clarence." She placed the call on speaker. "It's Genesis."

"What do you want, Genesis?"

The tone of his voice told Genesis that he was still upset. She understood and hoped that by the end of this phone call he could see her point of view as well.

"I wanted to let you know that I'm at your dad's house."

"What are you doing there?"

Genesis ignored the accusatory, non-trusting tone. She told him about the accident and being on crutches. "I'm sure someone can come get me next week, but I'm stuck here for now."

"How convenient. Tell you what. You'd better not touch one thing in that house. I don't give a damn what that lawyer says. It doesn't belong to you."

Maybe this conversation wasn't the best idea. His comments hurt more than her ankle. Clarence being upset was understandable, but he wasn't the only one who'd lost a loved one.

"It doesn't sound like this is a good time. I just called to let you know what happened and to ask about funeral arrangements."

She heard Clarence heave a sigh. When he spoke, the edge was gone. "I spoke with Daddy's pastor before leaving town. The funeral and repast will be at the church. We'll finalize everything else next week. Right now, Cleo and I are trying to process how Daddy could have done what he did, and how you're going to correct it."

"I don't know. I'm still as shocked and confused as you. I had nothing to do with Uncle Cyrus's decision. If he'd asked, I would have said to leave everything to y'all. But I wasn't and he didn't. Now I'm in the impossible spot between doing what you and Cleo believe is right and honoring Uncle Cyrus's wishes."

"You have any experience with a farm?"

Do you? It took everything in her to keep from asking the question but knew it would start a fight.

"None."

"See there? Daddy didn't think this through. How are you, a single girl from the city with no farm experience, going to know what to do with the land, besides sell it? Cleo and I are the rightful heirs! That's our stuff in that house."

"What's here belonged to Uncle Cyrus. You're welcome

to it. I don't want to argue. At the end of the day, we're family. I hope something can get worked out."

"Me, too. Let me know what's going on."

"I will. Same about Uncle's funeral. If there is anything at all I can do to help, please let me know. I used to work for a printing company and can get the programs done for free. I could also write the obituary. I've read dozens of them and written a few. Editing and proofreading was part of my job.

"It's probably hard for you to understand, Clarence, but I truly loved your father. Uncle Cyrus was the connection to the dad I didn't know, the only connection to his side of the family along with Tiff and Kayla. He treated me like a granddaughter. Like family. Given my father's rejection, that meant a lot to me."

"Well, yeah, I can understand that."

The rest of the conversation wasn't overly warm, but it was civil. The call ended with Clarence accepting the offer to help with the programs and agreeing to send the information she needed to write the obituary. She went to sleep on the couch thinking of her uncle Cyrus, smiling at memories of them playing checkers and smelling his sweet pipe tobacco.

The next morning, she woke up groggy and disoriented to the sound of a loud barking dog. For the first few seconds she wondered how it managed to get close to the door of her condo. Then she moved her ankle. Pain ripped through her leg. The pain-pill fog lifted. Memories from the past twenty-four hours flooded in.

Nipsey continued barking. What could possibly have him

this excited so early in the morning? Another dog, maybe? The next sound caused even greater alarm. Gunshots. Several of them. She switched on the lamp beside the couch, grabbed one crutch and hopped to the window still wearing Jaxson's sister's warm-ups. Another shot rang out, but that wasn't what set her soul to stirring. No, what started the flame at her gut that quickly spanned to her chest was the sight of a pair of long legs leaving an unknown truck, rounding the corner of her uncle's house and she imagined heading up the stairs of the front porch.

A series of soft taps caused her to jump, followed by a round of louder knocks.

Jaxson!

"Hold on a minute!"

Genesis looked around for a look at her reflection. Not a mirror in sight. Did these country folk know anything about calling before coming by someone's house? Especially before eight in the morning?

She reached the door, ran a hand through hair that refused to be tamed, and opened it.

"Sorry about the disturbance," Jaxson said in a rush, before she could go off. "We were just dropping off your car. I sent a text. Did you get it?"

"That's right. The car. No, I didn't see the text. I just woke up." If her unruly hair hadn't given that fact away, the frog in her throat surely did.

"I figured you might be asleep, which is why I sent the text letting you know the keys were under the mat. Probably wasn't a good idea to let my dog, Butch, ride along. That's

Nipsey's homeboy, but I didn't expect their greeting each other to be so loud."

She looked beyond Jaxson's shoulder and saw Nipsey and a beautiful brown pit romping across the yard. Jaxson dangled the keys in front of her.

"Thanks for getting my car unstuck and driving it over. That was very considerate of you. But you didn't have to get up so early, as I won't be driving for a while." She nodded toward her foot.

"It was no problem. I'm up early most mornings and wanted to check on you anyway. I also had help pulling your car out from an even earlier riser."

Genesis heard footsteps. A tall, burly man came into view and up the steps.

"Mornin', miss lady."

He tipped his cowboy hat. Endearing.

"Good morning."

"I'd say I was sorry to disturb you, but it's those dogs that need to apologize." He held out a hand the size of a small ham. "Name's Granville."

"Genesis."

"Pleased to make your acquaintance."

"You're Hazel's husband."

"Don't ever confuse me with that joker. I'm her lover when he's out of town."

"Oh." Pause. "Excuse me." Genesis tried and with effort wiped the shock off her face.

"Go easy on her, Granville." Jaxson offered a smile and

a wink that sent a squiggle through her vagina. "She's new around here."

"Well, in that case, I guess I'd better come clean. Hazel is my beloved wife of almost half a century."

"I see everyone around here has jokes," she said to Jaxson.

"And bulls." Another smile. Another wink. With his scruffy, barely-there shadow, the man managed to look even better this morning than he did last night.

The sound of another gunshot pierced the air.

Genesis jumped. "I thought you said this area was safe."

"It is."

"Then what's with all the gunfire?"

"That's what makes it safe, young lady!" Granville laughed at a joke Genesis didn't find funny.

"I have a little shooting range up on the mountain. Are you good with a pistol?"

"I've shot a gun before." She'd been twelve and Uncle Cyrus had helped absorb the kickback, but…whatever.

"What kind is it?"

"I…don't own one now."

"Cyrus has a few. Did Jax tell you about the bears?"

"Jaxson! I thought you were kidding."

Seeing her expression, Granville held up his hands, his gray eyes twinkling. "Oh, that's right. I forgot. You're new in town. In all seriousness, though, if you're going to live out here you need to know how to shoot. Is your family moving in with you?"

"I'm…just here until my ankle gets better."

Granville noted the boot before turning to Jaxson. "Alone

and injured? Son, that's a recipe for disaster you don't want to get cooked. Teach your girl how to handle a firearm, pronto."

"I'm not his girl."

"She's not my girl."

Said simultaneously. In harmony. With conviction. It may have been the first thing they agreed on since Jaxson found her in the mud.

Granville ignored them both. "I'd invite you to the hill, but seeing as how you're on crutches and all, it will be easier for Jaxson to teach you down here. Don't be like these modern women who feel they don't need help from a man. Can't find one better than Jaxson for firearm training."

He straightened his back and squared his shoulders. "Now, listen here. Cyrus owned several firearms, including shotguns. You need to know your way around a gun, and you need to know how to shoot."

"Granville, I've offered my assistance several times. Genesis has made it clear that she's fine on her own. She's very independent."

"Uh-huh. So are those coyotes." He trained a stern eye on Genesis. "I may be retired from law enforcement, but out here my badge is still good. That means you need to pick up what I'm putting down, understand me?"

Genesis couldn't help but like the old codger. "Yes, sir."

He headed down the steps. Once at the bottom, he eyed her with the warmth of a beach in Jamaica. "Jaxson is one of the best shooters I've ever taught. You'll be in good hands with him.

"I'd better get a move on. Hazel's waiting. I don't want to hear her mouth."

Granville continued to his truck. Within seconds, they heard the engine.

"Guess that's the end of the conversation," Jaxson said.

Genesis deadpanned, "Bang, bang."

Jaxson left soon after. Rather than go back to sleep, she found coffee—thank God!—and after a bird bath donned one of her uncle's long flannel shirts and a pair of boxers from an unopened package still in the discount department store's bag. She checked her dwindling bank account, one that wouldn't be replenished with the usual weekend of DoorDashing, then scrolled through various social media accounts. An hour later, the early wake-up caught up with her. Grabbing the throw from her uncle's chair, she curled up on the couch and drifted off to sleep thinking about guns. Not the ones Granville had mentioned were in her uncle's arsenal, but the one she remembered existed between Jaxson's legs.

Eight

Jaxson stood in the living room of a three-bed, two-bath flip he and Blake had purchased at a recent auction. It was his first participation as a partner and Jaxson had to admit having that title rather than independent contractor felt good. The single-family home had good bones, just needed updating and a good dose of TLC. They would start by highlighting the footage with an open-concept layout. Fortunately, tearing up something was perfect for Jaxson's mood. He aimed a sledgehammer at the X on the wall and swung with abandon. The drywall exploded, creating a two-foot hole in the partition that currently separated the living room from the kitchen/dining area. He imagined the wall of this latest flip as the cause of his frustrations and swung again, harder this time. The drywall gave easily. He wished that his conflicting emotions regarding Genesis Hunter could get solved as quickly. That she was living rent-free in his mind didn't sit well at all.

He couldn't figure her out. That was the problem. She

didn't follow past scripts written by other women in his life. Usually, the women he dealt with came in two categories— the obvious gold digger or the ones that feigned disinterest. Jaxson had become a master at spotting both.

Genesis was different. She honestly disliked him. Though he felt the blame and anger were misguided, the feelings were real.

She was the most independent and stubborn woman he'd ever met. She seemed fine with the person she saw in the mirror, unafraid to be her natural self. She spoke her mind, even when doing so was sure to piss him off. In short, Genesis didn't seem to want or need anything from him.

When it came to women and the pro athletes they went after, that was a trait he hadn't often experienced. Being fed up with superficial women and the games they played was what had sent him running from Phoenix to the comfort of Holy Mound. That and the near scandal that could have cost him his reputation and possibly his freedom. The business partners he'd been involved with then had used his trust and naivete to their advantage. In the small place he once again called home, people said what they meant and meant what they said. Big cities could learn a thing or two from small towns.

His ex was another cause for frustration. On the way to Memphis, he'd called Abby to speak with his daughter. Instead of offering a civil greeting and handing over the phone, she had gone into a list of complaints that were none of his business. Of the four billion–plus women on the planet, why had he picked her to have his child?

Oh, that's right. He hadn't. But he'd engaged in sex without a condom or a gun to his head, so he shouldered half the blame. He wished their situation was less contentious. It killed him not to raise his daughter full-time, to know another man enjoyed the moments that were his by right. Their weekly video chats and holiday visits were not nearly enough. He did what he could—paid a hefty amount of child support, had Jazz on his insurance and set up a trust. But as Susan told him when discussing her children's father's inconsistent visits, children craved presence, not presents. Jaxson resented having to fight to stay connected to his child.

He raised the sledgehammer to another piece of drywall and swung for the proverbial fences. Ah, yeah. Hitting that wall felt like making a great tackle.

Back in the day, most of the frustration and angst from Jaxson's problems got left on the field. Until partnering up with Blake and learning construction on the fly, he hadn't realized how much he missed hard work. He spent time in the gym, but that didn't compare to breaking something down with your bare hands and building it back up again. He tossed aside the sledgehammer to pull the rest of the material from the wooden beams. He could already see the difference tearing down the wall made. Natural light flowed from the living room to the kitchen, making the space look much larger than it had moments ago. He pulled out his phone to take pics to send to Blake and realized he'd missed a text from Genesis.

What time are shooting lessons?

He smiled, wondering whether it was Granville's stern-
ness or a fear of coyotes, or maybe Randy, that had moved
her to call. He also realized he was probably happier than
he should be at the chance to shoot a gun.

In Memphis, working. Back around six. Will that work?

He waited awhile, but when the answer wasn't immedi-
ate, he figured she was away from her phone. When his rang
just a few seconds later, the screen flashed Unknown Caller.
"Hello?"
"Hey, it's Gen."
"Who?"
"Genesis Hunter."
"Naw, I heard that. You said Gen. I called you Genny
and you were quick to correct me. Have I moved into the
friend zone?"
"We're not friends. We're neighbors."
"Can I call you Gen?"
"Absolutely not. You're still in Genesis territory."
Said so seriously and quickly, her retort made Jaxson laugh
out loud. "Using the nickname is a privilege, not a right."
"Exactly."
"Duly noted. What's up, Genesis Hunter?" With great
emphasis placed on her proper name.
"Where are Uncle Cyrus's guns?"
"In the trunk."
"The one that doubles as a coffee table?"
"And a gun case."

"Good Lord."

"You might want to wait until I'm there before you start messing with them. Cyrus kept his guns loaded, and probably locked. But I wouldn't want you to chance finding a safety off."

"I think I know enough to be careful."

"Okay. Just looking out for your well-being. You've already got a twisted right ankle. If you shoot off your left toe, don't come crying to me."

With an informal date with Genesis later that evening, and a chance to finish the conversation that had started in his bedroom, the rest of Jaxson's day flew by. Blake arrived with a crew midafternoon, increasing the manpower and providing Jaxson the camaraderie he missed most when he wasn't working with a team. Blake's running commentary about the upcoming baseball season was also a nice distraction from thoughts of Genesis, Abby and working out an amiable arrangement to spend more time with Jazz. He left the house and, on a whim, headed to a well-known BBQ spot to pick up dinner for him and Genesis. She'd have a hard time saying no to food from the local favorite that had placed first in several cooking contests and gained national attention on a Food Network show.

Traffic was light. He made it back to Holy Mound in record time. Nipsey was the first to greet him. He picked up a stick and tossed it before continuing up the steps.

He knocked on the door and, just to be ornery, hollered, "Gen!"

The front door was open. He tried the screen. Locked.

"I should leave you out there!" she yelled. "What did you call me?"

"I've got Papa Joes!"

He heard shuffling noises, followed by the muffled sound of rubber on wood. Genesis appeared in the hallway and quickly made her way to the door.

She unlatched the screen and headed back in. "Papa Joes is about the only thing that would get you in here," she said, over her shoulder.

"Good thing I had the code."

He followed her into the living room and was hit with a strange sensation—like coming home after a hard day's work and having your woman greet you. The way he imagined Granville felt with Hazel. Or his grandpa Dixon with his grandmother Essie when he was still alive. In an instant, he imagined Jazz on the worn rug with Mario, and maybe Jazz playing dominoes or checkers or putting a puzzle together. Jaxson shook off the feeling, blamed it on an empty stomach. The long day working had obviously affected his senses. He needed to eat.

He walked over to the sofa and held out the bags. "BOB or PAPA?"

"BOB! That burnt-ends-on-brioche is my favorite."

"Got any soda?"

"In the fridge."

He headed toward the kitchen as though he lived there. A feeling of familiarity followed him down the hallway. Almost like déjà vu.

"You want one?"

"No, thank you. The doctor's office called, reminded me to drink a lot of water while on pain medication. Wish I had bottled, though."

"Did you check the back porch?"

"No, I didn't."

Jaxson opened the back door and pulled a bottle of water from the case Cyrus kept there, then returned to the living room and handed it to Genesis.

"So that's where he keeps his stash."

"Yep, there's nearly a full case out there."

"Thank you." She unscrewed the cap and took a long, satisfying drink.

"Is there still a lot of pain?"

"Not when I take the meds. But they make me sleepy, so I'm only taking a half dose at a time."

"It's good to be careful."

He sat down and watched Genesis gleefully taking a bite of her sandwich and following it up with a thick, hand-cut fry. After that she licked her fingers like a pro, sent Jaxson's mind straight to the night when another kind of licking had been their main focus.

He settled into the recliner, opened his bag and pulled out the PAPA, pulled pork topped with a slaw containing the fresh apple, pickle and avocado slices that helped create the name. He dug into his own order of fries and set the bag on the side table.

"I bought wings, too," he offered. "Wasn't sure which you'd want. Now you have lunch for tomorrow as well."

"I'll pay you back."

"Damn, woman. I think I can afford to buy you a sandwich. I'm not in the pros anymore, but my hustles pay pretty good."

"What hustles are those?"

"I lease part of my land to a small cattle rancher. In exchange, I get cash and a cow for slaughter that I split with the mayors. Another piece of land is used to grow Christmas trees."

"Hmm, that's different. Is there good money in that?"

"There is from October to December. Last year one of the neighbors tried to sell pumpkins but that business didn't do as well. Too many larger retailers priced her out of the competition.

"After retiring, your uncle tried growing soybeans. Too much trouble for too little reward. He made himself content to live off retirement and Social Security, and the money he made doing odd jobs here and there."

"Is that why this place is in such disrepair?"

"That's part of it. I didn't get into his personal business, but it appeared funds were tight. I think after his sons made it clear they weren't coming back, he lost interest in making big changes. What he had was enough for him to get by and be content. The world doesn't appreciate old folk like Cyrus, who probably forgot more about truly good living than younger generations will ever learn."

"I don't remember Uncle Cyrus ever trying to grow anything. He worked at the assembly plant for as long as I knew him."

"Up until the lockdown," Jaxson said, reaching for his

soda. "Then they cut the workforce and forced him into early retirement. He didn't like that experience. Said he never again wanted to be in the position where another man dictated his paycheck. That's when he started growing soybeans and tried to get his sons interested in the land. He wanted to create a family business. But you probably already know about that."

"I know he missed his sons and grandkids and wanted them to visit more often. And I knew he'd stopped working. I'd assumed by choice."

"Why didn't I ever see you? I was over all the time."

"Until a few years ago, I lived in Charlotte. Moved back right before the pandemic happened and the world changed. The last time I saw him was six months ago. Meant to come back but got caught up helping a friend with a project and then…Uncle Cyrus was gone."

"He appreciated you checking in on him."

"He told you that?"

"I didn't know it was you. He mentioned a niece in Memphis who kept in touch and always thought about him during the holidays. But he never said Genesis or Genny. I think he called you…"

"Peaches?"

"Yeah."

Genesis smiled. "I've always loved peaches. One of the neighbors used to can them."

"Miss Alma."

"You knew her?"

He nodded. "They were a cabinet staple. Barely through the front door, and I'd start begging."

"He never mentioned you to me."

"There was probably never a reason. Cyrus was a baseball man. We didn't talk much about my career. That he treated me like a regular Joe—"

"Or regular Jax."

"Touché. That was one of the things I loved most about him, Granville, Hazel, all the folk around here."

Jaxson finished his sandwich and sat back in the chair. "Can I ask you a question?"

"It's a free country."

"It's really none of my business, and I know you're Cyrus's niece, but...are you also the executor of Cyrus's estate? I ask because that day at the restaurant you seemed to be in control."

"You're right. It's none of your business." A quick smile softened the words. "Let's just say I'm helping out with his affairs, making sure that his wishes are followed."

"Like not selling the farm."

"Correct."

"Just so you know, buying the farm wasn't my idea. Clarence asked if I was interested. Knowing what pride Cyrus took in owning that property, I was surprised the question came up."

"That's no doubt why Uncle Cyrus...made sure his business was in order. He knew that no amount of money would make me go against what he wanted."

"I see."

Genesis didn't know it, wasn't even trying, but she'd just scored major points in the attraction game. Once betrayed, loyalty became an invaluable asset. Her pros were pulling ahead of the cons. For Jaxson—duly noted.

"How are you Cyrus's niece? It's not through Clarence or Cleo. Is there another sibling?"

"I'm his great-niece, technically. My father is, was, his nephew."

"Oh, right." Jaxson remembered that Granville had shared this. "Does your dad still live around here?"

"No." The way Genesis answered put a special type of period at the end of that complete two-letter sentence. Jaxson got the memo.

"Who named you Genesis?"

"My grandmother." She finished her sandwich and reached for her drink. "Who named you Jaxson, and was it always spelled that way?"

"Believe it or not, my grandfather. He spelled it with an x with a nod to his name, Dixon."

"Did you grow up here in the country, or in town?"

"I grew up where you were last night. Moved in with my grandparents when I was fourteen."

"And before then?"

"Here and there," Jaxson replied. "My mom was military before she remarried. We moved around a lot."

"Did you get along with your stepdad?"

He shook his head. "Not at all. That's how I ended up here."

"I heard your grandfather died. Is your grandmother still with us?" she asked.

"She was in love with Papa and couldn't live without him. Less than a year passed before she joined him."

Genesis nodded, took a drink of water. "Did you like moving here as a teenager?"

"I wasn't happy at all. But then I enrolled at Holy Mound High and became a Hornet. Being a part of that team gave me focus, something to believe in. I was popular and well-liked for all the right reasons. Probably saved my life."

It had been a long time since Jaxson had thought back to his troubled childhood, even longer since he'd felt comfortable enough to share it with someone, even in the guarded way he'd done so with Genesis. Keep that up and she might discover his sensitive spot.

"When'd you stop playing for the Cardinals?"

A slow smile spread across Jaxson's face. "You followed my career?"

Genesis gave him a look. "Slow your roll, Jaxson. I don't watch much football. You couldn't live in Tennessee and not hear talk about your career."

Jaxson frowned. Shook off the discomfort her comment caused. He'd paid big money to keep his name out of the papers. So far it looked like the tainted business venture that happened in Phoenix hadn't followed him home.

"I hear ya." He stood. "Ready for shooting practice?"

"Is your big head the target?"

As a former pro athlete who was often worshipped, he loved her dismissive sense of humor.

Without hesitation, he replied, "Maybe tomorrow. Today I'll settle for the side of a barn."

Genesis slowly lifted her ankle off the pillows. He watched her wince with the effort.

"I'll bring one of those dining room chairs outside if you want. Learning to shoot from a sitting position will make you an ace once you stand up."

He wasn't surprised when she refused his offer to be helped down the steps. For him that was a good move. It gave him a chance to fully appreciate how sexy a man's flannel shirt could be on the right female body. Some of the memories from that night had faded with time. He wouldn't mind getting an updated picture. He set down a chair in the driveway, then went back inside for another one to elevate her foot.

He returned with the chair.

"When it comes to guns, it's safety first." He offered his hand. "Let me show you a few things."

He went over how to properly handle and hold the gun, how to release and lock the safety, the correct way to aim and a few other details. Then he nailed an old farmers market poster to a nearby fence and stepped away.

"Okay, let's see what you've got. Aim for the biggest target, right in the middle."

She closed one eye, focused the other on the watermelon and missed the whole poster.

"Let's try again. Aim for a little higher than your actual target."

A few more attempts. A few more misses.

"Here, let me show you."

Jaxson knelt next to Genesis's chair and walked her through

the steps. Eyeing the target. Holding and aiming the weapon. "Then take a breath," he instructed, "and shoot."

The poster contained all kinds of fruits and vegetables. He hit a pea in a pod.

"Show-off." Genesis shifted her weight in the chair and reached for the gun. "Give me that."

"Here, let me help you line it up."

Jaxson moved behind the chair where Genesis sat and reached around her to grasp the gun. He knew immediately that he was in trouble. From this position, he could feel the softness of her flyaway curls against his face. Could smell the subtle scent of a citrusy floral combination, something both harmonic and contradictory, like Genesis. He aligned his arms with hers and covered her hands. The movement pressed his forearm against the side of her breast. Inappropriate thoughts assailed him. The weighty breast being cupped in his hand, or the nipple gently sucked into his mouth. The pressure of her soft tit against his hard forearm created an undeniable sensation. She felt it, too, and stiffened.

He squeezed her shoulder. "Relax. Take a breath and concentrate on the middle of the poster."

For once, she didn't argue. Instead he felt her shoulders rise and fall against him. She had no idea how dangerous that simple move was, how the gentle pressure affected his groin. How his dick began to think with a mind of its own. As her fingers tightened on the trigger of the gun, he took a deep intake of air, leaned back and broke contact.

"Ready?"

She nodded.

"Aim… That's it. Steady. Now…fire."

The gun went off. Genesis jumped. The plank of wood he'd nailed the poster to splintered into a thousand pieces. The poster, still secured by a nail, swung from side to side.

Genesis did a little jig in the chair, then, Jaxson supposed, remembered they weren't quite friends like that. "I hit it." The statement was subdued but her eyes gleamed.

"You damn sure did," Jaxson responded, even though the poster and not the fence holding it was the target. But her excitement was sexy. He couldn't take her joy away.

"I destroyed the fence."

"That plank of wood for sure. No worries. There are more in the barn. I'll replace it."

Jaxson felt his phone vibrate. He checked the screen. Abby. Hopefully whatever she wanted could be handled in a civil conversation. Since it was a toss-up, he decided to take it in private.

"I think that's enough for your first practice," he said, after renailing the target, having Genesis practice for another ten minutes and actually hit the poster. Once done, he picked up the pieces of wood scattered on the ground. "Let me help you inside."

"Go ahead. I'll be okay."

"You can get yourself and the chairs up the steps?"

"Oh. Right. Guess I could use a little help."

Once inside, Jaxson lingered. Even with her wishy-washy attitude, there was something about Genesis that made him want to stick around.

"Have they set a date for your uncle's funeral?"

"This Saturday."

"If you need anything—"

"I'll let you know. Thanks for dinner, and the lesson."

"We'll set up another one next week and add a shotgun to the lineup. Around here, that's the weapon used the most."

"I'm not sure I'm ready for that. With my aim I might blow out a window."

"Practice makes perfect. You'll get there." He headed for the door. "Oh, one more thing. If you're going to be staying out here for any length of time, you might think about getting a set of security lights. And a camera."

"You really think that's necessary?"

He did. Despite Genesis's independent streak, or maybe because of it, Jax felt the need to protect her.

"With Nipsey, I don't imagine any strangers sneaking up on you. But I think it will help you feel safer."

"For sure. It's a good idea. Thanks."

"You're welcome."

Jaxson hopped into his truck and headed for home. His phone rested on the seat but he didn't call Abby right away. His thoughts were on another woman. One selfless enough to brighten up an old man's life, as she'd obviously done with Cyrus. One fearless enough to begrudgingly trust a stranger, though getting there was like pulling teeth. A woman who was fiery, smart, independent, loyal, who turned a man's flannel shirt into a minidress and smelled like jasmine and oranges. She'd joked about her potential of being dangerous with a shotgun, having no idea that when it came to him, Genesis Hunter was a weapon all by herself.

Nine

The melancholy strains of the gospel classic "Precious Lord" filled the small Baptist church as friends and family gathered to celebrate the homegoing of Cyrus Lee Perry. Faced with still not being able to drive and having no appropriate black dress in her closet anyway, Genesis had gone shopping online and bought a few things, including a short-sleeved black maxi with small flowers on the hem that mostly hid the black fracture boot she'd paired with one of a pair of black ballet flats she'd also ordered. Her normally wild curls were tamed into an Afro puff at the top of her head. Makeup was minimal, a good thing since the morning had come with more than one bout of unexpected tears. Not only because of her uncle's death, but because of how alone she felt. She hadn't heard from her mother, nor from Lance. She sat in the front row with her brother Habari, who'd thankfully agreed to join her for moral support, and a couple of distant relatives she barely remembered.

On the other side of the aisle, Clarence and Cleo and their wives, her cousins Tiffany and Kayla and other siblings rounded out Cy's next of kin. The McCormicks were there, and the attorney who'd surprised her and Clarence and Cleo just over a week ago with the contents of Cy's trust. A smattering of older people dotted the pews. Whether neighbors, longtime friends or members of the church, Genesis didn't know.

What she was very aware of was how the atmosphere changed when Jaxson arrived. Not that he'd ever gone far from her mind. His accidental touch on her breast during the shooting lesson had scorched her like fire. She'd felt it for days. Memories of that interaction—his thoughtful dinner purchase, patient instruction, prolific gun skills—had all worked to lessen the animosity she was already finding hard to hang on to. The incident with her brother that in her mind had cost him a college and pro ball career now seemed far away and irrelevant, like holding on to an item well past its expiration date.

She observed the somber expression now highlighting the square of his jaw and watched him approach the casket. After a quiet goodbye to his friend and neighbor, nods at those in the front row, he scanned the pews. For her? It looked that way. He passed the second row, where she sat, made eye contact and squeezed her shoulder. His touch brought comfort, a brief balm over her sadness, something that hadn't happened earlier when she saw her cousins for the first time in years.

That reunion hadn't gone well. Kayla ignored her, but

Tiffany, always outspoken, had bypassed courtesies and cut straight to the chase.

"You know you're wrong."

"Hello to you, too, cousin. Long time no see. About ten years, right? Where's my hug?"

Genesis had taken a step forward. Tiffany, a step back.

"It's behind you doing the right thing. What Grandpa did wasn't right at all. I can't believe you're going for it."

"I'm not going for anything, nor am I going to argue over what Uncle Cyrus owned with his casket on the other side of the door."

That comment had not only shut Tiffany's rant, but it had glued her to the spot long enough for Genesis to walk around her and enter the church. Whispers had been followed by daggers flung in her direction, but once the first note from the organ sounded, it was all about Cyrus Perry.

The service was short and heartfelt. She'd braced herself to have to defend her mother's absence, but no one said a word about her not being there. The hugs from Clarence and Cleo were perfunctory, but those from their wives felt sincere. Tiffany finally came around, and so did Kayla. Neither apologized for their earlier actions and incorrect comments, but when they hugged and thanked her for how she'd written the eulogy, it felt genuine. At the repast, the mood was more relaxed and somewhat cheerful. Amid platters of meat loaf, ham, sliced turkey and roast beef, and bowls of spaghetti, green beans and candied yams, and the obligatory macaroni and cheese, Genesis enjoyed catching up with her cousins, swapping stories about Cyrus and reminiscing about good times on the farm.

"Which one of you got chased by the pig?" Tiffany said, laughing at the memory.

Genesis and Kayla pointed to each other.

"It was you, Kayla," Genesis said.

"Genesis, you know you clocked a sprinting record trying to outrun that pig. I was the one who almost went vegetarian after finding out about the chicken."

Genesis nodded. "Right, that was crazy. You absolutely loved that chicken-and-vegetable soup until you learned the bird that tasted so delicious had been running around the yard that afternoon."

"You still ate the soup, though," Tiffany reminded Kayla.

"I couldn't help it. That food was so good. I always hoped Grandpa would marry Miss Margaret."

"Me, too," Genesis agreed. "I loved her cooking."

"Yeah, unfortunately for us, the skills that his other girlfriend Miss Jackie lacked in the kitchen were clearly made up in the bedroom."

"Ooh, stop!" Kayla said, play-punching Tiffany's arm before lowering her voice to a whisper. "I can't unsee that from my imagination!"

The laughter Genesis enjoyed from her cousins' teasing dissipated when she took in a scene across the room. Clarence and Jaxson had their heads together in what looked to be a serious conversation. Clarence's animated gestures suggested being passionate about whatever it was he was sharing. Jaxson's furrowed brow was evidence of his intent listening.

Genesis knew how badly Clarence wanted to sell his father's farm. Jaxson knew her position, but was he really on her side? She watched as he pulled out his phone, punching in keys while Clarence continued speaking. Cleo walked over with his wife and sister-in-law. Jaxson shook Cleo's hand and bowed slightly for the ladies. They conversed quietly until Cleo said something that made all of them laugh and Clarence slapped Jaxson on the back as though they were old pals.

Genesis's eyes narrowed. Standing there, watching him, watching *them*, every interaction she'd had with Jaxson became suspect. How had she allowed her guard to fall, to not remember that the guy now over there conspiring with her cousins was the same one who'd slept with her on a dare, then robbed her brother of a state championship and a glorious pro ball future? What else from her family was he trying to snatch away?

In that moment, the opportunity to find out presented itself. Clarence turned and waved Tiffany and Kayla over. Genesis, hot on their heels, almost led the charge. She forced herself to act nonchalant when inside her blood was on a low simmer. All this supposed wheeling and dealing with the dirt not yet shoveled on Uncle Cyrus's grave. The nerve!

"This is my beautiful daughter, Tiffany," Clarence said, presenting her as though cameras for *The Bachelor* were rolling and the host was nearby. "And my niece, Kayla."

"Nice to meet you," Jaxson said. His expression was appreciative yet respectful. Genesis tried to tell herself she didn't care one way or the other. She did, though.

Damn, damn, damn!

"Kayla is married and has two sons. Tiffany is single, smart and thinking about moving back to Tennessee. Right, Tiff?"

Genesis barely concealed her surprise. At one time she and Tiffany had shared the deepest of secrets, but not a word of this possible move had been uttered.

"I'm thinking about it," Tiffany admitted, looking at Jaxson with a flirty expression on her face. "Being back here and reminiscing has me thinking it might be the right time for a move. Keep the house in the *immediate* family. Pass it on to the next generation when the time comes."

At least a half a dozen sarcastic responses danced on Genesis's tongue. She practiced restraint. She wouldn't remind Clarence about his comment of no one wanting to marry his single, smart daughter, nor bring up the fact that until this moment, Cyrus's "immediate family" had said nothing regarding relocation plans.

Genesis wasn't left unaffected. The immediate-family comment stung more than Tiffany could know. Another reminder that once again she was with a group where she didn't quite fit in. An outsider. Where she wasn't an official or actual member. Not a daughter, but a stepdaughter. Not a niece, but a great-niece. An outsider the way Tiffany would likely feel in the country. In Genesis's mind, her Vegas Strip–loving, club-hopping, lights/camera/action, citified cousin had about as much chance of being happy in Holy Mound as the German shepherd Nipsey had of turning into Garfield the cat.

"I guess you and Genesis will be roommates," she heard Jaxson say, as she refocused on the conversation.

Tiffany turned accusatory eyes toward Genesis. "Are you living there?"

"Only temporarily."

"I didn't know you'd already grabbed a broom and swooped right in."

"Your dad knew," Genesis said, feeling defensive and becoming increasingly angry that she felt that way. "I was at Uncle Cyrus's house when this happened." She held out her leg. "I can't drive right now."

A grunt was Tiffany's response.

She waited for Clarence to cosign her statement. His glare was as hard as Tiffany's. She thought there was empathy in Kayla's eyes, but her cousin stayed quiet. The animosity from them made one thing abundantly clear. The only real family she had in Holy Mound, Tennessee, was no longer there to protect her. She decided to protect herself.

"I'll talk to y'all later."

She walked away without waiting for a response but didn't get far. A hand grasped her arm.

"Genesis."

She stopped at Jaxson's voice behind her. "What do you want?"

"Are you okay?"

"Do I look okay?"

"Look, I apologize if I spoke out of turn. I assumed your cousins knew you were at Cyrus's house."

"You know what they say about people who make assumptions."

"This guy bothering you?" Habari walked up, filled with

the heightened bravado and macho testosterone of a man who'd just turned twenty-one. Genesis noted the added bass to his voice.

"My brother Habari," Genesis offered. "Bari, this is Jax King."

"I know who he is, the fool who stole the championship from my brother and ruined his career."

"Your whole family believes that story?" Jax calmly asked. "And you're all still angry?"

Habari tried to stand taller than his average five-nine height. "You got a problem with that?"

Genesis stepped between them. "Okay, Habari, that's enough." Said even though a part of her had appreciated Habari standing up for their family. There was already enough tension in the air. Clearly, before the service someone had passed around a big bag of argu-mints!

"Jaxson was Uncle Cyrus's neighbor, helped around the farm after he got sick. They were good friends."

The words rolled out of her mouth unbidden. Even as they made their way to the air, Genesis questioned her taking up for this man.

Habari's expression calmed as he lost some of the attitude. "I guess that explains why he's here." He looked at Jaxson. "I would have figured you for more of a West Coast dude. Especially after you got that analyst spot on the Sports Network. Why'd you move back here?"

"Family matters."

Genesis heard that end-of-story punctuation mark. Bam! She would never admit that misery loved company, but it

looked like she wasn't the only one in Holy Mound with
land mines of the bloodline kind. She didn't know much
about Jaxson beyond his connection to football and being
her uncle's neighbor. She wanted to, which was something
she'd rather not think about. When Hazel caught her eye,
Genesis was more than happy to make her exit.

"Habari, come meet another neighbor."

With that, she pulled her brother away and made sure both
of them steered clear of Jaxson for the rest of the afternoon.

The next day, Sunday, Genesis sat at the dining room
table trying to figure out her life. She hadn't worked for several days, and though she'd regularly sent out résumés, she
couldn't seem to buy a job. Next month's rent would just
about clear out her savings. And Lance had flat out told her
moments ago he didn't know when he could pay back the
loan. Hard decisions had to be made.

Borrowing money was out of the question. Her mother
and stepfather could easily afford it, but Genesis wouldn't
ask. When told about Cyrus, Lori had barely reacted to the
news. She felt obligated to let her mother know what she'd
inherited. Lori's only comment was a question. "How much
is it worth?"

Ironic that doing what Clarence wanted would solve a lot
of her immediate woes. The paperwork showed the land and
home to be valued in the low six figures. Split three ways
between her, Clarence and Cleo, it would still leave enough
money to get her life back on track. There was only one
problem. Selling the farm was not what Cyrus wanted. Her
uncle would get the last word.

She wouldn't ask Hank either. He had responsibilities, a fiancée and child, and was doing better than he had in a long time. Most of her friends had little discretionary income. Bottom line? She'd have to figure life out by herself.

The familiar sound of a certain truck interrupted her thoughts.

"Don't these people know how to call first?" she said out loud, though, truth be told, she'd had worse distractions.

She reached the porch, put a hand on her hip and adopted what she thought was an appropriate scowl to show her displeasure. Jaxson slowly unfolded himself out of the cab, offered a quick wave, then retrieved a box from the bed of the truck. He looked all sexy and mysterious with his ball cap, airplane shades and a smile, and Genesis found it hard to hold on to the act. But she tried.

"Have you ever heard of calling before driving over to someone's house?"

"Have you ever heard of the phrase *Do drop in*?"

"What?"

He sauntered by her just as unaffected as you please. "Leave your attitude outside, Hopalong Cassidy, and come in the house. I've got a gift for you."

Did he just? I know he didn't. "Did you just call me…?"

"Hopalong Cassidy? Yes. I did." He laughed as she hopped inside. "You're always copping an attitude with me. I'm trying to get you to lighten up."

He pulled a box cutter out of his pocket and cut the tape. "Your uncle got me watching those old-time Westerns.

Country classics, he called them. *Gunsmoke. Bonanza. The Wild Wild West. Hopalong Cassidy* was one of his favorites."

Genesis knew he told the truth. She didn't even know television used to be shown in black-and-white until visiting her uncle.

"What's that?"

"A security system. I tried to talk Cyrus into getting one years ago. This model comes with five cameras, including one for a doorbell, and motion sensor lights."

"It looks expensive. You shouldn't have bought it. That kind of money won't be in my budget for a while."

"Consider it payment for being an ass the other day, sharing information with your family that you didn't want them to know."

"You didn't have to do that." But he had, and Genesis was touched by the gesture. She couldn't remember the last time Lance or anyone she'd recently dated had done something to help keep her safe.

"I was joking earlier. I wasn't really that angry at you for coming here. I do remember the 'do drop in' kind of casualness out here. When visiting Uncle Cyrus, people were always stopping by."

"I admit it takes getting used to."

"It's actually refreshing. I've lived in my condo for three years and have people living close by that I still don't know."

"Around here everybody knows everybody. But times are hard. The world is changing. Just in case someone you don't know comes around, I want to make sure you're protected."

He wanted to protect her. Genesis's heart fairly swooned

at the words. Men their age seemed more focused on themselves. She'd encouraged Lance to follow his dreams of opening a blues-and-BBQ spot in Little Rock, Arkansas. Had
invested her last dollar to help make it work, along with her
blood, sweat and tears. She knew the restaurant world was a
hard code to crack, but had faith when Lance swore to repay
her. They'd been friends before they became lovers. She
knew he cared. But could he protect her? Would he put her
well-being before his own? With Lance, there was no way to
be sure. But when it came to Jaxson...she knew the answer.

Ten

"I need to grab a few tools," Jaxson said, once he'd removed the myriad of parts that made up the security system and scanned the instructions. "Be right back."

"Shouldn't you be at work?"

Technically, yes. While getting supplies for the business, he'd seen the cameras and bought one. The sunny sky helped shape his decision to stop by and install them. He could see the appreciation in her eyes, maybe even a hint of admiration. But when she opened her mouth, suspicion tumbled out. She did a good enough job of trying to stir up a cloud when the sun was shining. He decided to keep things light.

"I am working. Later I'll be installing this same system on the bungalow we're flipping in Memphis. If it makes you feel better, consider this the pro bono stuff I do to stay on good terms with God. And Granville."

A smile chased away Genesis's doubt face. He loved it when she smiled. It hinted at the sensitive side she tried hard to hide, reminded him of the young woman he'd met at the party. She'd smiled like that. Jaxson took in those soft-looking up-turned kissers and suppressed a groan.

"The God thing I'd question, but Granville, I can believe."

Their laughter further lightened the mood in the room. Satisfied, Jaxson retrieved his tools and went to work. He continued to add up the qualities about Genesis that he liked—her practicality, sense of humor, love and loyalty to her uncle, and overall, the way she made him feel. That she was gorgeous only highlighted the other attributes. He pondered this while placing cameras on the porch, above the back door, atop the shed roof and in a tree that faced the driveway. All the while he was überaware of Genesis sitting at the dining room table wearing an oversize hoodie and a pair of baggy shorts she'd somehow fashioned from what looked like a cutoff pair of Cyrus's long johns.

Earlier, he'd taken in the sight of her sipping coffee with those incredible lips. Had forced his eyes to not linger on the leg being elevated by a chair beside her. The muscled shin covered by smooth, soft skin. The dip just below the knee that he could imagine licking. The thigh that suggested a memorable journey to other, more private places.

He told himself it meant nothing when she turned on a smooth jazz station and a saxophone oozed notes like wet kisses into the atmosphere. He recognized the song. A classic by Norah Jones. He banished the thought that he was on her mind as the singer encouraged her lyrical lover to come away, focusing instead on the chance that smooth jazz songs and old-school music was something they had in common. Though the weather was a bit chilly, he felt relieved to go outside and mount the cameras. Better to focus on something tangible, like hanging security cameras, rather than a fantasy like Genesis, a woman he'd likely never be intimate with again.

When he returned inside, Genesis was in the kitchen. Her crutches were propped up against the countertop filled with ham slices, salad, cheese and condiments.

"Would you like something to eat?" she asked, surprising him yet again.

Yes, he would, and not anything in the kitchen.

"I don't have any peanut butter and jelly but know my way around a ham sandwich."

He told himself the reference to the meal he'd prepared meant nothing, but the comment touched his heart nonetheless.

"The church generously gave me a nice basket of leftovers from the repast. There was enough food to feed all of Memphis."

"Miss Hazel and those church mothers throw down in the kitchen! I'm good, though. Before coming here, I ate a big breakfast but could use a bottle of water."

"Cold or room temp?"

"Cold, please."

She reached for her crutches.

"Wait. I'll get it." He walked over to the fridge and pulled out a bottle. "Good thing the mothers helped out. Other than their basket, I don't see very much food."

"Stop being nosy."

"Wouldn't want you to starve. Come over here in a week and find a skeleton rocking on the porch."

He should have been gone five minutes ago, but once again, the pull of his attraction kept him planted on Cyrus's worn linoleum tiles. He opened the water and took a healthy swig.

"Have you heard from your cousins?"

"Cleo called. He said he reached out to see how I was doing but managed to also ask if I'd spoken again with the lawyer." She spread mustard on one slice of bread, mayo on the other. "I hadn't, which made for a very brief conversation."

"Sounds like good cop, bad cop."

"I didn't think about it like that. You could be right."

He watched as she built a masterpiece, using the salad in the sandwich with slices of ham and cheese.

"Excuse me, but this is breakfast." She cut the sandwich in half and took a bite.

"Help yourself. Here, let me take it to the table for you."

"Thanks."

He set the plate in front of her, next to a partially filled glass of juice, then leaned against the wall.

"Thought you had somewhere to be."

"I've got a couple minutes. FYI, the electrician will be out sometime this week to hook the wires to the pole. The system itself is wireless, but it has to be plugged in at the base. Oh, and you need to get those front steps fixed ASAP, especially with you on crutches. Those planks should have been replaced years ago. I'm surprised Cyrus didn't break a leg."

"I'll add that to my growing to-do list."

"Put it somewhere near the top."

"Okay, boss" was her sarcastic reply. "Dang, I forgot my chips."

"Where are they?"

"In my *almost empty* cabinets."

"Ha!" He'd rarely catered to a woman this way, but something about the damsel in sprained ankle distress had him bringing out and buckling on his armor. "Here you go."

She eyed him as she opened the bag. "Thanks for the DDI."

He cocked a brow.

"Do drop in. That's my customized abbreviation."

"I like it."

Genesis plopped against the dining room chair. "I never dreamed I'd be living the country life."

"Things could be worse. You could be here all alone with no one caring about you. No one calling. No one stopping by. Even Nipsey turning up his tail and moving to my place. Is that what you want?"

Her laughter, he decided, was like a perfect set of chimes letting you know the wind was blowing at just the right speed.

"Well, put like that, I guess I'm grateful for people who feel they can stop by whenever they feel like it."

"Exactly." Said in a way that mirrored her response when

it was explained that calling her Gen was a privilege, not a right.

"I can't stand you!" she deadpanned. But her eyes were warm.

"You're welcome."

There was a companionable silence as she focused on food and he focused on her.

"I want to ask you something," she said.

He nodded.

"At Uncle Cyrus's funeral, what were you and Clarence talking about?"

Jaxson chuckled. "Your cousin was low-key trying to become my father-in-law. And the farm, of course." He paused, wondering how much of their conversation he should share. His loyalty was to Genesis, not Clarence. He decided to tell it all.

"He told me about Cyrus leaving you the farm, and that the family questioned his mental health for making that decision."

"You spent time with my uncle. What do you think?"

"I played chess with Cyrus a few weeks before he died. Wasn't anything wrong with his mind."

"Did you tell that to Clarence?"

Jaxson nodded. "I told him in no uncertain terms that Cyrus seemed fine to me."

"I don't know why they're in such a hurry to sell, to the point of offering up his firstborn."

"That didn't matter. No shade to Tiffany, but I'm not interested."

"Is it because…? Never mind." She sighed and looked away.

"No, go ahead. You want to know my status."

"Your personal life is none of my concern."

"I'm not involved with anyone right now—not seriously, anyway. Haven't had a committed relationship since my daughter, Jazz, was born four years ago. Thanks to her mother, and another betrayal, it's hard for me to trust."

"What happened?"

"Long story. But since we're not friends yet, I can't tell you."

He watched different emotions skitter across Genesis's face. "It's not fair to judge us all based on a couple bad experiences."

"Probably not. But that's where I'm at. Are you dating anyone?"

"My personal life is none of your concern."

Her nonanswer was an answer. If she was dating, or had a man, Jaxson believed he would have met him by now.

He spent the rest of the day working and thinking of Genesis. That night found him at the bar section of Holy Moly, nursing a bourbon neat and going over conversations with her in his head.

The regular weekend bartender, a young blonde who reminded him of a girl he'd briefly dated in high school, came over wiping down the bar with one hand and holding a menu with the other.

"Figured you might want some wings or a couple sliders to settle down that alcohol."

"Not a bad idea." He reached for the menu even though he ate at the restaurant enough to almost know it by heart.

"I don't think I've tried the fish tacos."

"That's a new item."

"Any good?"

"Delicious but not something I'd recommend with brown liquor. Plus, that's your second beverage. You need grease." She dug a dipper into the ice and filled a glass. "And water."

Jaxson pushed away the tumbler of bourbon and reached for the water. "I'll take an order of sliders, half a dozen spicy wings and home fries."

"Now we're talking." They both laughed. "Coming right up."

Jaxson downed half the water and made small talk with the couple sitting next to him. The later it got and the more patrons poured into the place, the more he questioned whether placing the order was a good idea. He usually stayed away from the square on weekends, when it got taken over by high schoolers, Memphis travelers and every single person within a thirty-mile radius. Just as he was about to make his order to go, a familiar face entered the bar.

Susan saw him and made a beeline to the bar.

"Hey, stranger!"

She gave him a hug and a kiss on the lips. He pulled back without thinking.

"Whoa, it's like that, huh?"

"I didn't mean... Sorry, you caught me off guard."

"It hasn't been that long since we've gotten together." Susan motioned to the bartender. "Longer than I'd like, but not long enough to forget me. Right?"

"How could that ever happen? You're unforgettable."

"Yeah, said like a man who's trying to distract from his secrets. Like who you've been spending time with these past couple weeks."

"Why can't I just be busy flipping houses and being a good uncle and long-distance dad?"

"Because I know how much you like sex. Thank you," she said to the bartender who gave her a drink menu. Scanning the choices, she casually added, "I hear there's a new girl in town. I hear she's your neighbor."

"You've got big ears."

"And an even bigger nose for sniffing out juicy gossip."

Jaxson gave Susan the side-eye. "Who'd you talk to, Miss Hazel?"

"I went one better. Her hairdresser."

Jaxson pulled back for a more thorough look. "That's what's different about you."

"Thought I'd add a few extensions again." She twirled in the chair. "You like it?"

"It looks nice. A lot of money to pay for information you could have gotten for free."

"It was an informative beauty-shop visit, but not all about you. I'm here to meet a date."

Jaxson raised a brow. "Seriously? On a Sunday?"

"Yep. After hearing all about Mr. Perry's cute niece, the bull incident and you playing doctor to heal her boo-boo, and even more being evasive when I asked about it point-blank, I figured it was time for me to stop settling for benefits and go for a whole package."

"Wow, you really do know everything. There's nothing

going on there, but I'm sorry for not coming clean when you asked. Forgive me?"

"Always."

Conversation paused as the bartender delivered Jaxson's food and took Susan's drink order.

"You said there's nothing going on. Would you like there to be?"

"Maybe."

"Meaning definitely. What is it that has you so interested?"

Jaxson chuckled. "Probably the fact that she can't stand me."

Later he'd conveniently forget admitting he was interested at all. While munching on his dinner, he reminded Susan about his and Genesis's shared history, minus the one-night stand, and why she looked at him as an enemy.

"I remember that championship game," she said.

"Were you there?"

"Yes, and if you'll remember, I had a traitorous crush on Hank Hunter. It almost got me kicked off the drill team. In fact, that night I… Hold on." Susan checked a text on her phone. "My date is pulling up in ten minutes. It's crowded. I'd better grab a table."

"There's a seat." Jaxson tipped his head toward a nearby bar stool. "Why don't you invite him over so I can check him out, make sure he's a good match."

"Probably for the same reason you've tried to keep your neighbor hidden. Hey, if you're into her, go for it." Susan slid off the bar stool and grabbed her drink. "Wish me luck."

Jaxson finished the sliders, polished off the wings and was casually wiping his hands on a napkin when Susan's date came in. Bald head, athletic build, not bad-looking and, thankfully, no one he knew. She definitely had a type.

He reached into his pocket, peeled off some bills and tossed them on the counter. A few people recognized him as he snaked his way through the unusually thick Sunday night crowd. He was cordial but kept it moving until he reached the cool springtime air.

Not yet ready to drive to his empty abode, he began walking around the square, peering into shop windows, enjoying the music spilling out from the bars. At the corner near his truck, a street vendor was in the process of closing a cart selling flowers and knickknacks. He eyed a bouquet similar to the color of the hoodie Genesis had worn earlier that day. The nice arrangement in a crystal vase would brighten up Cyrus's old wooden table. Still, he quickly nixed the idea. Genesis would probably look for an ulterior motive or feel it an inappropriate gesture. The bottom of the mobile cart was metal and covered with magnets. He scanned one with a message that made him laugh out loud.

He immediately pulled it off the metal. "I'll take it."

As it turned out, Jaxson had a type, too. Her name was Genesis.

Eleven

Genesis threw back the covers, unable to sleep and unwilling to take a pain pill to aid rest along. The pain was becoming manageable, felt mostly when she moved too fast or tried to walk without a crutch. She reached for it and maneuvered from the bedroom to the living room. At the time it sounded hokey, something she wouldn't be caught dead doing, but when Hazel called to check up on her, maybe she should have accepted the invite to join the church ladies for bingo night. Or her brother Habari's offer to come get her. Hanging with either of them couldn't have been more boring than the way she'd spent her evening—watching an unfunny romantic comedy that took ninety-three minutes away from her life that she could never get back. Habari had suggested he might come spend the weekend. Genesis knew it would only take a cute woman or a jamming party for him to forget all about big sis. As it was, it felt like the walls were closing in.

She walked to the window and peered into the darkness. It was so quiet, even lonely, in the country. At times she loved the serenity but at others she missed city noises, loud neighbors and the occasional sound of a car speeding down the boulevard. Even more, she missed the company of a man and was only mildly surprised when the one who came to mind was Jaxson, not Lance. Their engagements were cantankerous but also lively and fun. It was getting harder to remember she didn't like him, and even more difficult to justify why.

With her imagination beginning to fashion things that went bump in the night, she turned away from the darkness and decided to make a cup of chamomile tea. The water had just begun boiling when she noticed headlights turning into her uncle's drive.

Jaxson? The thumping bass of a hip-hop track nixed that idea. In the times she'd been around his truck, his music was never that loud. It was her brother Habari, a thought confirmed seconds later when he banged on the screen door.

"Coming!" She unlocked the inner door and then the screen. "Ooh, you smell like a whole blunt, like I could light a match to you and get high."

"Wasn't me. It was the fellas riding around with me. I was the designated driver."

"Yes, and I'm Meghan Markle married to the prince."

She locked the door and followed him into the kitchen, where he was scanning the scant contents of her fridge.

"You don't have a beer in this joint?"

Genesis remembered Jaxson had taken care of the last

bottle when installing the security system. "What you see is what you get."

He reluctantly pulled out a cola. "Dang, sis. You've got to do better." He walked into the living room, plopped on the couch and reached for the remote.

"Thanks for coming to visit, Habari. I didn't think you would." She sat on the couch beside him. "Given how many women you usually juggle, I appreciate the sacrifice."

"How's the foot?"

"Ankle. Healing."

"Still can't drive?"

Genesis shook her head.

"You're not working?"

"Can't make cash if I can't DoorDash."

A reminder that once again she needed to keep on Lance about repaying the loan. It was time for him to give her something, even if he had to borrow money from someone else to do it. Given the circumstances, it wasn't too much to ask. People like the friends around her had been robbing Peter to pay Paul for most of their adult lives.

"How long are you planning to stay out here? It's spooky."

"Hopefully not too much longer. I just had a security system installed. It will get turned on next week."

"That's good to know. I'm not trying to scare you, but seriously, do you think being out here by yourself is a good idea?"

"I have protection."

"You talking about that mangy dog? Earlier tonight, I saw a squirrel that looked older than he did outrun him."

"Careful how you talk about Nipsey. His bite is worse than his bark. There's nothing mangy about him. When I said protection, I meant guns."

"Girl, shut up. You know you're not down with the Second Amendment."

"Maybe not, but I'm learning to use a Glock 19 and a Remington shotgun."

"Damn, sis. I didn't know you were packing like that!"

"I'm not, silly. Uncle Cyrus was. The trunk beneath the glass your feet are resting on contains an arsenal."

"Word?" Habari moved his feet and reached for the glass.

"Please don't mess with them, brother. Not tonight, okay? I'd rather not have them around at all, but knowing I do makes me feel safer."

"No worries. I can check them out later." He sat back, placed his foot back on the table. "Where are you practicing, a firing range? And how are you doing that with a busted ankle?"

"One of the neighbors is helping me."

Habari frowned. "That neighbor wouldn't happen to be Jax King, would it?"

"Why would you think it was him?" Genesis asked, giving off a vibe that suggested Habari had hit the nail on the head.

Habari snickered. "Because of your reaction. I sure hope you don't end up with that dude again."

"You don't have to worry about that."

"Good, because it was bad enough when him and Hank were in high school. Now it would be even worse. Guys like him are used to smashing their cake and eating it, too. Along with the cookies and everything else on the dessert menu."

"I didn't know who he was when we got together, if you'll remember. After finding out, I never met up with him again."

Habari shrugged. "That's water under the bridge of a dried-up river. Nobody cares about him."

"That's not how you acted at Uncle Cyrus's funeral."

"Yeah, I was feeling myself. Probably overreacted."

That her brother admitted to ego was impressive. The boy was turning into a man. "Move over. I need to put my leg up."

Habari reached for a throw pillow and helped elevate her ankle.

"Ah, that's better. Thank you. Now, tell me what happened."

"When?"

"Back in the day. With Hank and Jaxson. I know he sabotaged Hank's chances for a college scholarship, and I hated him for it. But remember, I was living in Charlotte and never knew the details."

Habari shrugged. "I don't either. The story Hank tells is different from the play I remember seeing that night."

This got Genesis's attention. "What did you see?"

"Two determined competitors going up for the ball."

That was what Jaxson said. She honestly didn't remember. Everything had happened so fast that night, the hit followed by brief yet complete pandemonium. While her brother lay writhing on the ground, Jaxson ran the ball in for the touchdown that won his team the state championship.

"I was in the stands. Hank's viewpoint was different. He's the one you need to ask about it." Habari reached for the remote. "And hate the dude because he's an asshole, not because of something you know nothing about."

Genesis looked at Habari with a sense of respect. "Are you my little brother or my guru?"

"Both."

The two half watched a crime show and talked until Genesis became sleepy. She gave Habari the couch and slept in the guest room. For the rest of the night, Habari's words haunted her. Which was why the next morning her first call was to Hank. It was just after seven thirty. Oh, well. If she couldn't sleep, then her brother couldn't either.

"Gen?" Hank's groggy voice suggested that he had indeed been in dreamland.

"What happened between you and Jaxson?"

"Jax King?"

"Yes."

"Back in high school?"

Genesis began to second-guess the importance of calling so early. Or at all. "Yeah. Habari came over last night. He said I should ask you what really happened."

"Hold on."

She heard him mumbling, presumably to his partner Xenia, then a few more sounds that suggested he was getting out of bed.

"Okay, sis. What's going on? Why are you waking me up to ask about this dude?"

She filled him in on her fall, staying at her uncle's house,

Jaxson's neighborly interactions and the conversation she'd had with Habari. "I feel disloyal for liking him," she explained. "But it's hard not to when he's been so helpful and kind. I guess what I'm saying is…he may indeed be an arrogant asshole, but from what I've seen, he's not a bad guy."

There was a long pause before her brother asked, "Are y'all fucking?"

"Hank! What the hell?"

"Don't act shocked. You sleeping with the enemy has happened before."

Genesis paused to gather her thoughts and quell the rapidly growing indignation inside her.

"Hank, trust me when I tell you that I didn't call to talk about my sex life. I called to get some clarity about Jaxson breaking your arm that night."

"What about it?"

"How'd it happen? Did he grab it, twist it? What did he do?"

"I don't remember."

"An event that changed the whole trajectory of your life… and you don't remember."

Hank remained silent. Genesis frowned, as an uncomfortable theory began forming in her head.

"Habari said, from what he saw, both of you went up for the ball, but admitted his viewpoint was from the stands, not on the ground, like yours."

"I don't even know why this shit matters, Gen."

His flippancy pissed Genesis all the way off. That and what her roiling gut now seemed to be telling her, that the hell her family put her through for being with Jaxson might be based on a lie.

She spoke calmly, clearly, enunciating every word. "Did Jaxson somehow purposely break your arm, or was what happened an unfortunate accident?"

"Either way, it ruined my chances of playing pro ball!"

"That's not what I asked."

His silence screamed.

"When you found out I'd slept with Jaxson, you went off on me, remember? Blamed me for not knowing who he was. Made me feel like a whore because I didn't have a full-blown got damn history on the man I'd slept with."

"Was I lying?"

"That's not the point, and you know it. I was grown and on my own with the right to do whatever the hell I wanted. You were still in high school. I was too upset to pay attention to everything back then, especially when what happened got back to Mom and the whole family turned against me."

"What's this all about, Gen? Are you wanting to date him again?"

"We never dated. And now, like then, my love life is none of your business."

"Back in the day, it was my business. He only slept with you to get back at me!"

Hank's comment slapped her in the face. After they'd slept together, Genesis thought about the guy she remembered as "Jack" and sometimes wished she'd given in to his pleas to exchange numbers. That night, though, she rationalized not doing it. She'd moved to Charlotte and had her eye on a businessman who lived there she'd recently met. What happened at the party was supposed to stay at the party. She'd had no intention of spending two nights with what was supposed to be a one-night stand.

The day after the championship game, everything changed. She learned that Jack was actually Jaxson King. Her brother's rival. The enemy. By the time she made her next trip home, a rumor had traveled from Holy Mound to Memphis. Jaxson had slept with her on a dare, and because she was Hank's sister. That weekend, she saw him at a popular mall. He'd broken away from his friends and strolled over to the table where she sat.

"Hey, Genny, you're looking good."

The glare she gave him could have caused spontaneous combustion.

Jaxson had the nerve to act confused. "What?"

"Seriously? You're going to stand there and act like you didn't know."

"Know what?"

Genesis huffed, exasperated. "Hank Hunter is my brother."

"For real? Genny, I promise you I didn't know."

"You broke his arm."

Jaxson held up his hands. "No, I didn't. We were both focused on the ball and collided. I hate what happened, but it wasn't my fault."

"That's not how Hank feels."

"But it's the truth." After a pause, he continued. "It sounds like y'all are blaming me for what happened. Hank knows that getting injured comes with the territory. It's unfortunate, and like I said, I hate that it happened. But any one of us could have gotten hurt that night. It's part of the game."

He took a step forward. She stepped back.

He sighed, dropped his head, then eyed her with an intensity that made her body react and remember. The deep, thorough kisses...and so much more.

"I hope this doesn't mean you and I can't be friends. As important as that game was, I kept thinking about you. If possible, I'd really like to see you again."

Genesis listened to the sincere-sounding words coming out of his mouth, watched the same thick, well-formed lips that had given her so much pleasure. Once again, the act was impressive. She almost believed him. Then she remembered what she'd heard. The dare or bet or whatever that quite likely had fueled his flirtation. Her brother, and how the broken arm changed his future situation. The family fallout. Jax King was as electrifying in the bedroom as he was on the field, but there would be no follow-up fuck. She lifted her chin, looked into deep brown bedroom eyes and stated clearly and emphatically, "Go straight to hell."

The next day, there had been another family blowup, a huge confrontation. She returned to North Carolina. Didn't speak to them for two months. Later she read that Jaxson had accepted a scholarship to USC. She began dating the businessman. When that relationship fizzled out, she moved back to Memphis, reconnected with her good friend Lance. She'd definitely never meant for them to date. Then, after almost a year of celibacy and a night of partying, it had just happened. Because they were such good friends, she thought it might work. For a while, it did.

But loving and being in love were two different things. Their friendship survived. The romance didn't. And here she was.

Genesis heard the sound of tires on gravel. She frowned, threw back the covers and hobbled over to the window. Her mouth dropped.

"Hank, I've got to go."

"Okay, but, Gen—"

Their conversation could be finished later. It looked like she had about two minutes to throw something over her naked body or give the mayors the shock of their lives. In haste, she hopped over to Cyrus's room and grabbed his plaid robe from a hook on the back of the door. A knock sounded, just as she tied the sash.

"I'm coming, Miss Hazel!"

She opened the door. Hazel carried a casserole dish. Behind her, Granville held two bags of groceries. Beyond them, in the back of a truck even bigger than Jaxson's or the one Granville had driven the other time he came over, was what looked like an ATV.

"Good morning."

"Excuse us for dropping by so early." Hazel lifted the casserole dish. "May we come in?"

"Of course." Genesis recognized the value of a DDI. The neighbors had unknowingly rescued her from an unpleasant conversation and distracted her from fixating on exactly what knowing the truth meant.

She stepped back, then closed the door behind them. Hazel sailed down the hallway like it wasn't the first time. Given her uncle's lack of cooking skills, it probably wasn't. Granville followed dutifully behind her. Genesis did the same. They reached the kitchen. Hazel placed the dish on the stove.

"I told Granville last night, that girl down there needs some help. Cooped up in this house. No way to get around. About to worry me to death. We were preparing to eat before going to volunteer at the church. Pulled out this big ole casserole and thought of you. You hungry?"

Without waiting for an answer, she continued. "This dish was one of Cyrus's favorites and my husband's, too. Easy to make, I can assure you."

She lifted the lid. A bouquet of aromas escaped. Genesis's mouth watered.

"What is it?"

"A breakfast casserole made with frozen hash browns. Didn't know whether you liked sausage or bacon, so I used 'em both. Same with the cheese—American, Swiss and cheddar. Go on and put some clothes on while I dish up the plates."

Genesis went into her uncle's closet, warmed by her neighbors' thoughtfulness. They'd not only rescued her from Hank's excuses, but also from Cyrus's lean pantry and being left stranded by Habari's late-night rendezvous. She'd planned to ask him to give her a ride to her place to pick up some clothes and go to a grocery store but had awakened to a text that said he'd left "to help one of his boys." In the middle of the night? She didn't think so. More likely he drove straight to a booty call. Genesis may have been born at night but it wasn't last night.

She went into the guest room and pulled on one of the maxis she'd ordered after Cyrus's funeral. Because it was chilly and the maxi was sleeveless, she pulled the robe back on as well. Once done, she walked out to find Miss Hazel placing the last plate on the table.

"Sit down, child. We bought juice. Do you want orange or apple?"

"Orange is fine." Genesis sat. "Where's your husband?"

"Out there getting your ride off the truck."

"My… Ma'am?"

She returned with two large glasses of orange juice. Heading back for the third, she said, "You need to be able to get around down here. One of our church members had that." She nodded toward the window. "I call it a scooter. The gas and brake are operated by hand."

"Really?"

The door opened and closed.

"Come on, Granville! Your food is getting cold!" Hazel yelled as though they were in a mansion, instead of a home boasting just over a thousand feet.

"Lewis, our church member and head usher, found out about them when an accident temporarily paralyzed that poor soul from the waist down. God heard our fervent prayers, though, and granted a miracle. Lewis was back walking in six short months. Went back to work as a truck driver, a job he has to this day."

They washed hands, bowed heads for prayer and dug into one of the best simple breakfasts Genesis had ever tasted. Raisin bread, another first, rounded out the delicious meal.

Granville belched, pushed back his chair and stood. "C'mon, now. I've got about five minutes to show you how to operate that contraption out there before me and the missus have to be at church."

The three of them went outside. Genesis learned the jeep-like car was a UTV, a utility terrain vehicle. In less than five minutes, she was ready to ride. She didn't even return to the house. When the McCormicks pulled off, she waved goodbye, then set off to finish the adventure interrupted by rain and a bull. It was time to clear her mind and reconnect with the country. It was time to check out her land!

Twelve

Jaxson hopped in his truck and set out down the back road to Cyrus's place. He'd been in Memphis all morning finishing a project with Blake, then stopped by the hardware store in Holy Mound for a couple of specific items this store carried. Their latest flip was 95 percent complete. Even though it was early afternoon, he was ready to celebrate. He remembered the days when that would involve Kobe steak, Maine lobster, caviar and expensive champagne. Instead, a box of tacos from his favorite food truck occupied the seat beside him. On the floor of the cab was a bottle of wine and a six-pack.

He thought about the irony or maybe serendipity of working with Blake and how different it was from the last time he'd ventured into real estate. In Phoenix he'd been the celebrity endorser of a project that promised great, affordable homes for deserving families. What followed their trusting investments was a travesty equal to all-out theft. Some people lost homes put up as collateral. Others, their life savings.

Jaxson had had no idea what was happening until a detective knocked on his door. After finding out, he'd felt horrible about his unknowing participation. He vowed to never again have his name associated with anything without proper and thorough research. Thankfully, that was how Blake liked to do business—everything out in the open and aboveboard.

He turned up the volume on a Willie Jones joint and tapped the wheel in time with the rhythm. Country music had been one of many things that connected him to his grandpa. When Dixon died and Jaxson moved into the house, he rediscovered that love through his grandfather's old-school collection—Willie Nelson, Charlie Pride, Glen Campbell, Patsy Cline, Loretta Lynn, and anything by Johnny and June. There were even a few sounds from the '80s and '90s thrown into the mix, probably courtesy of some of the younger men who'd helped Dixon while Jaxson was away. Since returning to Holy Mound, Jaxson had discovered some faves of his own. Willie Jones, with his unique style of country soul, was one of them.

Jaxson pressed on the gas, enjoyed the way his truck tackled and conquered the dirt road. A flash of color caught the corner of his eye. He slowed before turning to check out the movement. Thought about driving across the field to investigate, but the smell of grilled meat and fresh tortillas helped change his mind. He'd take a gander, Dixon-speak, before returning home. Once he'd checked on Genesis.

After pulling in next to the Kia, he reached for the tacos, opened the door and bounded up the steps. The front door was open. He hollered out through the screen.

"Genesis!"

All was quiet inside. No TV. No music. Maybe she was sleeping.

He rapped on the wood. "Genesis!"

Remembering how pain pills made her sleep, he tried the screen and found it unlocked. He walked in.

"Gen, where you at?"

He set the tacos on the trunk in the living room, then continued down the hall. He checked the room to his right, then continued to the end of the hall and the master bedroom. Cyrus's room. The door was closed. He knocked. No answer. He eased the door open. The presence of Cyrus assailed him. For a moment, he stood there, taking it in. He could almost hear Cyrus's voice.

"Rest easy, Pops."

He closed the door and went to the third bedroom. It was empty but looked like where Genesis slept. Jaxson became concerned. Where could she be? He pulled out his phone, about to panic, then realized the obvious. Someone must've come to get her. He should have called. Oh, well. Wouldn't be the first time he'd devoured a taco-truck family meal by himself.

Back outside, he was just about to get in his pickup when he heard the sound of a revving engine. He looked up to see an ATV cutting across Cyrus's yard. He searched his mind for whose kid this was, and how they'd gotten through the fence. He set the bag on the truck's hood, then began walking toward the vehicle steadily coming his way. He squinted his eyes as it neared him.

Well, I'll be damned.

Gen.

She reached and passed him. He turned in full curiosity mode. How was she driving that thing?

She stopped near the steps. He grabbed the bag off the hood and walked over.

"Hey, there."

"Hey."

Her greeting was subdued. He let it pass. She reached for her crutch.

"Looks like someone's doing better."

"Yeah." She paused and tapped the hand controls he hadn't noticed.

"Ah. Nice. Great idea." He opened the door and helped her out of the vehicle. "Was that you I saw by the pine trees?"

She nodded, then slowly took the steps and crossed the porch.

Puzzled by her mood, Jaxson walked to the other side of his cab, retrieved the beer and the wine, then used those pro footballer hands to expertly carry it all into the house.

Genesis had sat on the living room couch, eyeing him with an expression he couldn't quite identify. "What's all that?"

He set everything down on the trunk and sat down, too. He was careful to not encroach on her personal space. She wasn't being her usual fiery self. Something had happened. Something was on her mind.

"Lunch. I brought enough for you."

"I appreciate it, but thanks to my first set of DDIs, I'm completely full."

"Let me guess. The mayors."

Genesis nodded.

He reached for a beer. "Granville and Hazel finally made you official, huh?"

"I guess."

"Oh, for sure. That's what happened. Their coming by is like christening your home. *Now* you're a part of the valley clan."

He pulled out the bottle of wine. "Would you like a glass?"

"Not right now."

"Are you sure? I'm celebrating."

"What?"

"I recently made my partnership with Blake official." He unscrewed the cap. "We're just about finished with our first flip under the new company."

"Congratulations."

He stopped, the bottle halfway to his lips.

"You okay?"

She shrugged. "Lot on my mind."

"Your first time seeing the land since Cyrus passed?"

"Yeah."

"Remember those pine trees I saw you by? That grove forms the boundaries for our properties on that side. Surprised you were out that far."

"My Randy radar was on high alert."

"That explains it. How far did you go?"

"I saw a pond that I didn't remember. Very peaceful atmosphere and a nice addition to the farm."

"I noticed it when leasing the land out. Cyrus said it had been dried up for years. I asked if he wanted it filled and restocked, one of many projects we worked on together. It's kept us supplied with bass and catfish nearly year-round."

Again, that look. "You fish."

"Yep. A requirement if you live in the country. Along with the acceptance of DDIs."

Genesis failed to respond to his attempt at humor. "Are you sure you're okay?" he asked again.

"Not exactly. I found out something today that was rather upsetting."

"Want to talk about it?"

She looked at him a long moment, then looked away. "No."

Jaxson thoughtfully sipped his beer. Sometimes silence was all the room people needed to share what was on their mind. A few seconds went by. Then a few more. The tacos remained untouched.

"The last six months have been hectic," she said, her eyes to the floor. "My job downsized. After searching unsuccessfully to find new employment, I decided to take a risk and invest in a new business venture. Took the time off to help them get off the ground, and began DoorDashing for a little extra income. The money was supposed to be repaid in thirty days. I'm still waiting for it."

"What kind of business is it?"

"A restaurant-slash-lounge. A blues music theme featuring live bands on the weekend. The kitchen specializes in wings, offering like more than a dozen different varieties. The concept looked really good on paper. Great corner location. Easy freeway access. Catchy name. I bought into the dream."

"Is it in Memphis?"

"Little Rock. It's called BB Wings."

"A play off of the blues great BB King. Very creative."

"I think so, too. They chose Little Rock because, unlike in Memphis, there wasn't another business exactly like it in the city. People who've visited have left good reviews. Honestly, I think in time it will catch on. The question is whether the owners can sustain it until that happens."

"The restaurant industry is one of the toughest markets to break into. I know a few players who stepped into that field thinking their name would bring in easy money. All of their spots closed in less than three years."

"Gee, thanks."

"I apologize. Those are the facts, but maybe you didn't need to hear them right now."

Jaxson wanted to ask how much she'd invested but heard her likely "none of your business" answer float through his mind. He wasn't a wealthy man, but he wasn't poor either. If Genesis needed financial help, he'd jump in without hesitation and with no strings attached.

"Do you need money?"

She glanced at him, then away. "I can take care of myself."

"That's not what I asked. Life is filled with ups and downs. Everyone needs help now and then."

"That's true. Life has a way of working itself out."

"That's also true. Thing about it is, you can choose to be a participant or a spectator. The latter tend to go with the flow and react to whatever happens. Participants are creators who shape their own destiny or at the very least give it a damn good try."

From Genesis, no comment.

"Hey, what're you doing for the rest of the day?"

She shrugged.

"Why don't you let me get you out of this house? Take you wherever you want to go. Have you been back to Memphis?"

"Not yet."

"Would you like me to drive you home?"

She looked him squarely in the eye and smiled. "Actually, I'd like that very much."

While Genesis exchanged the flannel robe she wore over a maxi for the warm-up top he'd given her, Jaxson wrapped up the uneaten tacos, beer and wine to take with them. Then they hit the road.

Jaxson could tell that something about Genesis and the way she viewed him had shifted, and that the change was likely the reason for her earlier mood. On the way to Memphis, she lightened up, returned to her more playful self. He tuned in to a station playing songs from their high school era, which brought out lots of reminiscing and seat dancing. About halfway to their destination, a song came on that shifted the mood again. A slow-grooving love song that conveyed the sizzling sexual undertones that Jaxson felt between them. He sang along, as if to her. She flirted, subtly, but enough to make him comfortable enough to flirt back. This shifting dynamic happened organically. Effortlessly.

Jaxson's attraction to Genesis deepened. Being with her was fun and easy.

By the time they reached the condo, kissing the luscious lips that had sung along with those sexy lyrics was the only thing on Jaxson's mind. As soon as they were inside her place and closed the door, he decided to do something about it.

He kissed her. Then waited. Genesis looked into his eyes, hesitated for only a second and then kissed him back—opened her mouth and slashed her tongue against his lips. What else could he do but welcome the wet tip, to suck her into his mouth and give in to the moment? What was happening felt not only right but inevitable. She was a perfect fit in his arms.

"I want to do more than kiss you," he whispered, his breath hot and wet against her ear.

She stilled. Jaxson silently cursed himself. He'd gone too far, too fast. "I'm sorry, Gen—"

"Do you have condoms?"

"Yes."

She stepped back, her look one of daring as she looked him squarely in the eyes. "Then do it."

He was more than up to the challenge. "Take your clothes off."

"Let's go to the bedroom."

"No, here. Now."

He pulled the button-down shirt she'd earlier admired over his head, then stepped out of his shoes. His jeans quickly followed. Then a T-shirt and briefs. Watching him strip, Genesis did the same. She pulled off the warm-up top, then slowly eased both spaghetti straps down each arm. Impatient, Jaxson took it from there. He slowly pulled the stretchy fabric down her curvy body, kissing parts of exposed skin along the way. Kneeling put his face directly in line with her thong-covered pussy. He buried his head in its delicious scent, kissed the lips and swept his tongue along the slit. Genesis moaned. Her nails dug into his shoulders.

"Ow." The moan was low but audible.

He stopped immediately. "You okay?"

"My ankle."

Jaxson immediately swept her up and walked them to the living room. He laid her on the couch and was about to finish what he'd started when she surprised him by sliding off the cushions and onto her knees.

Oh, shit.

"What about your ankle?"

She reached out and curled her fingers around his hardening dick. "It's okay if I'm not standing up."

Stroking the soft skin covering his hardened sex, Genesis winked. She tickled his nuts and smiled when he hissed. His hands sank into her hair, gently coaxing her toward his desire. But…um… Not. Quite. Yet. She placed her hands on each side of him, slid them around to his tight ass and squeezed. His dick bobbed up and down with a mind of its own, stroking her cheek. She licked the hair covering his groin, and the sensitive skin near his thigh.

"Damn, Gen. Got. Damn!"

She nipped the tip of his rock-hard shaft. His fingers held her hair tighter. She sucked him into her mouth, kissing, licking, nibbling his meat. Both hands ran up and down the sides of him while she took him in as far as she could, slowly pulled back until only his tip was between her teeth, then eased her lips back down. His hips began moving to her rhythm. He was definitely picking up what she was putting down. Jaxson was a disciplined man, but Genesis's mouth was so wet and soft he'd explode if he didn't stop the madness.

He pulled away, raised her back to the couch and continued what had begun in the hallway. He parted her lips with his fingers, then sucked the sensitive pearl that greeted him into his mouth. She ground her hips against him as he licked and sucked and finger fucked. Mewling sounds escaped her lips as the hips swirled faster and faster.

"Ah!" she whispered, as though surprised to have gotten to this point so quickly. Then…she exploded.

Jaxson prepared for the encore. He strolled to the pile of clothes in the hallway, retrieved a condom, then, after shielding himself, returned to see Genesis's half-lidded eyes drinking him in. He eased her off the couch.

"Where's your bedroom?"

She took the lead, walked them down a short hallway to a door on the right. He crawled in bed behind her and reignited the assault by licking his way up her body as he rubbed himself against her. He placed his massive member between her juicy lips, rubbed it against her still-quivering jewel.

"You want this, Gen? You want to feel all this dick I've got for you?"

"Yes."

He eased himself about two inches in. "You want it right now?"

"Uh-huh." Four inches. "Ooh. Shit."

"You want me to fuck you?"

"Oh my God, Jaxson."

She tried to push down on him and deepen the connection. He chuckled, pulled a nipple into his mouth and stroked her pearl, while halfway in.

"You're driving me crazy."

"I know."

He was going crazy, too. Time to take this party to the next level. He repositioned himself, lifted her leg, entered her fully with one long thrust and gave her everything she asked for. He pounded her punanny, at first slow and steady, then deeper and relentless. Her second orgasm was more powerful than the first. A few more thrusts and he joined her and found his release.

Exhausted in the best possible way, Jaxson pulled Genesis against him. He kissed her ear and whispered, "That was amazing."

She pulled his arm tighter around her. "Yeah."

Sweaty and satiated, Genesis was asleep within minutes. Jaxson, not so fast. He lay awake gently stroking her arm, thinking back to that last time, the first time they were together. So much had changed. Genesis was going through a lot. He wasn't a kid anymore. He didn't want to overthink the moment but for whatever reason felt there was a lot on the line. She was the great-niece of a man he'd admired and respected. She could become his neighbor. Jaxson wasn't sure she'd be down for a casual relationship and, quite honestly, wasn't sure he'd want to think about her being with somebody else. There were so many variables, but one thing he knew for sure. He didn't want what had happened to be a onetime thing. He already wanted to be with her again.

Thirteen

When taking Jaxson up on his offer to drive her to Memphis, having sex hadn't been on her mind. However, the combination of emotions from Hank's nonadmission to lying, to her conflicted feelings, to Jaxson's actions all along, culminating in that hallway kiss, obliterated all her defenses. The night spent making love with Jaxson was a game changer.

Somewhere in the back of her mind, Genesis had always known it would happen. She'd felt the decision would impact her beyond the bedroom. Maybe that was why she'd fought so hard against the attraction, against the pull she'd felt ten years ago, and the energy flowing between them now. After ten years of waiting, their reunion was magical. His whole body was a weapon, but he'd made her moist using just his lips, then followed that opening act with equally talented body parts. His tongue was a precision missile. His hands should be registered as lethal weapons. His thick, ample dick could be enshrined.

As good as the multiple orgasms he produced were, it wasn't just the sex. It was everything about him. Their easy conversation. The way he made her feel protected and safe. His work ethic and respect for elders. His down-home sensibility and country charm. Jaxson was a very likable guy. She'd allowed, sometimes forced, herself to be too angry to see it. Though her thoughts about Jaxson still clashed, she didn't even try to convince herself that what she felt was simple lust. There was nothing simple about her connection with him. When they came together, it wasn't just fucking. No, Jaxson made slow, passionate love to her. And did it oh so well.

After that first round satisfied their sexual appetites, Genesis and Jaxson were ravenous. They'd heated up the tacos and a bag of fried rice from Genesis's freezer. She drank a glass of wine; Jaxson downed a beer. They talked about everything and nothing. The companionable silences were languages of their own. He'd spent the night. The next morning, Genesis decided to stay in Memphis. It was the first of the month. There was business to take care of, time-sensitive decisions to make. One thing Cyrus's death had taught her was the value of life and how to not take it for granted. You could be here one day and gone the next. Jaxson had taught her a few things, too. One particular statement he'd made the night before struck a chord:

In life you can choose to be a participant or a spectator. The latter tend to go with the flow and react to whatever happens. Participants are creators who shape their own destiny or give it a damn good try.

Without him knowing he'd done it—and without her

knowing she needed it—Jaxson had diagnosed her whole life. Not challenging her mother's distant personality. Taking a back seat to Lori's second marriage, and the sons it produced. Settling for jobs instead of building a career. Not standing up for herself in relationships. Dating someone she'd known for years because it was convenient. Living someone else's dream instead of her own. Basically, Genesis had fallen into the all-too-common trap of being okay with an okay life.

After a long, hot shower, then enjoying some of the food Jaxson had thoughtfully dropped off before leaving Memphis, Genesis got down to the business of figuring out her life. The first thing she focused on were her finances. Numbers had never been her strong suit. Math. Finance. Budgeting. None of that. After making poor choices in the early post–high school years, she'd worked hard to live within her means, pay her bills on time and raise her credit score. However, one look at her bank balance online and it didn't take a Wharton grad to know drastic changes had to be made ASAP.

She looked around her rented condo. She'd always liked the modern features and minimalist vibe, but after time in her uncle's ranch house, it somehow felt cold and oddly impersonal, even with pictures of friends and family and art she loved on the walls. She got up. Walked around. Standing in her stainless steel kitchen, she thought of the one at Cyrus's house almost fondly—with its cracked, faded linoleum, stained wood cabinets, and appliances that had seen better days about twenty years ago. She stepped out on the balcony.

The contrast to life in the country was stark. Had the buildings always been this close? The noise so loud? In the space of a few seconds a horn honked, music blared from a passing car and a siren sounded in the distance. Hard to believe that not even a month ago, this was her normal. Her first weekend on the farm, she'd missed the hustle and bustle. Until Cyrus had done the unthinkable and made her his heir, she couldn't imagine living anywhere but the city. Couldn't believe what she considered now. Tried to argue with the logical suggestions sounding off in her mind. What she didn't do was try to dismiss how in a very short time the country had changed her. She now missed the fresh air and wide-open spaces. The black night, bright stars and an insect chorus. She missed her DDI neighbors Hazel and Granville. And yes, she missed Jaxson. The woman who'd left the condo for a visit with Cyrus's attorney was not the same one in Memphis making decisions right now.

Genesis walked back into the condo and fired up her tablet. She opened the Notes app. For several seconds, her fingers hovered over the keyboard. Then she began typing.

Creating My Life To-Do List:

1. Send 30-day notice to vacate condo.

Just typing those words took her breath. Questions ping-ponged back and forth. *What the heck am I doing? Do I really want to leave the convenience of the city?* Memphis was where she'd been born and raised. Where she'd grown into adulthood. Where most of her friends and family lived. *How could living by myself in the country ever work? Am I moving there because of Jaxson? What if...whatever this is isn't really anything and doesn't work out?*

She deleted point one. Went back online and rechecked her balances against incoming expenses, then mentally assessed the big picture. It might be another week before she could drive. Rent was due now, utilities in a few weeks. If she worked seven days a week and used the rest of her savings, she'd only be good for the next couple of months before living paycheck to paycheck. On the other hand, if she moved to the farm, there would be no rent, only utilities. She probably wouldn't make enough money DoorDashing out there, so she'd have to find another source of income. But living out there for three to six months would give her enough time to replenish her savings account and think out her next move. As fast as time was flying, she could bounce back in no time. She returned to the Notes app, typing randomly as thoughts came to mind. Her fingers flew across the keys.

Creating My Life To-Do List:

1. Send 30-day notice to vacate condo.

2. Find cheap moving company for relocation.

3. Put rest in storage.

4. Find job working from home.

5. Call cousins.

Her hands stilled for a minute before she continued.

6. Clear out Uncle Cyrus's things.

7. Donate? Garage sale? Ebay? (Ask Hazel)

8. Put loan to Lance in writing.

9. Talk to Jax re minor renovation. Cost?

She paused again. Took a long look out the patio doors. Then wrote,

10. Talk to Jax about Hank...the TRUTH.

She read over the points. Poured herself a glass of juice. Read them again. The thought of making these major life changes was both exciting and terrifying. Going on the condo's property management website gave her butterflies. She pushed past the fear and submitted the notice, which gave her the courage to tackle another task she found difficult: calling her cousins. She decided to try out the news with the lesser of two evils.

"Hello, Cleo? It's Genesis."

"Oh, hi, there. How are you doing? How's the ankle?"

"Better, thanks for asking. How are you guys doing?"

"Oh, you know, taking it one day at a time. Are you still at Daddy's house?"

"I'm at my condo but will return to Holy Mound in a few days. It's why I called." When there was no response, she took a breath and continued. In for a penny, in for a pound.

"I've made a decision and wanted you and Clarence to be the first to know. I'm moving into Uncle Cyrus's house."

The pause was so long Genesis thought he'd disconnected. "Cleo? Are you there?"

"Genesis, I don't think you moving out there is a good idea. This issue about the farm hasn't been settled, at least not to our family's satisfaction."

Genesis's heart sank. She became nervous but refused to be intimidated. "Did you guys read over the will?"

"We read it."

"Have you spoken with Mr. Young, the attorney?"

"That's what you were supposed to be doing."

"I never said I'd speak to him. What am I supposed to say?"

"You need to contest the will on the basis of Daddy being incompetent."

"I've spoken with his neighbors, people who were around him at the end of his life. I spoke to him myself by phone not long before he died. All of us agree he sounded normal, like his usual self."

She thought about bringing up what Jaxson had told Clarence. Something stopped her.

"We've got people looking into the matter," Cleo said. "You need to hold off on making any changes until this thing is made right."

"With all due respect, cousin, I didn't call to get your permission. I'm being respectful by letting you know of a decision that's already been made, and to offer a chance for you and Clarence to go through Uncle Cyrus's belongings for anything you'd like to keep."

"You're making me an offer about my daddy's things? You sound crazy."

"I hope that one day we can have a more civil conversation, but on that note, Cleo, I'm going to let you go. Have a good evening."

Before Cleo's comments could make her second-guess her choices, she made another call.

"Gen!"

One word, and her world righted. "Hey, Jax."

"I can call you Gen, right? I'm now in the friend zone?"

"More like the lover zone, so watch yourself."

"At least you didn't say booty-call zone."

"Ha! I'm glad I called. I needed this energy."

"Why? What happened?"

"I just got off the phone with Cleo." She gave him a brief rundown of their conversation and what led to it. "Does my decision sound irresponsible or, worse, crazy, as Cleo said?"

"I think your decision is perfect, but I might be a little biased. When is this move happening?"

"By the end of the month."

"Then the only other thing I need to know is how I can help."

Over the next two weeks, Genesis worked on the list. Rather than get a truck and move all of her stuff to the country, she rented a month-to-month storage for everything she didn't currently need. She went online, found a simple promissory note template and sent it to Lance. He balked at first, but eventually sent back a signed copy. Best of all, she secured a work-from-home job in customer service. It wasn't ideal and the pay was crap, but it was steady income and mindless work. Just what the doctor ordered.

Speaking of doctors, she visited one in Memphis who assessed her ankle and delivered good news. Hers had been between a one- and two-grade sprain. X-rays showed the ligaments healing nicely. With no further complications she could ease off the crutches and remove the boot in two weeks. He advised that she still take it easy but cleared her to drive. Genesis began her transition from city life. Gave some of her stuff away to friends. Rented a small U-Haul for the rest. A week before Memorial Day weekend, Habari and a couple of his friends helped move her heavier items to storage. Then he stayed behind to help her pack what she'd take to Holy Mound.

As she drove into the driveway of Cyrus's house, a welcoming sight was there to greet her—Nipsey, Jaxson and his dog, Butch. The emotion she felt surprised her. They hadn't been apart long and had spoken regularly by phone, but she'd missed him being physically around. She'd barely put the truck in Park before he was there ready to open her door.

"Hey, pretty lady."

"Hey, you."

Genesis moved in for a passion-filled kiss. Jaxson stopped her with a brief, friend-like hug.

"These trees can talk," he said, stepping away. Hooded eyes filled with desire stared into hers. "Looks like you missed me as much as I did you."

"Probably."

"Want to do something about it?"

"I'd love to but I'm renting this truck by the hour and what I'd like even more is to not keep it overnight."

Jaxson unloaded the truck in half the time it had taken both her and Habari to pack it. He followed her back to Memphis so that she could drop off the U-Haul, and on the return journey, they stopped by Papa Joes before reaching Holy Mound just as nightfall approached.

"Those security lights make a huge difference," she said. "Uncle Cyrus's place is growing on me, rickety steps and all."

"Correction—*your* place is growing on you. Another move in the direction of what you desire is claiming out loud what belongs to you."

She squeezed his thigh. "Thank you for that. Now, let's go into *my* home."

"Hang on. I bought you a housewarming gift."

"Seriously, Jaxson? At the rate you're going, I'll be forever in your debt."

He smirked, pecked her lips. "That's the point."

He reached over, opened the glove compartment and pulled out a small bag.

"What is it?"

"Nothing that'll bite you. Check it out."

She pulled out a magnet, shaped like a house. "'Like a

Good Neighbor,'" she read, smiling, "'Stay Over There.' Ha!
Whoever made this is a person after my own heart."

"I thought you'd appreciate it. Bought it a while ago. Forgot to give it to you."

They went inside. Genesis walked directly into the kitchen
and proudly placed the magnet in the middle of the otherwise bare refrigerator door.

"Can I get you something to drink?"

"No." He picked her up, squeezed her ass and backed them
against the kitchen wall.

"What are you doing?"

He kissed her ear. "You'll catch on soon enough."

Then her nose.

"Umm…"

Then her mouth. Genesis gave in to the moment, feeling
Jaxson's hardening shaft press against her.

Without breaking the rhythm of their tongue dance, he
reached beneath her top and tweaked a nipple. She moaned
in his mouth. He eased along her body until a deep ebony-
colored nipple and his mouth were at the same level. He
sucked it in. She hissed her pleasure, squirming against him.
She was wet and ready. Long strides made quick work of
reaching the couch. Apparently Jaxson was ready, too.

He placed her down, knelt beside her and gently pushed
the minidress she wore up around her waist. His eyes, black
with lust, sent a clear message: *I'm going to make love to you,
and it's going to feel real good.*

Genesis lay back and spread her legs, sending a message of
her own. A small patch of flimsy material was all that sepa-

rated him from her shaved mound, the lips evident against the lacy triangle. She watched him kiss her shin, her thigh, the top of her heat. Her head fell back. Hips moved of their own volition. He kissed the other thigh, took his thumb and massaged her pearl. The friction from the lace and pressure of his thumb made her slick with desire. He leaned down and licked her stomach, then slid his thumb beneath the lace and down the slit of her heat. Genesis placed a hand on the back of his head, encouraging him to exchange his mouth for what his thumb was doing.

He didn't have to be told twice.

Instead of bothering to remove her undies, he pushed the lace to the side and covered her quivering lips with his own. He French-kissed her lower lips, thrust his tongue deep. He licked. Sucked. Kissed again. Genesis's gyrations, slow at first, became faster, more insistent. Her hips moved up and down as he made love to her with his tongue. He grabbed her ass, spread her cheeks and continued to assault her. At the height of her pleasure, she tried to pull back. He held her in a love grip, demanding she release her ecstasy and shower him with it.

"Oh. My. Gosh!"

Her hips bucked as she placed her hands behind his head and pushed him into her. The frantic bucking returned to the sensual grinding from the first time he'd licked her. The pants turned to moans, and then steady breathing. She closed her legs, opened her eyes and beckoned him closer.

"My turn," she said, easing to a sitting position and reaching for the buckle on his belt.

"No, wait." He sighed, heavily. "I've got to go."

"You're leaving? Why?"

"Because what's happening right now is new, and special, and just for us. While we're defining what this is, I think it should stay that way. Anybody sees my truck parked in your drive overnight and they won't ask questions. They'll draw their own conclusions. The mayors are probably up there now, taking bets on how long I'll stay."

She didn't want for Jaxson to be right. But he'd spoken the truth. She was trying to eliminate drama, not create more. The last thing she needed on her first night as a Holy Mound semipermanent resident was the makings of a small-town scandal.

"Okay." She buckled the belt and pulled down his polo shirt. He reached down and helped her up from the couch. Placing an arm around her shoulders, he walked with her to the door.

"Seems like I'm always thanking you."

He reached the door. Kissed the top of her head. "Know that you're always welcome."

Fourteen

It only took the short drive home for Jaxson to take back everything he'd told Genesis about being discreet. After parking the truck, he went inside and pulled several condoms out of the box beside his bed. He took a quick shower and changed into a light, loose pair of shorts and a cotton tee. He donned a pair of heavy sandals, then went to the garage to retrieve a ten-speed bike that hadn't been ridden in months. Butch ran up and reminded Jaxson he hadn't been fed. After filling the dog's food and water bowls, and with moonlight the only guide needed, he made his way back to the place he hadn't wanted to leave.

Just before he reached the driveway, Nipsey ran up to greet him.

"Shh, no barking," he said, giving him a friendly pat and rubbing his fur. Then he remembered the motion sensors. He pulled out his phone to send a quick text and prayed that Genesis hadn't turned hers off.

Gen, you there?

???

    He'd just left her at the house. Guess his text did seem a bit suspicious.

Go to the fuse box and turn security lights off.

Why?

I'll explain in a sec.

Where's the fuse box?

In the closet by the kitchen. Let me know when you're there.

OK.

    The waiting felt like forever. In actuality less than a minute went by.

Found it.

Good. There are three switches on the bottom right side marked SECURITY. Flip those to the other side.

Why am I turning the lights off? What's going on?

Jaxson knew he could show her better than he could tell her. There was one final message.

I'm outside. Unlock the screen door.

He pulled his bike around to the back of the shed that faced away from both the road and the McCormicks' eagle eyes. He continued walking on that side of the house, reached the porch and took the stairs two at a time. He opened the screen door. Genesis stood by the door in a silky-looking camisole top with matching ruffled short shorts, her beauty backlit by a lone hallway light.

He stepped inside.

"You came back," she said.

"Yes, I did."

For the next forty-five minutes, those were the only words spoken.

The next morning, Jaxson woke up first. He eased out of bed, checked his texts and emails, then went into the kitchen in hopes there was some coffee around. As he stood watching the black liquid puddle into the carafe, a pair of arms snaked around his waist.

"Good morning."

He turned for a proper hug. "Good morning, beautiful. Did I wake you?"

"I smelled the coffee. I see I didn't need to tell you to make yourself at home."

"You already did."

"When?"

"Last night. Several times."

"Touché." She yawned, leaned against the counter.

"How are you feeling?"

"What do you mean?"

"Us. This. Any second thoughts? Questions? Regrets?" Jaxson reached into the cabinet for two coffee mugs.

"Maybe."

He set down the mugs and turned around. He'd honestly not expected that answer.

"What is it?"

"Let's sit."

Each silently dressed their coffees, then sat at the dining room table.

Genesis took a couple of sips, then set down her mug. "There's a couple things you probably need to know about."

"Okay."

"My cousins aren't happy about me being here. I'm almost certain they're seeking legal counsel on how to fight the will."

"Have you spoken with Cyrus's attorney about it?"

She shook her head. "Maybe I should."

"Has the deed been transferred into your name?"

"Yes."

"Then let them spend their money and spin their wheels. You have nothing to worry about."

"The other matter…is about Hank. I think you're telling the truth about what happened."

Jaxson released a relieved breath. In that moment it felt like ten years' worth of heaviness fell away.

He reached for her hands. "Thank you, baby. What happened to change your mind?"

"An honest conversation, well, sorta kinda. Hank basically admitted he lied about that night. It wasn't what he said but what he didn't that convinced me.

"I went through hell for being with Hank's rival. You were the enemy, and even though I didn't even know who you were at the time, it was like I'd betrayed an unwritten, unspoken oath. It caused a lot of problems. I held you responsible. It didn't help to later hear it had all been part of a dare, that you'd slept with me just because I was his sister."

"That's a lie."

"I believe that, too. But when you hear a lie so long, the truth becomes unbelievable."

"Thank you for sharing that with me, for believing me."

"You're welcome."

Genesis's smile reached across the table and wrapped around his heart.

"Okay, it's my turn. There are a couple things I want to talk to you about."

Genesis looked skeptical. "Do I want to hear what they are?"

"Doesn't matter because I'm going to tell you anyway. First off, and I know it's early and I don't want to scare you, but I could get used to having coffee with you first thing in the morning."

She leaned over and kissed him. "You're right. It is early."

"No risk, no reward."

She didn't respond but Jaxson could tell when a woman was happy. He was no one's psychiatrist, but it seemed a lot of Genesis's life had been one lacking emotional security. He wanted to change that. Starting now.

"What's the second thing?"

Jaxson waved a hand around the room. "It's this house that Cyrus loved so much. Since you've decided to live here, we need to make it safe."

"I don't have any money for major repairs."

"Then start with minor ones. As my grandfather often told me, if you never start, you're sure to never finish."

An unexpected out-of-town trip delayed Jaxson's reno plans. No complaints. He'd spent time with his beloved daughter, Jazz. When Abby phoned and was actually pleasant, he knew something was up. She and her husband, Sam, wanted to take a trip with just the two of them before the new baby arrived. Jazz had one last week of preschool. Could he come to Phoenix and take care of her? Could birds fly? He'd rented an Airbnb and jumped into Daddy duties. For one unexpected and glorious week, he had another chance to be a real, full-time father. He never took visits for granted. To be the first face she saw every day and the last one at night was enough for him to die happy. During Memorial Day weekend, they flew to Los Angeles and hung out with one of Jaxson's best friends, another former pro baller who was also a single dad. They treated the kids with amusement parks, child-friendly movies, too much sugar and a day at the beach. Back in Phoenix, father and daughter relaxed with nonstop videos, games and books. He took her shopping and bought too many clothes. They did not drive to

Paradise Valley, the location of his former luxury home and where a near scandal almost cost him everything. The guilt he felt around what had happened followed him like a ghost.

The day Jaxson left Phoenix was bittersweet. He hated leaving his daughter. While he'd had no choice in the matter, Jaxson loved being a dad. He wanted to be that constant, positive influence for Jazz that his parents and grandparents had been for him, the way he watched his best friend be to his kids. On the positive side, he was returning home to the arms of a good woman, one who'd finally taken him off her enemy list. Did Genesis want children? Jaxson shook off the question. He was getting way ahead of himself.

Back in Holy Mound, Jaxson jumped back into work. He and Blake spent most of the week in Memphis. They'd won a hard-fought bidding battle and secured their most ambitious project yet—turning a neglected eight-unit apartment building into desirable two-bedroom condos. While working, he told his partner about Cyrus's outdated farmhouse in need of repair. He stopped short of telling Blake he and Genesis were dating, but being Jaxson's longtime friend, Blake added one plus one and got two.

Summer came early. Above-average temps hovered over the valley, bringing that much-anticipated sunshine and humidity Jaxson could do without. He'd stripped down to a simple tee, shorts and sandals for his visit to Genesis's house, where they'd just finished an assessment of repairs needed both inside and out. With each area Blake suggested for renovation, he saw more worry lines crease Genesis's face.

"How much are we talking?" Jaxson asked, once they'd

returned to the porch and sat in chairs that looked as old as the house.

Blake stroked his chin. "On the conversative side, I'd say twenty-five to thirty. More like fifty to bring the whole place up to speed."

"Fifty?" Genesis almost croaked. "As in thousand?"

"That's considering the likelihood of outdated wiring and pipe systems," Blake explained. "And addressing any foundational issues."

Jaxson rocked back on his chair's hind legs. "We'll probably find some. Cyrus didn't spend money. This place probably hasn't been updated in twenty, thirty years."

"At least. Which means, given how often they change, there are coding violations. Starting with the exposed wire snaking across the yard."

"That's on me," Jaxson admitted. "I installed a security system and got called to watch Jazz before having a chance to hide the wires."

"You're doing that later today, right?"

"Yes, boss," Jaxson jokingly replied.

Genesis ran a hand through wild, natural hair. "You guys have given me a lot to think about. I knew things looked bad but had no idea the place is basically falling down around me."

"It could be a lot worse," Jaxson said.

"Repairs can be done over time," Blake offered.

"Blake's right. You don't have to get them done all at once."

"Considering my limited resources, I can't repair anything right now."

"Have you considered a loan?" Jaxson asked.

Genesis shook her head. "Thanks to financial misman-
agement, my credit score isn't the best."

"Owning this farm will give you leverage to counter that,"
Blake said. "I'm sure there's equity in the house and the land.
You can borrow against it."

"We could go through my bank," Jaxson added. "I have
a contact there who knows and trusts me. On my word, you
could borrow what's needed, no problem."

He watched Genesis as this option sank in. He could almost see the wheels turning inside of her head.

"Baby, this is a viable option you should consider. Right
before I left for college, my grandparents took out a loan
for a new roof, driveway and storm windows. They tried to
talk Cyrus into renovating back then, but, as I remember,
Cyrus's response was something like—" he adopted the old
man's tone "—*I don't want to owe nobody nothin'!*"

Genesis chuckled. "That sounds like Uncle Cyrus."

"Sounds like you" was Jaxson's quick retort.

"Who asked you?"

"Okay, you two," Blake said. "If you keep on fighting
like that, someone is going to mistake you for an old married couple. Jax, how much wood do we have in the shed?
Did we use those planks we'd purchased for the duplex before being outbid?"

"They're still there, and some fencing wood. Why?"

"They might work for fixing this porch and the steps."

Blake's idea was almost perfect, the only problem being
it wasn't Jaxson who'd thought of it first.

"That's a great idea, Blake. We could start that repair as early as next week."

"Or I could finish the assessment on the apartment building, and you could start tackling this porch ASAP. The last thing we need is someone's foot catching in those unstable boards and Gen getting sued."

"Did she tell you it was okay to call her that?" Jaxson asked.

"It's fine, Blake. Call me Gen."

The thundercloud on Jaxson's face made Genesis laugh out loud. A second later, he joined her.

The lighthearted teasing gave way to number crunching. Jaxson would start on the repairs right away. With the wood they already had on hand, he told Genesis that a hundred dollars would buy the other materials needed to reinforce the porch, replace rotting boards and build new front steps. What he didn't tell her was that amount was all she'd pay. He'd make up the difference. But since she'd let the moon fall before that happened, he kept that minor detail to himself.

Jaxson left Genesis's house and headed for the hardware store. The next morning, he was up with the roosters, heading to the warehouse for a truckful of extra wood. He figured it would take at least two trips to transport enough to complete the project, which was why he'd started early. There was something to be said, though, for what Susan called *circadian rhythm*, rising and setting with the sun, tuning your body with nature and going with its flow. Thinking of his friend made him realize he hadn't heard from her since they'd run into each other at Holy Moly. The guy he'd seen her meet hadn't looked like a serial killer, but neither had Ted Bundy. He pulled into Cyrus's driveway, the cracks running across the cement like veins seeming even more prominent since noting them yesterday. He cut off the engine and sent Susan a text with a smiley face thanking her for letting him know that she'd made it through the date alive.

He got ready to text Genesis but, after looking at his watch, decided to call instead. She wouldn't be happy about the early hour. Having an attitude with him was nothing new, even though it was mostly smoke with very little fire. No one could look at him the way she had the first day they reconnected and feel anything less than adversarial. Thank goodness, that all had changed. So much so that Blake referred to them as an old married couple, and Jaxson had spent enough time with not only his grandparents but partners like Granville and Hazel to know the comment held more than a kernel of truth.

He exited the truck with the phone in his hand and was surprised to see Genesis on the porch, looking lovely. The shorts she wore showed off a pair of sexy legs that he knew firsthand were as soft as cotton and as smooth as a Boyz II Men love song. He forced his eyes away from the vision of beauty long enough to reach into the truck bed, grab a toolbox and head her way.

"Hey, Gen! What are you doing up so early? I was just getting ready to call."

Her brow lifted. Even with the progress they'd made, she remained cautious.

"Still acting like we're casual, huh?"

"Aren't we?"

"We haven't put a definition on what we're doing, but I'd say it's way past that."

"I'm surprised you're up. Did I mention last night that I'd be by early?"

"No. Miss Hazel called to tell me that, and to suggest it would be a nice gesture if I offered breakfast. I thought she'd have two heart attacks when I told her I didn't cook."

"Ha! As good as she knows her way around a kitchen, I imagine she did."

"I'm wondering how she even knew you and Blake had come by to visit."

"On the way home last night, I stopped by their place. I'm going to need some help with this, and with Blake tied up in Memphis, I asked Granville to lend me a hand."

"I wish you hadn't. It's enough to owe you for the work you're doing. Now I have to add Hazel's husband to the list."

"Tear up the list. You don't owe anyone anything. However, if you're determined to contribute, you can grab a plank of wood."

Jaxson got back to work stacking the wood close to the porch they were replacing. Granville joined him a short time later.

Hazel arrived midway through the rebuild, bringing a tuna casserole and fresh green beans in a hot-and-cold tote and complaining about "these newfangled women," Genesis included.

"I don't know what it is with young women today. Priorities are all twisted. Your whole generation is confused!"

"You're from a different era, Miss Hazel."

"When it comes to what matters, child, not much has changed. But it's like young girls these days don't know about what's important in life. I see them on TV looking flawless. Nails done up. Every hair in place. But if anything happened and they couldn't call delivery or reach a drive-through, their families would starve."

The men worked outside finishing the porch and steps. Hazel left to attend a meeting at the church, go grocery shopping and run errands. It was night before she returned to pick up Granville in her Cadillac Eldorado, their "Sunday-go-to-meeting" ride.

When Genesis brought a lemonade out to where Jaxson rested on the new wooden steps, he looked tired but pleased.

"You want to come in?" she offered.

He shook his head. "I need a shower and sleep, in that order. If I come inside, that's not going to happen."

"The porch and steps look beautiful, like they were done by a professional."

"Hey!"

"Just kidding."

"I walked right into that." He eyed her for a moment before pushing an errant hair behind her ear and offering a quick kiss on the lips. They sat in silence and watched the sun go down.

Just like an old married couple.

Fifteen

Amazing how a person's whole life could flip in less than two months. Surprisingly, what was happening didn't totally freak her out. The winds of real change had started when Genesis's company downsized and she found herself out of a job. Then, she hadn't been worried. There was money in the bank to cover almost six months of expenses and she hadn't thought work would be hard to find.

She'd been wrong.

The economy was on a downturn. Companies tightened their purse strings. When Lance came to her with grand plans for a great business, one where she'd receive her initial investment back in thirty days along with a future percentage of what was destined to be the next great franchise, think Hard Rock Cafe, the timing had seemed perfect. Until it wasn't.

Cyrus dying and leaving her the farm hadn't felt right either. Still didn't, but what could she do? Most of her apprehensions about country living had been eliminated, thanks to her DDI neighbors. And Jaxson, the biggest surprise flip of all.

Genesis glanced at her watch, stretched and got up from the dining room table that was also where she worked. She grabbed a bottle of water and retrieved her tablet, then went outside to sit on the sturdy new porch, now one of her favorite places. She opened her Notes app and pulled up the list she'd made last month and felt pleased to cross most items off the list.

Creating My Life To-Do List:

1. ~~Send 30-day notice to vacate condo.~~

2. ~~Find cheap moving company for relocation.~~

3. ~~Put rest in storage.~~

4. ~~Find job working from home.~~

5. ~~Call cousins. Update?~~

6. Clear out Uncle Cyrus's things.

7. Donate? Garage sale? Ebay? (Ask Hazel)

8. ~~Put loan to Lance in writing.~~

9. ~~Talk to Jax re minor renovation. Cost?~~

10. ~~Talk to Jax about Hank...the TRUTH.~~

She wanted to completely cross out item number 5. Since announcing that she'd be moving into Cyrus's home, she hadn't heard from her cousins. Wishful thinking suggested they'd decided to honor their dad's decision, but common sense told her those chances were slim to none. She reached for the cell phone and called Clarence, then Cleo. Both calls went to voicemail. Continuing down the list to items 6 and 7, she scrolled through her contacts list and called Hazel.

"Good afternoon, Miss Hazel. It's Genesis. How are you?"

"If I was any better, they'd have to hog-tie me." Both women laughed. "How are you doing, baby? I meant to call you last week and invite you to church. But I got a call about one of our members being in the hospital and the thought slipped my mind. When you get my age, child, there's a lot of slipping going on."

Genesis laughed. "I think that sometimes it's not age. I forget things, too."

"That ankle still acting right?"

"So far, so good."

"Continue to be careful. From what Granville tells me, there's still a lot of work over there to do. Don't get ahead of yourself. Let Jax take care of the heavy lifting. Speaking of my play son, is he over there?"

Hazel was fishing and Genesis smelled the bait. "No, ma'am. I think he's in Memphis."

"Oh, that's right. Working on houses now with his friend from school. What's his name?"

"Blake." Genesis smiled. The woman couldn't help but be nosy, bless her heart.

"That Jaxson King is a go-getter. I think he has a little money coming in from those football years, but he doesn't rest on his laurels. At any given moment, he's got three or four irons in the fire. That's the way you want to do it. Never know which one will get hot.

"But you probably didn't call me to talk about Jaxson," she continued, with a little chuckle. "Did you?"

"No, Miss Hazel."

"Well, darn. I told Jaxson the two of you needed to get together, combine households. You could live in one place and rent out the other. Lord, here I go, getting all up in your business. What can I do for you?"

Hazel was quickly becoming one of Genesis's favorite people, like the grandmother she never had. "I have a question. Do you think it's too soon for me to get rid of Uncle Cyrus's belongings?"

"That depends, Genesis. What are his sons' opinions on the matter?"

Good question, and a tricky one to navigate. Hazel had a good heart but a mouth for gossip, so Genesis trod carefully. "I've called and left messages" was her vague answer. "They haven't called back."

"Give them time. They're still grieving. Clarence and Cleo didn't spend much time down here. Can't imagine they'd want everyday items such as clothes, shoes and things not sentimental to the family. I don't see any harm in boxing up those items and storing them in the shed, just to get started. Cyrus can't use them anymore—God bless the dead.

There's thirty or forty years of living in that house, though. Going through it is going to be quite an undertaking."

"That's another reason I called you, Miss Hazel. If you have time, I could really use your help. I was also wondering if your church accepts donations, or if you knew any local places that did."

"Absolutely! I'm so glad you thought of donating to the church. You know we run a thrift shop on the outskirts of Memphis."

"No, ma'am, I didn't know that."

"We can pretty much take anything you don't need off your hands."

"That would be great, as there is likely to be quite a bit to donate. I'm going to try and sell some of the larger items myself, the farming equipment, his truck, stuff like that. A lot of repair work has to be done on this house. Whatever money I make from those sales will help cover the cost."

"Of course, baby. Go ahead and do what you've got to do. Cyrus would be happy to see how you've stepped up and are handling everything. And while he wasn't a regular church attendee, I know he'd be pleased with having some of what he owned helping to do the Lord's work."

"I think so, too."

"I've been to Cyrus's house a time or two and know that cleaning it out will be no small task. Don't you worry. I'll put the word out to some of my church sisters who will be more than happy to pitch in. Let me know when you want to get started."

A beep sounded in Genesis's ear. She looked at the phone screen.

"I've got a call coming in, Miss Hazel. I'll get back with you, and really appreciate the help."

"All right, baby. If it's Jax, tell him I said hello."

Her neighbor's radar was right on the money. She answered the phone, laughing. "Hello."

"What's funny?"

"I was talking with Miss Hazel. When I told her I had to take another call, she thought it was you."

"Miss Hazel is psychic."

"She also shared a rather interesting suggestion…that you and I should move in together and rent out whichever house is vacant."

"Trying to play matchmaker again, huh?"

"This isn't her first time?"

"Not at all. She's tried to hook me up with every single church member under the age of fifty, and a couple who've topped that milestone."

They shared a laugh.

"To Miss Hazel, living together means marriage. She's old-school. It doesn't matter what year we're in and how times have changed. She doesn't believe in shacking up."

"That's what she calls it?"

"Yep."

"Ha!"

The conversation shifted to Cyrus. Jaxson told her not to worry about hearing from her cousins. Everything Cyrus had left belonged to her now. He encouraged her to do what she wanted.

"What are you doing this evening?" Genesis asked, changing the subject again.

"Going fishing down at the pond. That's why I called. I want you to join me."

"Um, let me think about it. No."

Jaxson laughed. "You said the area was peaceful and nice."

"I love the water's tranquility, and the view of trees and pines. But the only fish I want to see are already cooked pieces served on a plate."

By the time the call ended, they'd reached a compromise. Genesis agreed to join him at the pond, but she'd be watching, not fishing. Turned out it was a pleasant way to enjoy the mild weather. She could see why people liked it, yet marveled at the patience it took to sit quietly and wait for a bite. All kinds of thoughts swirled in her mind as she watched the man who just months ago hadn't been a blip on her radar, and an enemy at that. Most of what she knew about him dealt with the past. What made up the man he was now?

"Hey, Jax." She liked how the name Hazel preferred popped off her tongue.

"Yes, Gen."

She also liked the way her nickname sounded on his lips.

"Tell me more about your daughter, Jazz."

At the mention of his daughter's name, she saw a smile that seemed to light up his whole body.

"She's amazing," he said simply.

"Chip off the old block?"

He glanced over and caught the twinkle in Genesis's eye. "She's way better than me."

"Did you name her?"

"No, that credit goes to her mom. It's crazy because before Abby got pregnant, I was adamant about not having children. Having my daughter changed all that. Now I can't imagine not having Jazz in my life."

She was surprised and pleased that Jaxson spoke openly, from the heart. He seemed genuinely happy to spend time with his daughter. Some little girls weren't as lucky.

"Don't get me wrong. I love kids. I'd just planned to be settled, more mature, done with football, married. I know firsthand how pro sports can wreak havoc on relationships. Abby knew it, too, and that I didn't want kids yet. But the second Jazz looked at me with those big bright eyes, my whole world shifted. The love was instant." Jaxson repositioned a rod. "I'd climb a mountain, fight a lion, take a bullet for that little girl."

It wasn't lost on Genesis that the closest she'd come to having that feeling was with the man holding a fishing rod in his hand.

"How often do you get to see her?"

"Not often enough. We video chat almost every day, but there's no chat or video app in the world to replace physical presence. That's why I was so grateful to spend that unexpected week with her. She'll be here in August and stay for a month."

"I'm happy for you," Genesis said, and meant it.

He nodded. "Me, too."

His line jerked. Genesis watched as the bobber, her new word for the day, went under water. Jaxson moved the fishing line right to left, all the while turning the handle attached to it. He took what he labeled a "small catch" off the hook, threw it back in and rebaited.

He pulled the second lawn chair he'd bought toward the water's edge and sat. "What about you? Do you want children?"

Genesis shrugged. "My answer used to be a definite no. Over time that turned into a maybe. One thing for sure, though. I'd want to be married and for the pregnancy to be planned. I wouldn't want to bring a child into the world who wasn't wanted. I know from personal experience that's not a good place to be."

It was also a topic she didn't want to talk much about. "Any plans for the Fourth?"

"I'll be in town," he said. "There's a concert happening on the town square lawn. A casual affair. Picnic baskets, folding chairs, blankets, that sort of thing. You ought to come with me. Silence all the wagging tongues by publicly showing up as a couple."

"Are we a couple?"

"At the very least, we're friends and neighbors. People with less in common have gotten together to have a good time."

"Who's going to be there?"

"Some of my favorite country singers."

"Country? You're kidding, right?"

"I take it you're a hip-hop head."

"Not just hip-hop. I like R & B, and some jazz and pop."

"You forgot the blues."

"Too many sad stories. Just like country."

"But told so eloquently. And they're not all sad." Jaxson reached into the small cooler he'd brought down, took out a beer for himself and gave Genesis the sparkling water she'd requested.

"Did you know that country music came out of the blues?" he asked.

Genesis watched a butterfly float across the pond. "No idea."

"True facts. A combination of the blues and traditional sounds created by the banjo, an instrument brought over from Africa."

"Well, I'll say. You learn something new every day."

"I was just as surprised as you. Turned my nose up at my grandfather's favorite genre until he schooled me on the history. I began to listen with a different ear. Hear the stories. Feel the pain. Same cooking as the blues, but a different flavor. I think you should try it," he said. "You might like it."

Last year, she and Lance had gone to Atlanta for the Fourth, to hang out with Hank and his family. This year, celebrating with family was all but out of the question. Especially her brother who'd technically admitted that the whole story about Jaxson breaking his arm had been a lie, then minimized what telling it had cost her. Though still angry at the deception, she'd tried to help him make it right by texting him and demanding an apology. He didn't respond. They hadn't spoken since.

"I attended the event last year," Jaxson told her. "It's not just the music. It's the atmosphere. Like a big party. A family reunion. Almost everybody knows everybody. People are friendly whether they know you or not."

Jaxson's offer was tempting, especially given the Hunter family dynamic. Hank was and always had been the star child. That he was angry with her meant that by default the rest of the family would have attitudes as well. Spending the day with Jaxson sounded like more fun.

"Okay, I'll go with you."

"Nice! Now come over here and help catch your dinner."

Genesis didn't bait a hook or catch a fish, but the afternoon of the Fourth found her engaged in something equally foreign, attending a country music concert. Jaxson had purchased her a cowboy hat for the occasion. At first, she'd balked about wearing it, but once she saw how cute it looked on, she thanked him.

From the time they arrived and connected with Blake and his girl, Pilar, beyond the VIP ropes until after the concert, when they met some of the acts backstage, Jaxson made sure that Genesis felt included. She met some of his former classmates and others he'd worked with since returning home. While listening to a list of talented acts that included the Chicks, Darius Rucker, Chapel Hart and, to Genesis's delight, Kane Brown, they feasted on Hazel's award-worthy spread of perfect finger food that would put any chef to shame: crispy fried chicken, BBQ meatballs, mac-n-cheese puffs, a green bean salad, homemade rolls and a container of fresh fruit. There was enough food for several of Jaxson's friends to enjoy the hearty fare.

Shortly after eleven that night, the two couples parted ways.

"Want to spend the night at my place?" Jaxson asked. "You haven't been back since I rescued you. I'm beginning to feel slighted."

"We wouldn't want that."

That night the love was slow and easy, like a country song. The fun-filled day and meaningful connections added to their friendship and intimacy. The foreplay was intentional— kisses deeper and more heartfelt, with lots of unhurried rubs and gentle squeezes. As the heat between them increased, Genesis took the lead. She straddled Jaxson's toned, athletic, naked body and eased down on a pole much thicker than the rods he fished with. Her body slid up and down his rock-hard shaft. His hands squeezed her butt cheeks and aided the rhythm. He pulled one nipple into his mouth, and then the other—licking, sucking, kissing. It wasn't long before the alpha in Jaxson took control of the dance. He directed her to her knees, pulled her to the edge of the bed, reentered her and slapped her ass.

"Ooh! Yes! Ride 'em, cowboy," she panted.

"Yeehaw, baby" was his raspy, whispered response.

He slapped her other cheek. The combination of light, un-expected, tingling pain with deep, thrusting pleasure threw Genesis into a frenzy. She pushed him away and flipped over. The quick action pulled off his condom. Genesis noticed but was too caught up in the moment to stop. She reached for his penis, guided it into her like a heat-seeking missile. He covered her, his pounding slow yet forceful, then fast and furious. Feelings of ecstasy coursed through mind, body and soul. The skin-to-skin, soul-to-soul action took the love-making to a whole other place. Their explosive orgasms left Genesis shaking and fully satiated. She fell asleep thinking only of how good it felt to be sexed by this man.

That was last night. As the morning dawned, Genesis woke to a different feeling about the unprotected sex. She and Lance had made a verbal commitment to exclusivity before having sex without protection. That hadn't happened with her and Jaxson. The reality didn't feel good. Jaxson began to stir beside her. Time for a conversation.

"Last night was amazing," Jaxson said, pulling her against his chiseled chest and squeezing her body's softness.

"I can't deny that. Something unexpected happened, though."

"Did I get a little rough, darlin'? I'm sor—"

"No, not that." Said with a smile in her voice. "I didn't know how much I'd like being spanked."

She eased out of his embrace. "The condom came off."

"Yeah, I know. That was part of what felt so good."

Genesis sat against the headboard. "That can't happen again, Jax, not with us being casual. And not without a serious talk about each other's sexual lives."

"That's easy enough. Let's talk." He sat up, too. "I'm not seeing anyone else, Genesis. I had a casual arrangement with an old friend, but the moment you came back into my life, the sex with her was over."

"Did the two of you have protected sex?"

"Always."

Genesis began rubbing her index finger, a childhood trait that only surfaced at the height of anxiety.

"Why are you nervous? Are you worried about getting pregnant?"

"No, I've got the patch."

"I'm STI-free, if that's a concern. My doctor's physicals are extensive, and include tests for sexually transmitted diseases, including AIDS."

Genesis's heart skittered. She clutched Jaxson's arm, her eyes alarmed.

"What?"

"I can't say the same, Jaxson. My ex and I went for checkups once deciding to become exclusive, but I haven't gone since he and I broke up."

"Have you been with anyone else since then?"

"No."

"Are you dating around?"

Genesis tsked. "Are you kidding? I haven't had time!"

"Is that what you want to do, explore your options, or are you ready to give us a shot?"

Genesis took a deep breath. "I think I'm ready to hang with you for a while."

"I don't want to be with anyone but you. So…we're good?"

She nodded. "We're good."

Just like that, they made being exclusive official. Later that night, the agreement was enthusiastically and thoroughly consummated—skin to skin.

Sixteen

Ten years after that first fateful meeting, Genesis was surprised yet delighted to be in a committed relationship with the teenager who'd been the first guy to use his tongue to make her booty tingle. He'd done it again last night. Nothing like a few rounds of good sex to stimulate the brain cells. That and time and distance away from certain other situations. With the security of this new exclusivity, everything felt better. The sun shone brighter. The future held promise. She remained cautious, tried not to have expectations, but being with Lance or any other guy had never felt like this.

She was thankful to have a great guy by her side, but life was not problem-free. Since speaking with Hazel about Cyrus's things, she'd tried several times to contact her cousins. Had left messages and texts. Neither had responded. She'd tried again today, twice, with the same results. After the day passed without hearing from them, she called Tiffany. Doing so was more than a notion because her once-dear cousin was ghosting her, too. They hadn't talked since the funeral. Yet, miracle of miracles, she answered the phone.

"Who is this?" was her reaction to the unknown number.

"Hey, Tiff, it's Genesis."

"Hey."

The usual effervescence whenever her cousin spoke was now replaced with a voice dryer than the Sahara.

"I've been trying to reach Clarence and thought you might know where he is."

"Out driving, I guess. He's had to double up on his limo business now that the money he'd expected didn't come through."

Clarence was in financial trouble? This was surprising news and valuable information. The upscale limo company he owned appeared to be successful. Cyrus had shown her pictures of Clarence with various celebrities. She'd seen pictures of his home, complete with a pool. Yet, from the few rappers she'd partied with in Memphis, Genesis knew what looked like wealth could be mere illusion. Maybe that was Clarence's story, that all that glittered wasn't gold.

"I guess you're doing all right," Tiffany continued, sarcastically. "Better than us."

"I'm doing okay. My ankle healed. I was doing DoorDash, but once that stopped, mostly because of the injury, I took a customer service job working from home."

"From Grandpa's home, you mean. Daddy told me you had the nerve to move in, even though that's not your house. Grandpa has two sons *and* several grandchildren. No way in hell he'd voluntarily leave it to you."

Growing up, during the times they were together on the farm, Genesis, Tiff and Kayla had been thicker than thieves. Time passed. Situations changed. The realization made her sad.

"Jaxson King, the football player you met at the funeral, spoke with your father and told him Uncle seemed fine. He was Uncle Cyrus's neighbor and saw him often. They'd played chess not long before Uncle passed. I never graduated past playing checkers, but from what I hear, chess is a very mental sport.

"The last time I saw Uncle Cyrus was six months ago, around the holidays. He was his usual spunky self. Two weeks before he passed, I called him. He sounded a little tired, but nothing that sent up red flags. Tiff, I can't tell you why your grandfather did what he did, but I don't think it's because he had dementia. Whatever the reason, it's placed me in the middle of an awkward situation."

"You should do the right thing, Genny," Tiffany said. "Daddy and Grandpa didn't have the best relationship, but at the end of the day, he's still his son."

"What do you think is the right thing?"

"Move out! Find somewhere else to live. Turn the farm over to Daddy and Uncle Cleo."

"Has Clarence explained the whole situation? Uncle Cyrus set up the trust in a way where it's not that easy. I suggested they speak with the attorney directly. Did that happen?"

"I don't know. What I am sure of is how weird it is for Grandpa to leave all of his stuff to you when he had two whole sons and grandchildren, his real next of kin."

Ouch.

Genesis worked hard not to react. The statement was hurtful, but true.

When Cyrus was hospitalized during the pandemic, Genesis was the only relative who'd bucked the system and gone to his house to make sure he was okay. That visit was when she saw how distant the sons were with Cyrus. They'd called but made no plans to actually see him. No one did, even after the lockdown was lifted. Not Tiffany, nor Kayla, nor their brothers, Uncle Cyrus's grandsons, who were also no-shows at the funeral. Maybe that was what he'd appreciated about Genesis, knowing someone cared enough to show up.

"Daddy and Uncle Cleo want to sell the farm and split the proceeds, as they should be able to do. Daddy's fair, Genny. I'm sure he'll give you something. Daddy and Uncle Cleo aren't getting any younger and aren't in the best of health either. Nobody needs this stress. Selling the farm, splitting the money and moving on is what works best for everybody."

Everyone but Cyrus. But Tiffany had a point. In her mind, Cyrus's sons were the rightful heirs. Was it really fair for Genesis to be the only one who benefited from her uncle's foresight and years of hard work? Even though keeping the farm was her late uncle's wishes, did that trump the needs of folk still alive?

"Do you think I should go against what Uncle Cyrus wanted and turn over the farm to your family?"

"Doesn't that feel like the right thing to do?"

Genesis sighed. "In a way. Most of the time, whatever belongs to the parent is passed down to the next of kin. Following the advice to sell the farm would definitely make my life easier. It would end this family squabble and give me a little financial relief. But the people closest to Uncle Cyrus, including the attorney who helped him create the trust, assured me that he was very clear about who he wanted to have the property, and that he didn't want it sold."

"Grandpa isn't here anymore," Tiffany countered. "He left the farm in your hands. You have the power to do the right thing by all of us."

"Tiff, please tell your dad that we need to talk as soon as possible. It would be great if he and Cleo could fly back one weekend to see the farm and all of what Uncle Cyrus left. In the meantime, I'll speak with the attorney again and see if there is a reasonable way out of this dilemma. I'll let your dad know what I find out when he calls."

The call was upsetting and then some. Genesis tapped Jaxson's number, looked at the clock, then decided on a drive-by instead.

He was out playing fetch with his pit bull. Until Butch, Genesis hadn't been fond of that breed. But Butch was a big ole baby.

"Genesis! What are you doing?"

"Running away from home."

She went in for a hug and immediately felt better.

"I'm glad you came by. Blake and I spoke earlier about the farm. He's particularly concerned about how long it's been since anything was updated, especially the wiring, which is likely not up to code. That and the plumbing system—pipes, water heater, sewer. Have you given more thought to taking out an equity loan? I could call my guy tomorrow and have the money in your hands next week."

"That may not be necessary. I just had a long talk with Tiffany."

"Who's that?"

"My cousin, the one Clarence was trying to get you to marry."

She looked for a smile at her attempt to ease the tension. Jaxson remained straight-faced.

"I think communication stopped because their position is the same. The farm should be theirs. At the end of the day, despite my uncle's wishes, I think they're right. When I get back to the house, I'm going to call Al Young. Find out how I can make that happen."

Jaxson reached out his hand. "Come on."

Instead of going up the steps, Jaxson continued to the side of the house. She almost gasped at the picturesque scene— a huge maple tree with a swing tied beneath it. They sat on the swing, and while he gently rocked them back and forth, she expounded on her talk with Tiffany. "I'm thinking about how I would feel in their situation. If it were my mom, for instance, and she left everything to Hank."

A definite possibility. She immediately shut down the uncomfortable thought.

"For instance, if I needed money and Hank had it but wouldn't give me any because it's what Mom wanted. Whether that was true or not, I wouldn't be happy."

"To me that's apples and oranges, but let's go with that scenario and look at the other side. What if you'd been a real bitch to your mother and she had every right to cut you off. What if she laid out, in no uncertain terms, that she wanted Hank to have the money because you had ignored her, all but deserted her, for the last ten, fifteen years. Wouldn't Hank's actions then be understandable, even honorable? Making sure that someone who wasn't helpful while the person was living didn't benefit once they died?"

Jaxson had a point. Genesis felt torn.

"Thanks for listening. I appreciate your feedback."

"What are you going to do?"

"The same thing I planned to do when I came down here. I hope Uncle Cyrus will forgive me, but life's too short to argue over money. I'm going to call the attorney and try to sell the farm."

Jaxson stopped the swing. "If you ask me, you're making a big mistake."

Every fiber of Genesis's being believed he was right. But this decision wasn't about him, or her either.

"Maybe," she finally whispered.

Jaxson hopped up. "Let's go."

"Where are we going?"

"I'm going to take you for a spin on my tractor."

"Oh, no! You want me to go all the way country for real!"

"Woman, you haven't lived until you've straddled a John Deere."

"Not only have I straddled one, I've driven one, thank you very much!"

For the next hour, Jaxson took Genesis on a tour of the

land that had been in their family for several decades. They went past a herd of cows, saw Randy in the distance.

"Those belong to the farmer who you lease land to as another stream of income?"

"Some of the profit but none of the pain, and the beef I get to eat is organic."

They reached the copse of pine trees she'd first seen up close on the UTV. Jaxson explained that by November they would have grown several more inches, ready for ornaments and lights. Jaxson used his land in a variety of income-producing ways, which not only handled upkeep but added to his annual profits.

"It doesn't pay as well as the NFL," he admitted, as they headed back toward his two-story farmhouse. "But working with my hands is just as satisfying."

"That's why you flip houses?"

Genesis watched Jaxson almost wince before covering the action with a smile. "That's one of the reasons. The other is to help people who typically can't afford a house be able to get one. Everybody deserves to live the American dream."

Jaxson suggested they have an impromptu picnic down by the pond. He'd make the PB and Js. She knew what he was trying to do. Connect her to the land the way Cyrus had been, to see its value and beauty and why he didn't want it sold. He was also trying to distract her from making the only decision that made sense.

It didn't work. She declined the picnic offer. Back at the house, she retrieved her phone and sat on the porch. It seemed an appropriate place to have the lawyer conversation. It was after five, later than she'd thought. She dialed the number anyway and planned to leave a message. Instead, to her surprise, Al answered.

"Hello, Mr. Young. It's Genesis Hunter, Cyrus's niece."

"Oh, hello, Genesis. How are you?"

"Good. Mr. Young—"

"Al. Please. Mr. Young is my father."

"Okay, no problem."

"What can I do for you?"

"It's about the farm. I want to sell it and split the proceeds with my cousins, Uncle Cyrus's sons."

"I thought we'd already gone over this, Genesis."

"I know."

"I also went over the will with your cousins Clarence and Cleo."

"They called? When?"

"It's been more than once. I explained as thoroughly as I could that the will was clearly and specifically written and properly executed."

Genesis was stunned. Either Clarence hadn't shared this info with his daughter, or Tiffany knew it but thought her coaxing Genesis would somehow lead to a different outcome.

"Al, I know it wasn't what my uncle wanted, but his decision has created conflict in the family and, honestly, made life difficult for me. Selling the farm is the only solution."

A prolonged silence preceded the attorney's response. "I'm afraid that won't be possible. Cyrus Perry was nobody's fool and he didn't suffer them lightly. He knew his sons better than they thought he did. Which is precisely why the trust was created with ironclad instructions on what he wanted to happen, and why a letter was drafted and notarized to combat any pushback. I didn't read it during the meeting and quite frankly hoped I wouldn't have to. The truth can be harsh and what's stated in the correspondence Cy dictated doesn't paint his sons in the best light. Genesis, that farm is your uncle's legacy. It must remain in the trust under your name for at least ten years."

"But if the land is legally mine, shouldn't I be able to do what I want with it?"

"Technically, yes, and after ten years has passed you can do just that. You might not be able to see it now, but your uncle believed you owning it might be a curse in the short term, but a blessing and a gift in the end. Cyrus was right about most things. I think he's right about this, too."

Needless to say, the phone call was not at all what Genesis had expected. It dampened her mood and made her feel as though she was back at square one. She immediately put a call in to Clarence, but, as usual, it went to voicemail. She left a message just short of showing her whole poker hand.

"Clarence, it's Genesis. I just spoke with Al Young about selling the farm and learned why there's no way that can happen, at least not right now. He said you and Cleo were told the same thing on more than one occasion. Deciding to sell the farm was stressful and, in the end, pointless. I wish you'd returned at least one of my calls or texts and told me what you'd learned.

"Given the situation, Clarence, I'm going to move forward, starting with clearing out Uncle Cyrus's personal belongings. There are decades of your father's memories stored here. It would be great if you and Cleo could come help go through it all. I'm planning to sell the larger items to help pay for much-needed repairs, some considered to be safety hazards. Any remaining items will be donated to charity, starting with the Baptist church where the funeral was held.

"I'm sorry this didn't work out the way your family wanted. Please call back and let me know if or when you think you can fly down. I'd like to get this project completed before winter, so...let me know."

Genesis called Jaxson.

"Is that dinner offer still good?"

"Sure. What do you have a taste for?"

"Where did you get those tacos?"

"A truck that's usually parked in the square. If not, I know a couple other places. Should I come now or give you time to make yourself presentable?"

"A little time, maybe."

"Like what...an hour?"

"Jaxson! You know what—"

She heard him howling with laughter while hanging up the phone.

The taco truck had left, so Jaxson took her to what he called a small-town staple, a place where he'd hung out as a kid.

She looked at the marquee. "Tastee Freez?"

"Ever heard of it?"

"Never."

"Then allow me to place your order. Prepare to be amazed."

Ten minutes later she tried what was called a pizza burger

for the first time. It didn't exactly taste like pizza, but it was different, and good.

"This franchise is one of the few who still serve it," Jaxson explained. "And not every location. I think the locals are addicted. If they ever tried to discontinue this item, someone might try and tear the place down."

Her fast-food diner experience was rounded out with a bite of Jaxson's chili cheese dog, onion rings, fries and a banana split she shared with Jaxson. They talked about the equity loan, with Jaxson providing valuable information on how it worked and why it was a good idea, namely increasing the property's value and improving quality of life while there. He pretty much talked her into an affirmative decision. He agreed to call his banker the following week. They returned to the valley appropriately stuffed and with Genesis feeling better about the future.

"My house or yours?" Jaxson asked.

"Mine, please. Now that I've made the decision to move forward, I want to start the process of really going through Uncle Cyrus's things, and cataloging them into categories of what stays, what's sold and what's given away."

"Sounds like a plan. Want some help?"

"I'd love some."

Jaxson used the private back road. As they neared the house, both were surprised to see a car next to the Kia.

"Do you know who that is?" Jaxson asked.

"I have no idea. Where's Nipsey?"

"I don't know." Jaxson pulled up next to the small white

sedan. A middle-aged man with graying hair and a full beard got out of the driver's side carrying a folder.

Jaxson cut him off before he reached Genesis. "Can I help you?"

"I'm just here to drop off papers for Ms. Hunter."

"After business hours?"

"Apologies for the lateness," the man said. "I came by earlier, then decided to enjoy one of those Holy Moly burgers before trying again and heading home."

The situation felt unusual, but the guy seemed friendly enough. Jaxson relaxed. A little.

"Yeah, those burgers are something."

The man patted his ample belly. "Try to get one every time I come this way. Was told this was an important document, an addendum to a deed or something. The attorney wanted to make sure it got delivered personally. I live in Covington. Before hitting the main highway, I followed through on my plan to swing by here again."

The explanation made sense, but something felt off. Very few strangers ventured into the valley. Jaxson decided he was being overly protective but was glad he'd made the offer to come over. What if Genesis had been alone? Who was to say the man, as nice as he appeared, was telling the truth? These days, unfortunately, one couldn't be too careful.

He reached out his hand. "I'll give her the paperwork."

The man hesitated. "Nothing personal, sir, but me getting paid is predicated on handing off my delivery directly to the client. May I walk over there with you, just to see for myself that she receives them?"

"We can do that."

Jaxson kept an eye on the guy as he approached the passenger door.

"This guy is from the attorney's office. Says he has an addendum to your deed for the farm."

"Thank you," Genesis said, taking the envelope. Given their earlier conversation, she assumed it was the letter Al had mentioned, the one that laid out exactly why she owned the farm and why it couldn't be sold for at least ten years.

"My pleasure," the man said. He started to say something else, but after looking at the scowl on Jaxson's face, he backed away and went to his car. When parallel with the truck, he rolled down the window and yelled, "Y'all have a pleasant evening. Ms. Hunter, you've been served!"

"What?"

The man took off before Jaxson could react. Still, he instinctively took off running after the car, hurling a string of expletives toward the retreating lights. He walked back to where Genesis sat reading the envelope contents, her cell phone flashlight moving back and forth across the stark white paper.

"I take it that's not the deed?" Jaxson asked.

She slowly shook her head. "It's a petition submitted on behalf of my cousins. They're contesting Uncle Cy's will."

Seventeen

Jaxson woke up feeling irritated. Days had passed since the process server situation. The memory still rankled. Genesis was upset, which meant he too had a problem. Something had happened to her that he couldn't fix or control. After another half hour trying to reclaim the sleep that had already left him, he reached for the cell phone and texted his barber, then jumped into the shower. When he returned to the phone, there was a message. The barber could try to move up his standing 2:00 p.m. appointment if he could be there by nine. After filling his thermos with java, he headed into town.

Jaxson hopped out of the car, ready to enjoy a cut, a shave, a healthy dose of trash-talking and brotherly love. Greetings rang out as soon as the chimes went off. Jaxson greeted the patrons as he offered one-shoulder hugs and fist bumps before taking a chair by the window. He listened to the men debate one thing after another and scrolled his phone.

While checking out renovations on a popular social media site, a video title caught his attention: Build Your Tiny Home for under 10K!

Jaxson was intrigued. For the next several minutes, he went down the tiny-home rabbit hole. Of course, he knew about them, but when it came to alternative living, he'd gravitated more toward container homes, some as luxurious as the homes in Paradise Valley. One video was especially inspiring. Two brothers in South Carolina had come together to form a tiny-house village. They set up plots with individual gas, electric and water hookups, then leased the plots to homeowners. Their plan had been immediately successful.

According to them, finding space to park tiny homes was a major challenge. The brothers had worked with the city for the proper permits and zoning. In less than a year, they'd leased all the spaces and were making a respectable profit. As he continued to scroll, an idea began to form in his head, one that could not only provide redemption from the fiasco in Arizona he'd unknowingly aided, but help Genesis make hers a profitable property. He loved helping Genesis and was prepared to support her. But he also respected her desire to be independent. A tiny-home village could help that happen. Perhaps they could even form a partnership and use some of his land as well.

He clicked on a few links to tiny-home articles. The more he learned, the more interested he became. He sent a text to his banker friend to request a phone meeting. If Genesis increased the loan to cover land preparations, or they created a separate loan as a joint venture, the groundwork needed to build such a village could get started right away.

There were also more personal reasons Jaxson found this project interesting. From the bits and pieces that Genesis had shared with him, and given her initial actions toward him, she hadn't had a lot of positive male interaction. Cyrus Perry was the only man she constantly mentioned in a positive light. She didn't talk about her biological father, and said her stepfather was kind but distant. Now her cousin was on her case to dishonor her great-uncle by going against his wishes and selling the farm. Genesis needed to see that not all men were jerks. That good, honest, solid men like Cyrus still existed, the kind who'd help her stand on her own and be self-sufficient until the right man came along. A man who deserved her.

Like you? asked the devil on his shoulder.

"Jax! Man, quit daydreaming. You're up."

Jax took the ribbing good-naturedly as he slid into the chair.

"What's up, Ronnie?"

"I can't complain. Wouldn't do any good if I did." Ronnie draped a cape over Jaxson's clothes, then began arranging the tools of his handiwork.

"What are we doing today?"

"The usual. Take some off the top and shape it up."

"What about this thing happening on your face?"

"I'm thinking about growing in a beard."

Ronnie grunted. "Brother, you need to make a decision

one way or the other, because the current situation is not a good look."

Guys on both sides of where Jaxson sat heard Ronnie's comment. The teasing began. For the next thirty minutes Jaxson enjoyed the special camaraderie only found in barbershops, where men felt safe to speak freely about anything. Where they could be who they were without judgment. Not much, anyway.

An older man sitting two chairs down leaned forward to catch Jaxson's eye. "Heard you have a new neighbor."

Jaxson turned toward the voice. "News travels fast."

Ronnie squeezed his shoulder. "Keep your head still."

"How'd you find out?" Jaxson asked, believing he already knew the answer.

"Ran into Granville at church last Sunday. Hadn't been there in a while, since going down to Florida to help my brother recover."

"How is Daniel?" one man asked.

"Ornery as ever, which means he's feeling better."

"Remind him to take care of himself. Those heart attacks are no joke."

"Anyhow, that's why I missed Cyrus's funeral. Hate that I did. He was a decent man and a longtime friend. He told me it was a nice service, and that the niece who wrote and read the obituary now lives in his house."

"When was the funeral?" the man sitting next to Jaxson asked.

Jaxson told him.

"That's interesting. I could have sworn I saw Clarence just this morning."

Jaxson's head shot up in surprise.

"Dammit, Jax!"

"Sorry, man."

"No, you're going to be sorry when I have to carve a map of Tennessee in your hair to make up for these crooked lines happening."

The men laughed again. Jaxson ignored them, relaxed back against the chair.

"I don't think it was Clarence. His niece has been trying to reach him about coming down here to help handle his father's…affairs. I'm sure if he were in town, he would have called her."

"How much you want to bet?" asked a man sitting in the chair by the window Jaxson had vacated. "Looks like either him or his twin across the street right now."

The man nodded toward the street corner, out of Jaxson's view. He resisted the urge to jump out of the chair, yet pondered this development. Was he here about contesting the will? Clarence wouldn't have had to fly from Phoenix to do that. Was the attorney he'd hired someone local? Jaxson knew a lot of the townspeople. Could it be a former classmate, one of their parents or someone else he knew? There were a lot of questions, but not a lot of answers. One way or another, he was definitely going to try to find out.

"We about done here?" he asked Ronnie.

"Except for the scruff on your face."

Jaxson reached behind him and untied the cape. "Next

time," he said, already up and reaching for his money before Ronnie could stop him. "I just remembered something that I need to do."

Jaxson acted purely on instinct. He went to his truck, grabbed the ball cap he'd left in the passenger seat and a pair of shades from the console, then headed down the sidewalk in the direction the barbershop patron had been looking when he spoke. At the end of the block was an office building that housed an insurance company, a real estate business, a mail service and at least two law firms. Fortunately for him, it also housed a mini-mart. He stepped into the cool confines of the convenience store and posted up next to a rack of magazines.

"Can I help you?" the owner asked, after Jaxson had been there for about ten minutes.

Jaxson reached into his pocket and handed the clerk a twenty. "I'm not loitering. Just trying to ditch a girl." He winked in a show of camaraderie. "You know how it is."

The young man laughed and half turned before spinning back around. "Hey, has anyone ever told you that you look like Jax King, the football player?"

Jaxson pulled his ball cap lower. "I get that all the time."

After five more minutes went by, Jaxson decided to end the stakeout. He walked to the back of the store and nabbed a water, then went down the snack aisle for two large bags of the cheddar popcorn he knew both Hazel and Nipsey loved. He looked up just as a very familiar face stepped inside the store.

Clarence Perry, Genesis's cousin, was definitely in the building.

"Would you happen to have those…what do you call them…burner phones?" Jaxson heard him ask the clerk. "The kind that can be purchased without an account?"

"No, we don't carry those."

"Okay, thanks. Hey, let me get one of those cigars."

Jaxson kept his back turned until Clarence left the store, then went to the counter to finish his purchase. His first thought had been to let Clarence know he'd been spotted, but again, acting on instinct, he decided to remain hidden instead. When he thought the coast was clear, he exited the building and reached for his phone.

"Did you know Clarence was here, in Holy Mound?" he asked, when Genesis answered.

"Is that why he hasn't returned my phone calls? Because he was here working with someone to get me served?"

"I thought the same thing but why fly all the way here to do that?"

"Good question."

"He doesn't know I saw him. But he's up to something. He asked the clerk in the convenience store for a burner phone."

"A burner phone?"

"Stay put. I'm coming over."

Jaxson flew like a bat out of hell down the highway, ignoring the speed limit and damn near his life. He pulled into Cyrus's drive like a man on a mission, not sure when the old man's wishes to keep the farm had become his personal struggle. Probably the moment Genesis started creeping into his heart. On the way home he called a few of his connections, made a few inquiries, received some info. Before getting out of the car, he took a breath to calm himself. Genesis needed his rational, steady support, and she was going to get it.

"Gen!"

"Come in."

Jaxson entered a quiet living room. "Where are you?"

"In here."

Today she wore a striped cotton maxi, her natural curls loose and floating around her face. The only thing that would make her more beautiful to him than she appeared right now was a smile. Lucky for him he felt he had a way to make that happen.

"Hey, there, beautiful."

He squeezed her shoulder, before sitting down beside her. She leaned into his arms.

"You okay?" he asked.

"Never better. I'm happy, delighted, just thrilled to know the cousin whose phone I've called and left messages on was quite possibly right here in town when I did it."

"I hear you, sweetheart. That's messed up."

"Completely."

"What do you want to do?"

Genesis picked up her phone. "Leave another message."

She tapped her screen. Lifted her chin. Jaxson could feel her back straighten as she waited.

That's my baby. Get 'em! They had no idea who they'd messed with.

"Clarence, it's Genesis. I know you're in town and why. I got served.

"I can understand you doing what you feel you've got to do, but ignoring me and continuing to blame me for something I had no part in is ridiculous. Since you're here, I'm hoping you can be mature enough to come over tomorrow and have a civil conversation and help go through your father's things. You know the address. I'll wait until noon. After that *I* plan to make a few legal moves."

She ended the call ready to box. "I can't believe these people! I've tried everything to handle this family-friendly and they—"

"Shh." Jaxson turned her away from him and massaged her tense shoulders. "I'm proud of how you handled yourself just now, the way you've dealt with this whole process."

"Thanks."

"The next move is on your cousin. Until you hear from him, I have an idea that would be a much more productive way to spend your energy. Want to hear it?"

She nodded, rolled her shoulders. "Um, that feels good."

Jaxson told her what had happened while waiting for his haircut, then showed her the tiny-house village video, along with a couple of others.

"Imagine having sovereignty by creating a village. No mortgage. No debt. And a community of handpicked neighbors helping you live your best life."

"It sounds good. Great, actually. Why are you going to these lengths to help me? What's in it for you?"

"I know you've been mistreated, not only when it comes to the farm but in other ways. And there's that part about me being a nice guy."

"A nice guy. Nothing more."

"There may be a little more to it. If you're open, we could partner and use some of my land, too."

"Aha! So the truth comes out."

"Don't you think we'd make good business partners?"

"I don't know. Besides, I'm still trying to recoup money from the last time I ventured down that road."

"I completely understand, Gen. I've been burned, too."

The thought still brought a twinge of pain to Jaxson's heart. His ignorance had been costly. And though he'd done what he could to help those who'd been affected, it hadn't felt like enough. He didn't know if he'd ever feel fully exonerated. But a thriving tiny-house village and a woman named Genesis might make him feel at peace.

Eighteen

Though she hoped it would happen, Genesis was shocked the next morning to wake up to a message from Clarence. Even more surprising and suspicious was its civil tone.

"Genesis, I received your message. We'll see you at ten."

The "we" part threw her, but just briefly. Of course Cleo would be with Clarence. He was an equal part of all that had gone on. Genesis was still very upset with her cousins' actions. They'd treated her like a criminal and a liar, while she'd been blessed by Cyrus's generosity. She was done feeling bad for her great-uncle's gift and wouldn't allow her cousins to take away the happiness his largesse had provided. Not long ago, she would have gotten down in the mud with them. Not today. Her life felt good. She planned to stay focused on that.

Hoping to somehow mend the rift that Cyrus had created, she decided to play hostess and treat her cousins as guests. Not in the homemade-from-scratch way Hazel McCormick approved, but in classic Genesis Hunter style. This meant a trip into town to the Holy Goodness bakery for a variety of pastries, then a stop at the store for a selection of juices and a fresh fruit tray.

Back home, preparations became more complicated. Cyrus was a man's man, a decided bachelor with no use for frivolous decorations. There were no nice pitchers to pour the orange juice or a tablecloth in sight. She wished for the time to pick a bouquet of the wildflowers that grew near the pond. In the end, she ditched all ideas of fancy. This was a farm, not a five-star. She set the apple, orange and lemonade cartons on the table, opened the box of pastries and set the fresh fruit in the middle. The small plates, cups and silverware were set on the end of the table. She looked around and almost became emotional.

"Wish me luck, Uncle Cyrus."

She heard the sound of tires on gravel, looked out the window at a full-size SUV approaching and walked toward the screen door.

Showtime.

She opened the door and stepped out on the porch. The SUV windows were tinted. She imagined Cleo and Clarence getting out, and maybe their wives. She was right about Clarence and Cleo. The wild card she hadn't expected was when Tiffany stepped out of the van's side door looking runway-ready, her shoulder-length hair flat-ironed, makeup flawless, wearing jeans and a crop top that emphasized her assets. A pair of faux designer glasses completed the look. Genesis had always thought her cousin was pretty. Still did. Meanwhile, her hand unconsciously slid up and touched the uncombed tresses she'd quickly tamed with a scrunchie. Her cousins were family. She hadn't dressed up. Jean shorts were paired with a retro-styled black tee bearing an iridescent peace sign emblazoned on the front. She hoped they'd see it and get the message. No need for drama here!

Clarence, Cleo and Tiffany crossed the yard like strangers on their way to a business meeting. Clarence's neck stretched here and there, taking in the house and surrounding landscape. Cleo's eyes were fixed on the steps and front porch. A blinged-out cell phone held Tiffany's attention as she finished a conversation that had obviously begun in the van.

"Talk to you later," she said, as she walked up the stairs and pulled off her glasses. Then to Genesis, "Hey, girl."

"Hey, Tiffany." The brief, obligatory hug. Genesis noted Tiffany smelled good, too. She'd looked nice at the funeral but nothing like this. Had her cousin snagged a man and was he back at the hotel chilling, patiently awaiting her return? Or did her plans in Holy Mound include snagging a local, one who just happened to live down the road?

"We just talked two days ago. Why didn't you tell me you were coming?"

"You're not the only one who can keep secrets." Tiffany slid her a side-eye look. "Daddy didn't want you to know."

She continued across the porch. "All this is new, huh? The porch and steps."

"Looks good," Cleo admitted. "Hope you haven't started borrowing money on the house."

"What's in that shed?" Clarence yelled from the side yard.

"Why don't we all go in the house and get comfortable.

When it comes to this farm, there are no secrets." She looked pointedly at Tiffany, who tsked and turned her head. "Ask me anything. If I have the answer, you'll have the answer."

Genesis led the way into the house and continued to the dining room and the breakfast spread.

"I didn't know if y'all had a chance to eat breakfast, so I picked up a few things. Help yourself."

Tiffany bypassed the dining room and went looking— snooping—through the house. Cyrus no longer lived here. This was her house. Genesis took a breath and ignored the rude behavior. She was determined to have at least one conversation about this property that didn't result in a fight.

"Do you have any coffee?" Cleo asked, picking up a caramel-and-nut-covered Danish and taking a bite.

"Sure. Give me five minutes."

"That's okay if it's not ready."

"It'll only take a sec."

When she returned from the kitchen holding a mug of steaming java, she found the brothers had turned the living room into a treasure hunt. Clarence had removed the glass from the trunk and had Cyrus's guns spread across the glass that was now on the floor. Cleo had found a stack of papers in a piece of furniture she didn't even know had a drawer. He sat in the recliner, looking through them.

Genesis ran a hand across the iridescent iron-on. Peace.

"Here you go, Cleo." She set down the mug. "There's sugar and cream on the kitchen counter."

"No, black is fine. Thanks."

Tiffany came into the room. "This place is smaller than

I remember. That back bedroom we slept in felt huge at the time."

"Did you see the pastries, Tiffany?"

"I'm losing weight, doing intermittent fasting. I'll take a cup of coffee, though."

"Mugs are in the cabinet. Spoons in the drawer. Sugar and cream on the counter. Help yourself."

Genesis poured herself a glass of orange juice and, with the rest of the contents from Cyrus's trunk now taking up couch space, pulled a chair from the dining room table.

"How long are you guys going to be here, Clarence?"

"We leave tomorrow."

"That soon? It's going to take days to go through the lifetime Cyrus lived here."

"I'm only taking anything of value, and what can fit on the plane."

With the strength it took to not open her mouth, Genesis could have lifted her uncle's beloved John Deere tractor. She told herself their feeling validated was worth more than any material possession. She had the farm, the land and a great idea. They could take everything not nailed down in this house and the shed. She would be just fine.

"I know it's been a while since you've been here and there's a lot to explore, but is there any way we can talk first? About the will, the trust, the deed, the lawsuit?"

After several moments, long enough for Genesis to need another glass of juice and this time bringing a doughnut along, the cousins gave her their attention. Tiffany moved over some of the items on the couch and sat down.

Genesis started the conversation by addressing the bull the size of Randy in the middle of the room. "I wish y'all hadn't felt the need to sue me."

"Didn't want to," Cleo said. "You left us no choice."

"Uncle Cyrus left you no choice," she corrected. "Tiffany, when we finished speaking a couple days ago, I called Al Young, the attorney." She looked at Clarence. "I told him I wanted to sell the farm and split the profits. He told me I couldn't for at least ten years."

"We're contesting the will on the basis of incompetency," Cleo said. "Daddy was in no shape to make major decisions. There was no one here looking out for him, speaking on his behalf."

"I have no idea who was or wasn't here when the will was drawn up. As I've said many times, I was shocked by what happened. I received and read the will on the same day as you."

"When you speak with your…attorney," Clarence said, with contempt, "he'll let you know an injunction has been issued that bars anything further from being done to this property or moved until this matter is corrected. I didn't know you'd already started spending money. Have you borrowed against the place? Is that how you're living out here without working and how those repairs got done?"

Genesis wasn't much of a praying woman but she literally called on Jesus. The blatant disrespect was next-level. If her relatives thought they were going to come in here and walk over her, they had another think coming.

"I resent your implications, Clarence. They are insulting. You owe me an apology."

"Don't hold your breath," Tiffany said.

Genesis stood up. This charade was over. Clearly, her cousins were incapable of acting like they had some got damn sense!

"I've tried to be understanding. I've tried to be patient. I've tried to be fair. None of that is working. My kindness is taken for weakness, and the more I try to be compassionate and sensitive about what's happened, the more I get treated like an enemy. So we're done here. Okay?

"For the record, and not that it's any of your business, I am working. As Tiffany knows, because I told her, it's a customer service job worked from home. Nothing has been borrowed against this home—my property, I might add, as stated in the deed you're contesting. Until that lawsuit is successful and Cyrus's will is deemed invalid, I will remain in the house Uncle Cyrus gave me."

Genesis felt herself getting emotional. She didn't care. When it came to this whole debacle, she was tired of trying to hide her feelings. She would speak from her heart and call a thing a thing.

"Clarence, Cleo, I have only vague memories of you coming around when we were little. You're practically strangers to me. But I loved your dad, my uncle Cyrus, like a grandfather, a father even, because he loved me when my sperm donor wasn't around.

"Tiffany, I can't believe how you're acting. Unlike your father and uncle, we have history. We've shared things. You know how not having my biological father around affected me. The insecurities. The low self-esteem."

A tear fell. Then another. "I stayed in contact with Uncle Cyrus because he loved me, and I loved him. I did it because I liked his company. I did it because he was a connection to the half of myself that I didn't know. That outside of him and those treasured times with you, Tiffany, and Kayla, memories that are now being tarnished with this bullshit, I couldn't connect. Except for a handful of visits from a man who called himself dad but never acted like one, I didn't experience what you, Tiffany, take for granted."

Genesis paused, wiped the tears off her face.

"I will not let you take away the fond memories of my uncle. And as of this moment, since you're determined to go there and make this a battle, know that I will not ignore his wishes and destroy his legacy. I'm done trying to bend over backward to please you. I will not be selling this house."

The silence that followed was deafening. Genesis, emotionally drained, dropped into the dining room chair.

Clap.

Genesis frowned, looked over at her cousin who'd leaned back against the couch. She straightened and clapped again. Slowly. Repeatedly.

Clap. Clap. Clap.

"That was good, Genesis. Award-winning performance." She halted Genesis's coming outburst by holding up a hand.

"I'm not trying to be mean, really, I'm not. You did go through it as a little girl. Not knowing your dad. Being chubby, thinking you looked cute in those oversize glasses.

We shouldn't have teased you. Those glasses were cute. Hell, they're back in style. But I remember how lonely you sometimes felt, like you didn't belong. Especially if our parents were here. I'm sorry about that. Whether or not you know it, we are protecting Grandpa's legacy. My dad and uncle, his heirs, are his legacy, Genesis, not you." She stopped and delivered a dramatic pause. "And not Jaxson King."

The comment came so out of left field that Genesis flinched. Felt like she couldn't breathe.

"What did you say?"

"You heard me. While here gathering information to help our lawsuit, talking to people who also knew and loved Grandpa, I just happened to stumble onto some juicy small-town gossip. I know all about your little secret, your little fling you've got going with your neighbor up the way. More importantly, I know what you don't know about him. He's playing you now like he did years ago."

Genesis couldn't hide her surprise. Or hurt.

"Oh, yeah. I know about that, too. You know I've always been a people person. And over the last couple days I've gone around and met a few people who knew Jax King when he was the big boy on campus in this little town. People that had you not been so…whatever…you might have taken the time to talk to and know who you're dealing with. Later, you'll owe me an apology. And a thank-you."

Suddenly, a picture began forming that became very clear. The peace that had fled away returned. She looked at her cousin with a new understanding. Tiffany had been both her friend and her enemy. She hadn't wanted to see it, wouldn't admit it until now. Tiffany had grown up with everything but was still jealous of her.

Genesis crossed her arms, taking in what she now knew was fake confidence from a woman who really didn't feel good about herself. Genesis recognized it because it was once in her mirror. Had she not been familiar with how it showed up, Tiffany's act would have sent her straight to the depression she'd felt when her family found out about Jaxson and turned against her. That girl back there was not this woman. Genesis eyed Tiffany's hair, nails, the cute jeans, flawless makeup and saw right through the whole charade to her cousin's real MO. Clarence and Cleo wanted the farm. Tiffany wanted her man.

Well, damn family.

Genesis chuckled and did a little faking herself. She was still reeling from the emotional jab straight to the face, but ignored the shock, pain, anger, all the emotions that had been seconds away from erupting. She'd deal with them later. Now she sat back…slowly crossed her arms and legs.

"Why don't you tell me, Miss Wikipedia, with all the information? Why don't you tell me about the real Jaxson King?"

A loud thump sounded in the hall. All eyes turned at once toward the heavy sound of approaching footsteps. Jaxson walked into the room—and owned it.

"Yes, Tiffany." He acknowledged the cousins. "Clarence. Cleo."

"Why don't you tell all of us who I really am?"

Nineteen

It took less than five minutes for Jaxson to clear out the house. Tiffany looked as though she'd seen a ghost and developed a sudden case of laryngitis. Clarence went into protective mode, ready to defend. Jaxson hadn't come down to fight anyone, especially someone with an arsenal of guns scattered around him. The brothers had looked at each other and done that telepathic thing unique to twins. As one, without a word between them, they began walking toward the door.

"We'll see you in court," Clarence said to Genesis, looking Jaxson up and down before making his exit.

"Remember the injunction," Cleo added.

Tiffany glided over to where Genesis sat, giving Jaxson a look before addressing her cousin.

"I'm not lying," she said, her eyes drifting to Jaxson again. "Ask him why he left Paradise Valley."

The comment sent a chill through Jaxson. *WTH?* He silently followed them out the door, waited until they'd pulled away before returning inside. Told himself to not react to the taunts, that there was no way Tiffany knew about...that.

He'd not intended to come in the house at all. He'd seen the van pull up, watched the cousins get out and hadn't liked the three-to-one ratio. He'd intended to stay invisible, in the periphery, to be near just in case Genesis needed his support. Looking now at a shell-shocked Genesis with silent tears once again streaming, Jaxson surmised he'd had the right idea.

He went into the kitchen, made a cup of chamomile tea and set it in front of Genesis. He sat down beside her, close but not touching. She needed time to gather her composure and her thoughts.

He sat back, waited.

Eventually, Genesis took a sip of tea. She began talking, looking straight ahead.

"Why would my cousin say what she said?"

"I don't know."

"How did she find out about...what happened back then?"

"I'm sorry for that." Jaxson reached out to rub her shoulders. Genesis pulled back, ever so slightly. Jaxson tried to not take it personally, but it was obvious that the doubt, questions, suspicions planted in Genesis's mind had taken root.

"Maybe a high school classmate who still lives in town. Quite of few of them do. Or someone who heard the rumor from someone else. Small-town gossip has a hundred ways to get around."

Jaxson could no longer resist touching her. He could see the insecurity completely absent yesterday creep back in, could almost feel the suspicions she'd initially had about him being reignited.

"We've already been down this road," he gently reminded her, placing his hand over hers and giving a gentle squeeze. She didn't pull back. He exhaled.

"We separated the lies from the truth. There is nothing to the rumors about me, including the supposed dare."

"Started by an ex, right?"

"Yes. The girl I dated off and on all through high school. We were each other's first…sexual experience, something that happened way too young. She never accepted that we were truly over, that leaving for California marked the end of our dysfunctional, yo-yo existence. She moved to Chicago years ago, but still has ties here, still comes back to visit family."

"When was the last time you saw her?"

"Two years ago, when her favorite aunt died. It was a cordial enough interaction where she swore the past was the past. But Deidre has always been messy, and spoiled, used to having her way. I wouldn't be surprised if she was the link.

"But again, bae—" he picked up her hand, kissed it, held it between his "—let's not get pulled back into the illusions that lies created. What's important is the present, the man you know now. The man who helps you. Protects you."

Loves you.

"Okay?"

"Okay." Genesis sat forward and turned to look him in the eye. "Tell me about Paradise Valley."

For Jaxson, this was the moment of truth. One he'd hoped would never have to happen and definitely not this way. It was not a secret he planned to keep from Genesis forever, but one he wanted to divulge in his own way, on his own terms. Even though he didn't know what was happening at the time it went down in Arizona, ignorance didn't exonerate him. He looked beyond the room into the next moments and saw a crossroad. He could tell the story crafted after he left Arizona. Or he could stand ten toes down and trust this woman's ability to hear the lies, yet know the truth beneath them.

"It's an upscale suburb of Phoenix, where I used to live."

"What happened there?"

"I pleaded no contest to a crime I didn't commit."

"A crime? That sounds serious." Genesis turned fully toward him. "Did somebody die?"

"No, but it's funny you ask that, because my reputation was killed. My character was assassinated."

"Did it involve a woman?"

Jaxson sighed. *Here we go.* "Unfortunately."

Genesis looked away. He could almost feel the weight of the bricks in the emotional wall she was busy rebuilding.

"Gen, listen, I'm going to tell you everything. It won't be easy. I worked hard to put this situation behind me and wouldn't revisit it for anyone but you.

"I'd just gotten my multimillion-dollar sign-on bonus and moved to Paradise Valley. Loads of money. Nice cars. Beautiful home. I met a young lady, Cyan, whose dad is big in real estate there. She studied interior decorating and staged his houses, including the one I bought. She was young, had just turned nineteen when I met her, and honestly, when I found that out, I was shocked. She was very mature for her age, very professional, definitely didn't act like someone in her teens."

"I felt the same about you when we met," Genesis said. "When I learned you were five years younger, eighteen, still in high school…"

She heaved her shoulders, shook her head, unspoken words released in a sigh.

"Five years? I didn't know that. I thought maybe a year or two. Wow, that's deep." Jaxson paused as his mind traveled to the past and back. Whoever said hindsight was twenty-twenty had been spot on the money for real.

"Cyan was a year out of high school but very poised, knowledgeable, confident, well traveled. We had a lot in common. Both liked to party. I was twenty-two, twenty-three, and, I'm not going to lie, I was living the single, rich, pro athlete life. I was wilding in those streets. I loved women. Fast cars. Good cognac. Nice weed. When she and I hooked up, I didn't think anything about it. I've always respected women, no doubt about that. I felt when a woman jumped in bed at the drop of a hat, often with me not even knowing their last name, it was understood that what was going on was just about getting it on. Banging a stranger. I mean, what else could it be?

"I hate to say it and am definitely not proud about it, but anywhere money or power flows in abundance, casual sex is rampant—pro sports, entertainment, politics, all of that. Most women who hang out in those environments know the code.

"Anyway, Cyan and I, we're hooking up fairly often. Hitting the party scene. She's flying to some of my out-of-town games, borderline stalking. At the same time, I'm dating Abby, right? And a few others. I'm practicing safe sex with all the women I'm dealing with. I'm telling them all I don't want a child. I'm not ready to get married. I'm not looking to be exclusive, make commitments or settle down."

"If you're practicing safe sex, what happened with Abby?"

"I have my theories." Jaxson shrugged. "Let's just say she was determined to get pregnant and leave it at that."

Fortunately, Genesis didn't press the issue on what for Jaxson was a touchy subject.

"Meanwhile, Cyan's dad and I are becoming friends as well. He's giving me the game on real estate, investments, the whole nine. He pitches this particular real estate investment venture, a way for people with limited funds to invest in real estate as part of a collective and eventually, if desired, own their own home. The concept sounded good. I had no reason not to trust it. He's one of the top Realtors in the country. His client list is mad crazy. He asked me to be the spokesperson, a celebrity endorser, the recognizable, friendly face of the venture. A common marketing tactic and why so many celebrities are seen pushing product on TV.

"Saying yes is a no-brainer. I'm a star pro baller. The city's darling. Not bad-looking. I attracted a lot of people with very little effort. Especially women. Everyone's excited. The money is rolling in. What I didn't know, and wouldn't find out until it was too late, was that the investment group was a scam, a Ponzi scheme, defrauding thousands of people out of millions of dollars. Again, I don't know this yet. I'm still counting the cash like Monopoly money, living the dream, thinking everybody's getting paid. Only those of us at the top were raking it in like that, but I'm off playing football, none the wiser. I'm not in the business meetings, have no idea about the day-to-day. I think he counted on that. I'd fly in, learn whatever script, shoot the videos, attend a few parties. I was ignorant. And naive. But I wasn't a thief."

He looked beyond the living room at the dining room table. "Mind if I get some of that juice?"

"Help yourself. The doughnuts, too."

Jaxson poured a glass and sat down, this time across from Genesis.

"Around this same time, Abby gets pregnant. Cyan finds out and goes all the way off. Sets out to destroy me or break us up or whatever. What did I need with that kind of madness? I'm young, popular, successful. Juggling women from coast to coast. So I stopped seeing her. Decided to do the right thing by Abby. Bought the ring. Proposed. The whole nine.

"Little did I know that when I broke it off with Cyan, she'd run and tell her dad. All of a sudden, I'm not as cool as I used to be. I've hurt his little girl. At the same time and for the next several months, I hear murmurings of what is really going on with the business. People losing money, not getting new homes as promised. It was crazy. The timing sucked because it turned out her dad was already being investigated. He had his hand in a bunch of illegal shit. Long story short, the Ponzi scheme got uncovered, and I got thrown under the bus. Cyan and her dad made it look as though I personally encouraged homeowners to borrow off their equity so they could invest. I never personally talked to anyone or signed people up. I just made it look like the right thing to do."

"You talked me into doing that very thing."

Jaxson looked over and was devastated to see the accusation in her eyes. "I made that suggestion from what I learned from the banker and attorneys who helped me survive that mess. Taught me how to use home equity the right way, and leverage it correctly, the way people who know how banks and finance work do all the time."

"Why didn't you marry Abby?"

Jaxson stood and paced the room. "Believe it or not, as bad as all of what I just told you was, it got worse. Abby had been sleeping with a good friend of mine, a teammate. We all ran in the same wild circles and weren't exclusive, so it wasn't a total shock. But I'd asked this girl to marry me. I started questioning whether or not the child was mine and demanded a DNA test. The fighting started."

"Did you get the test?"

"Yes. But I'd been betrayed. The trust was gone. The final nail in my Paradise Valley coffin came when the Ponzi scheme was publicly exposed, around the same time I busted my knee. I got cut from the team and moved back here. Needless to say, I was done with the baller life. The trial came a year after that. Because of Cyan's father and both his political and shady connections, he was able to float above the indictments. Those went mostly to the second-tier guys. I got charged with fraud, a felony, for something I had no idea about. But I didn't want all the publicity that would come with me fighting the charge and I damn sure didn't want a criminal record. It's hard enough for a Black man in America, but throw in a felony and it's a wrap. I paid out a lot of money to several people to keep my name out of the papers and have the charge expunged, but to this day feel bad for the people who were affected, people who were as innocent and trusting as myself."

He stopped, drained, much as Genesis had sounded earlier when she poured her heart out to Tiffany.

He observed Genesis sitting as still as a statue. "Say something."

A second passed. Then another. Her shoulders heaved. "What is there to say?"

"I'd never run a game on you, Genesis. You believe me, right?"

"We had so many conversations. Why didn't you ever share this?"

"It's a chapter of my life I've tried to bury. I never wanted anyone here to know what happened."

"I'm exhausted, Jaxson. My cousin's visit, your story…"

"I get it, baby. And I'm sorry. Do you want company later?"

"No. I'm going to need time alone to digest all of this."

He hugged her but, given the tension in her body, didn't attempt a kiss.

"Call me tomorrow?"

"I'm not making any promises. Can you lock the front door on the way out?"

Do not pass Go. Do not collect $200. Jaxson had been clearly dismissed.

Twenty

For the next couple of days, Genesis was numb. She didn't go anywhere, talk to Jaxson or anyone else aside from her job in customer service. She texted a Call you back later to Habari. Even Miss Hazel's calls went to voicemail. The morning after his revelation, Genesis woke up to several texts from Tiffany with links to a few articles on the PV Ponzi scheme and subsequent trial. The ugly truth in black and white. Jaxson hadn't lied. In reading the article, she saw how his money had shielded him. He wasn't named directly. They didn't even list the sport. Phrases like "charismatic professional athlete" and "former high school and college standout" were used.

The story itself was devastating. There were instances where instead of cash the deed to homes had been held as "security," only to be quietly placed in the scammer's name, then sold for fast money. Eviction notices were how some of them found out their house had been sold. People had lost homes, life savings or both.

Genesis didn't want to think the unthinkable, but she couldn't unhear what she'd heard or unsee what she'd seen. Jaxson King had been involved in a Ponzi scheme, using home equity loans as investment capital. Jaxson King had been convicted of fraud. Jaxson King had urged her to use his banker to handle the loan for the home repair. Had this whole interest/attraction been a setup with a particular purpose in mind? Rather than wrestling with the green-eyed monster, had Tiffany been right? Was the lawsuit a way to protect Uncle Cyrus's land and legacy? Had dating Genesis been an easy, inexpensive and legal way to get his hands on a neighboring farm?

In times like this, Genesis wished she were close with her family, especially Lori. Or had a couple of BFFs. She almost called Lance. He was a great listener. He was also the one who'd talked her into investing her savings on the promise of a thirty-day payback. Promissory note aside, she felt she'd been scammed, too, like millions of people all over the world.

A few days after the family-farmhouse fiasco, a call came in that Genesis answered.

"Hello."

"Genesis, Al Young. I've been trying to reach you."

"Okay."

"It's regarding the contesting of Cyrus Perry's will. I believe you were served...last Friday night?"

"Something like that." Genesis had lived a lifetime since then. The days blended together.

"The petition has been filed in county court. As the attorney on record for Cyrus's estate, I received a copy. Did you read the document?"

"Not all of it. What do I do?"

"First of all, don't worry. As I've shared with you and Cyrus's sons multiple times, his fully executed will is within an ironclad trust, with very specific instructions on how its contents can be disseminated. Unfortunately, Cyrus's sons have opened an ugly can of worms. I will now have to include the notarized letter I mentioned to you as a counter to the petition and further evidence of his express desires. I've already submitted paperwork to the judge. His docket is usually not that full during the summer months. We should have a ruling in thirty to sixty days."

"It will take that long?"

"Hopefully not, but possibly."

"I have a question. I've already begun minor repairs on the house and was preparing to clear out Uncle Cyrus's belongings. Do I have to stop all of that until a ruling is made?"

"How extensive are the repairs?"

Genesis told him.

"Finish anything that's already in progress, but don't start anything else for now. That extends to anything outside or on the land as well. As I stated, Cyrus was very clear about how he wanted his estate handled and, because of how well he knew his sons, took extra precautions to ensure that his wishes would be granted. Be prudent. Don't worry. Once this is out of the way, you'll hopefully be able to enjoy your new home."

A week went by without speaking with Jaxson. He texted

every day—a greeting, positive quote, motivational message, GIF or meme. Not talking and no resolution made Genesis feel that her life was in limbo. That Sunday, a week and a day after she'd last seen him, she gave him a call.

"Bae. It's good to hear your voice."

"You, too." Genesis felt herself tearing up. She'd never been so emotional.

"I miss you."

She had no response. Their connection had changed.

"I want to see you."

"I need more time to think, process and make decisions. Not just about…what you told me. About everything."

"I wish you wouldn't shut me out. We could go through this better together."

With your name on my deed?

"Have you spoken with your attorney?"

Bad timing for that question.

"Has the lawsuit been filed, or did your cousins grow a conscience and withdraw it?"

"I spoke with Al. We have to go through the process."

"Jazz will be here soon. I want her to meet you."

"I don't think that's a good idea."

It was Jaxson's turn to be silent.

"This is hard, Jaxson. I really like us together. But if you look at it from my perspective, you'd know that there's no way I can keep seeing you. Not right now. Maybe not ever. I don't know what to believe, who to trust, what to think. I need time. We're likely going to be neighbors. Maybe some-

where down the line we can be friends. I need a break, so…
I'll reach out when things change…if they change."

"And if not?"

"Take care of yourself, Jaxson. Goodbye."

After that phone call, and about an hour of off-and-on
well-deserved tears, Genesis retrieved her tablet from the
bedroom. She sat and pondered for a moment. It was time
to make another list.

Do Me To-Do List:

1. Organize uncle's things/move to spare bdrm/shed

2. Make this my home—within circumstances

3. Work on myself (who am I, what do I want???)

4. Volunteer somewhere—Hazel

5. Lance—pymt plan

6. Call family/Hank/Tiffany

Writing that one hurt. Once again, because of Jaxson, she
was on the outs with her immediate family. Uncle Cyrus
had her at odds with her cousins. It was the middle of summer but the holidays would soon arrive. She'd thought she'd
spend them with the man she was falling in love with. Now
she wasn't sure where she'd be.

7. Reconnect with friends/Memphis

The next thought that popped in surprised her and made her feel good. The idea had come from Jaxson but it was a good one. And, if necessary, she could do it on her own.

8. Research tiny homes

As soon as the list was done, Genesis jumped right in. Al had told her she couldn't get rid of any of Uncle Cyrus's things. He didn't say they couldn't be rearranged, boxed and stored. She had to do something to change what had become a claustrophobic atmosphere. Memories of her dear uncle had been replaced by those from "that day." The energy of Clarence, Cleo and Tiffany's invasion permeated the space. After a walkaround, she came up with a game plan. On an impromptu drive to Memphis, she called Habari. He play-cussed her out for not calling back sooner. Asked about Jaxson. She said he was fine. She also reached out to Brea, the friend who loved New Orleans. They ended up doing a little shopping together and grabbing a bite. It felt good to hear someone else's story, someone who knew nothing about the dramas playing out in her life.

It took three days and dozens of boxes, but the farmhouse that once belonged to Cyrus began to transform. She completely cleared out the master, the other bedrooms and what she wouldn't need in the living room. The smaller of the two guest bedrooms became a storage unit, completely full, worthy of a sign saying DANGER: KEEP OUT or simply DO NOT ENTER. She splurged and hired a cleaning company. She swore they wiped away dust and dirt that had sat undisturbed for thirty years. She pulled down curtains. Opened all the windows. It made a world of difference just to let the sunshine in.

Throughout the month of August, and following her uncle's spirit vs. the lawyer's advice, the transformation continued. She missed Jaxson every day, replayed his confession constantly. One day he was an asshole, guilty of everything. The next a brother who'd been misrepresented, deserving of the chance to prove he was the man who'd picked her up from the mud. She tried not to think about him but gave herself room to process, analyze and absorb her feelings. To replay the conversation without emotion. To try to have an unbiased point of view. Some days were better than others.

One afternoon, in the middle of her fluctuating feelings about Jaxson and the unexpected break from dating they were on, Lance called.

"Gen, what's up?"

"Not much. What about you?"

"I've got good news."

"How much good news?" Genesis warily asked.

"A thousand."

Less than she needed but better than nothing. "I appreciate it, Lance."

"No, Gen, it's me who's appreciative. I'm sorry this took longer than I thought. It's obvious now my quick turnaround repayment timeline was unrealistic."

"Does you having a little extra mean business is picking up?"

"We've got a long way to go, but yeah, word is getting out. We're beginning to see a regular clientele. And we finally got a couple solid investors."

"Is one that rapper you mentioned?"

"Naw, these are real businessmen with degrees and shit."

"Ha!"

"They're out of Texas with a strong business portfolio—car washes, Laundromats and other passive income. They were in town on business and dropped by on a Friday night when a party of birthday revelers had the place jumpin'. They liked the concept, loved the wings and agreed to come on as silent partners. In time they'd like to open up a second spot in Dallas."

"That sounds good, Lance. I'm really happy for you."

"Thanks, Gen. I'm happy for me, too. What's going on in your world?"

Genesis gave him the *Reader's Digest* version of recent events, minus the Jaxson portion. "I can't believe Uncle Cyrus left me this property. Even with all the drama going on, I'm glad he did."

"Are you living out on that big spread of land all by your lonesome?"

"Uh, Lance, are you trying to get all up in my business?"

"Damn right!"

The conversation continued a while longer and helped lift Genesis's mood. Before they were lovers, she and Lance were good friends. Even though they didn't work out as a couple, she was glad their friendship had survived.

Later that week, Genesis phoned Hazel, apologized for not returning the call earlier and began volunteering at the church's thrift store. The humble abode that had once belonged to Cyrus began to look less like an old farmer's hangout and more like her—a combination of her uncle's ruggedness and her contemporary style. She was surprised at how well the two worlds came together. Knowing how much her uncle had loved the life he'd built here, she was happy to in some way keep his memory alive. One weekend, Habari came out and helped rearrange the heavy furniture. Later, Brea braved the country to see her place. When she arrived, her jaw literally dropped.

"Girl, you live in the country for real!"

Brea was a home-designing godsend, addicted to YouTube, DIY shows and HGTV. Genesis kept the trunk that doubled for a coffee table and a gun case but covered the glass with a colorful strip of kente cloth repurposed from a $10 muumuu purchased at the church's thrift shop. Pillows brightened up her uncle's well-worn black recliner and couch and complemented the strip on the table. At the thrift store, she purchased brightly colored curtains and a collection of wicker baskets. Other than items from her storage in Memphis, the living room and master bedroom were finished. The kitchen and bathrooms looked the same but were clean. It felt liberating to create the environment she wanted and not let others fully dictate how that happened.

Time continued to fly. One month bled into another, and

before she knew it, leaves had turned, turkey fixings lined the store aisle and Christmas music threatened to push another year out of the way. One or two times, she ran into Jaxson. It was awkward and amazing and her heart hurt after they spoke, but the exchanges were cordial. Hazel tried to talk to her about their situation, but she wasn't ready. Her wise words did lead to Genesis trying harder for a better relationship with Lori. She now made a point to call her mother once a week. The conversations were short and often one-sided, but Genesis felt better for making the effort, which, according to Hazel, was the point. She and Hank still needed to have an air-clearing conversation, but they'd started communicating again by text.

She watched self-help shows, especially those highlighting relationships, and journaled almost every day. She continued working on herself, too, which further helped generate compassion for Lori. Through an old *Fix My Life* episode where a mother and daughter were estranged, Genesis was able to look at herself through her mother's eyes. How it must have felt to have a fine brother wine and dine you, make all kinds of promises, talk you out of a preferred termination and beg you to have his baby, only to get back with and marry his ex before said child blew out her first birthday candle. To hear stories of their wedding and subsequent move to the East Coast. To have to fight for child support and endure verbal abuse during these confrontations. Genesis was sure Lori loved her. But Genesis also was the spitting image of her daddy, a daily reminder of a man Lori despised. It wasn't right, but Genesis began to understand, even empathize with, why Lori clung to Hank Sr., a good, no-nonsense, older man who adored her.

For his part, Hank Sr. did his best. He was clearly more comfortable around his sons than her, but in hindsight that might not have been personal. It may have been because he was an alpha male who gravitated toward activities like hunting, fishing and sports. Genesis was a girlie girl who wanted nothing to do with any of that. Like her mother, Hank wasn't affectionate. But he was a provider and a protector. From the time her mother married Hank Sr., all of them had everything they needed and most of what they wanted as well.

The weeks of self-improvement and difficult yet authentic relationship reflections softened Genesis's heart toward her family. Now she looked forward to spending the holiday with them. Just before she was to head to Memphis for Thanksgiving, Hazel called.

"Hello, Miss Hazel!"

"Hi, baby. You still going home for Thanksgiving?"

"Yes, ma'am."

"Good. I'm just making sure. Have you talked to Jaxson to see what he's doing?"

"Miss Hazel…"

"I know. You don't want to talk about him. But as your elder, I'm going to say what's on my mind.

"Sometimes things happen in life that are not all right or all wrong, all black or all white. We have to make sure the decisions made in those situations are coming from our heart, not just our head. That they're not being made out of fear, or what-ifs, or based on what happened yesterday, or with somebody else. Baby, I don't know the details. Those aren't my business. But I know Jaxson isn't just your neighbor. You love that young man. I saw it in your eyes. Take it from someone who has more years behind her than she does ahead. Life goes by in the blink of an eye. Don't look back later and wish for a do-over when there's a chance to have one right now."

Jaxson was angry at the world in general, and a few people in particular. From the night Genesis's cousin Tiffany had walked up and dropped a bomb, he'd been on a mission to find out who had his business in their mouth. He was never able to prove it 100 percent but felt his hunch was right. Deidre, his on-again, off-again high school ex, was the continuous thread through various aspects of his life's journey, and the only one messy and spiteful enough to not only keep tabs on his life but troll the internet and track down his secrets. A part of him badly wanted to confront her. He resisted. Attention from him was the prize she sought. Though he'd done it years ago, he blocked her again from all of his accounts and made sure they shared no mutual friends. It was a small step toward eradicating what had become like a cancer, but at least it felt productive and wouldn't land him in jail.

He missed Genesis. Plain and simple. Amazing how important she'd become in such a short time. Thank God for his daughter. Jazz arrived the week after the fallout. She kept him busy. Her constant chatter drove loneliness away. Once he flew her back to Phoenix, he treated himself to a much-needed break by spending ten days in Fiji. He returned home refreshed and ready to work. Good thing, because what followed were sixty-to-seventy-hour workweeks. The eight-unit apartment complex had come with unseen challenges, as often happened in an auction-style bid. Rather than be upset, he welcomed problems. Big ones. Complex ones. Next to repairing a one-of-a-kind relationship, fixing a wiring system, plumbing leak or reconfiguring a floor plan was easy.

He'd just gotten home, taken a shower and strolled into the kitchen when his cell phone danced across the quartz countertop. He looked at the caller ID and tapped the screen.

"Susan?"

"The one and only."

"Hey, stranger. What's going on?"

"Life. What about you?"

"Same."

It was good to hear from Susan. She hadn't reached out that much since meeting her new guy, Greg. They hadn't spoken since his fallout with Genesis.

"How's your baby girl? Back in Phoenix?"

"How'd you know she was here? Wait—let me guess. Miss Hazel."

"Of course. I'll work on forgiving you for not letting me meet her."

"You're right. I apologize," Jaxson said. "I should have arranged it. Next time for sure, okay?"

"Okay."

"How's your clan?"

"Bad. Smart. The loves of my life."

"Always."

"Speaking of love… You and that girl still dating?"

"Her name is Genesis."

"By now I thought you would have changed it to Exodus." Jaxson cracked up. "That was a good one. You're a fool!"

"I try. She's still around, huh? Must be serious. I hardly hear from you anymore."

"I could say the same thing about you. Life's been busy. Work is crazy." He gave her a rundown of his flips with Blake. "And Genesis and I are on a break."

"Seriously? Wow, Jaxson, I'm sorry to hear that."

"Are you really?"

"Honestly, I'd say around seventy percent so. She was different. I could tell you really liked her. What happened?"

"A misunderstanding. Long story."

"Any chance you'll get back together?"

"I honestly don't know." He paused to absorb the weight of that truth and picture its reality, a future that didn't include Genesis. Didn't look good. "Are you still with the guy from that night?"

"Greg? No."

"What? You've already chewed him up and spit him out?"

"He was too needy and controlling. It only took a couple months to see the red flags. He had some good traits, too, so I gave him a chance. But being with him took too much energy. I don't have time to help an adult grow up. Told him it wasn't him, it was me."

"Hang in there, friend. When you meet the right guy, it'll work out."

He heard his own words and wished it for both of them.

Genesis wasn't the only new thing from the past few months that stayed on his mind. So did the idea of a tiny-home village. The possibility of such a community sat well in his spirit, a type of retribution for past sins. In his spare time, he continued to research the project. Even ordered floor plans and got ideas from Blake. He was especially inspired by the two South Carolina developers who'd transformed ten acres of land into a welcoming village for those wanting to park their mobile abodes and had made attempts to contact them.

Through continued research, Jaxson learned that the tiny-home business was a growing, multimillion-dollar industry. A partnership with Genesis would have allowed a larger set of homes, but after walking his land and plotting out several possible configurations on paper, he decided on two acres that were flat and close enough to the road for his dream to begin. The land currently being leased for cow grazing could be added later if the plan took off. There were mature trees to provide shade and character, and maybe a swing for nice evenings. He knew people at city hall who could help with the zoning process. Running adequate lines for electricity, gas and sewer hookups and acquiring the means to accommodate both regular and composting toilets would probably take the most time and present the greatest challenges. But if he could help several families realize the dream of home ownership, even a tiny one, it would be worth all his efforts.

The additional work generated by opening his seasonal Christmas tree business kept him busy on the weekends, but not enough to erase thoughts of Genesis. He tried to get into the Memphis social scene and scrolled through images on a couple of date sites. None of the pics or profiles held his interest. He'd already found the woman he wanted. Once again, something from the past had messed it up.

Jaxson could reflect on one positive note—his relationship with Abby. Since agreeing to watch Jazz so that Abby and her husband could take a vacation, the atmosphere between them had shifted. Not as much friction. He and his ex would never be best buds, but for the past few months there'd been no major arguments or hang-ups. They'd had civil, albeit short, conversations and, even better, made compromises that worked for them both. The latest involved the upcoming holidays, which in the past had been problematic, because Abby had wanted Jazz with her family on all of them.

Yet recently, through an almost pleasant exchange, it was decided that Jazz would spend Thanksgiving with Jaxson and Christmas at home. Whether it was the new baby, another girl, finding happiness with her husband or time healing wounds, the changes he saw in Abby made him hopeful that they'd reached a stage of positive co-parenting that would provide the best for their daughter—the one thing they both wanted.

Most of November was spent in Memphis. The eight-unit building that was formerly an apartment complex had been completely renovated and now boasted eight unique two-bed, two-bath condos. With the sale of just four units, Blake and Jaxson made back their investment. Two more were in the closing phase, and the other two had multiple applications from interested buyers. Buoyed by the success of that multiunit venture, they'd purchased another, larger complex in Nashville. Renovations on it would begin after the first of the year. With the completion of the apartment building, he and Blake returned to Holy Mound to enjoy the Thanksgiving holiday. After Christmas, they'd give themselves a two-week vacation to be refreshed and ready at the start of the New Year.

It was a small yet lively bunch that gathered for Thanksgiving in Jaxson's sister's backyard. They'd enjoyed a feast of turkey, ham, duck and all the usual suspects for trimmings, and were now relaxing and enjoying each other. Some smoked cigars and other types of leaves. Others sipped a mixture of cocktails and nonalcoholic drinks. Jaxson bantered with everyone as he went from group to group, with one eye always on Jazz and the other children. He watched as two of his favorites among them broke away from those playing cornhole and other lawn games and ran in his direction.

Mario reached Jaxson first and threw himself into his arms. "Uncle Jax, when are we going to see the tree light up?"

"Yes, Daddy, and the fireworks!" Jazz half spoke and half whined as she jockeyed with Mario for premium positioning on Jaxson's lap. Her move was as if to make it clear that he was *her* dad after all. "Can we go now? Please! Please!"

Holy Mound never let a good holiday go uncelebrated. Tonight was the annual Christmas tree and town square lighting. Retail establishments usually closed at night would stay open to welcome early holiday shoppers. Food trucks would line the street. Vendors would be out selling every-

thing from spiced apple cider to tarot card readings. Every
building in the square and those surrounding had been out-
lined in white and multicolored lights. Neon, blinking an-
gels, stars and snowmen had been mounted on light posts and
tree branches. A seventy-five-foot Shasta fir decorated with
tinsel, lights and ornaments hand-made by various school-
children would anchor the festive setting from the center of
the square. A citywide choir comprising high school students
and seniors would provide the entertainment. The mayor
would give a speech. At just after dark, and usually with
great anticipation and flair, one lucky citizen selected from
a random drawing would get to flip the switch and turn an
ordinary shopping and business district into a winter won-
derland. Fireworks would end the affair.

Jaxson skillfully balanced a child on each leg and answered
the question for the umpteenth time.

"What did I tell you when you asked the last time?"

"Just after dark!" they chimed together.

"And we get to ride in the back of your truck?" For Jazz,
this was a treat, and probably something that would freak
Abby out.

"Yes, indeed. I'm throwing all of you hardheads back
there."

"My head isn't hard," Jazz said, running her hands across
her curls for confirmation.

"No, sweetheart. You're a softy."

"I'm not soft! I'm strong!"

An older cousin ran by and squirted the group with a
water gun, thankfully rescuing him from a debate he couldn't

win. Jazz was as headstrong as he was and as opinionated as her mother. If channeled correctly, the combination could take her as far in life as she wanted to go.

His sister Ruth joined him on the picnic bench. "Mario! Share with your sisters." And then to Jaxson, "They grow up fast, don't they?"

"It's incredible. Can't believe she'll soon turn five and enter kindergarten."

"She's been in preschool since she was, what, two?"

"Just about. But she's moving up to the 'big kids' school,'" he emphasized with air quotes. He continued mimicking Jazz's voice. "She gets to ride the bus and everything!"

"Ha. Enjoy it, brother. You'll blink and she'll be sixteen, wanting nothing to do with you."

"Like you were with Mama?"

"And like you were with all of us, Mr. Sports Superstar!" Ruth took a sip of her Arnold Palmer.

"Where's Susan?"

Jaxson shrugged. "Probably with family. Why do you ask?"

"That's who you brought to dinner last year. Y'all aren't still dating?"

"We never dated, really. Just friends from high school."

"Nobody special in your life?"

No, and pointing it out didn't help matters at all.

That evening, Jaxson enjoyed a quiet night alone. He'd finally given in to Jazz's begging and allowed her to spend the night with her cousin. He grabbed himself a beer from the fridge and had just settled on a sports channel when he heard a knock at the door. Couldn't be Granville. That loud contraption of a truck always announced his arrival. Either he'd borrowed Hazel's Cadillac or Susan had decided to drop by. Either way, he was glad for the company.

He hopped up and opened the door. It wasn't Granville, Hazel or Susan. It was...

"Genesis."

"Hi."

"Hi."

"Is this a bad time for a DDI?"

He smiled. Stepped back. "Of course not. Come in."

They walked into his living room. "Have a seat."

An awkward silence ensued, before Jaxson said, "It's good to see you, Gen. How have you been?"

"I've been okay. You?"

"Good. Busy. Jazz is here."

Genesis looked around. "Oh. I'm sorry. I didn't mean to—"

"No need to apologize. She's not physically here at the moment. She's at my sister Ruth's house, spending the night with Mario and some other cousins."

"I see."

"Did you have a good Thanksgiving?" he asked.

"Yes, surprisingly. In Memphis."

"You weren't expecting to?"

"I'd hoped so. Hank and I had only talked by text since I'd confronted him about lying and then not taking responsibility for how it affected my relationship with the rest of the family. He finally apologized. We all talked about it. More than a decade later, we cleared that stale air."

"Is that what brought you over?"

"That's one of the reasons. The other was a phone call from Miss Hazel. She helped me put...everything you shared with me that night in perspective and be open to a different conclusion than the one I drew."

"Which was...?"

"That you couldn't be trusted. On top of what you revealed, Tiffany sent me articles she'd found on what happened. Your name wasn't mentioned, but I knew the stories were about you and not told in the best light. The scenarios of how some of those people were scammed, taking out home equity loans and possible deed manipulation resulting in people losing their homes, felt too similar to be coincidental. That you'd kept encouraging me to work with your banker made trying to steal Uncle Cyrus's land out from under me even more of a possibility, very similar to what happened in Paradise Valley."

"And now?"

Genesis hesitated. "While that scenario is still a possibility, it's not so much a probability."

Jaxson nodded, afraid to voice any optimism about their future prematurely.

"Even though it's been proven that what Hank said was a lie, I'd lived ten years thinking you'd conned me, slept with me on a dare. That much built-up emotion doesn't leave overnight, even if it was a lie that started it.

"Miss Hazel's words of wisdom helped me see all that's

happened from another perspective, to do what I hadn't done, which was give you the benefit of the doubt. I refused to believe you were totally innocent. Then I ran across an article involving a crypto scandal where a bunch of celebrities lent their face to a scheme that looked legitimate and got caught in the cross fire. I made a business investment in blind faith. She reminded me that life doesn't fluctuate between good and bad or black and white. That there are variations and layers in between."

"Miss Hazel is a wise lady."

"Indeed," she agreed.

"That day after your cousins left, I told you the ugly, painful truth about what happened in Paradise Valley. It was a multimillion-dollar lesson. That's how much I paid to put that fiasco behind me and keep my good name intact."

Several seconds went by with neither saying a word. The television had been muted. Even nature was silent.

Finally, Jaxson took a chance and asked the million-dollar question. "What does your new understanding mean for us?"

"I hope it means that we can be friends again. I've missed you, not just as someone I dated, but as my neighbor, contractor and potential business partner. That suggestion you made about tiny homes has really stuck with me."

"Me, too!" Jaxson interrupted, excited that even while apart they'd been in sync.

"I've watched dozens of videos, even subscribed to a few series where people share their tiny-home journeys. I'm very interested in moving forward. It's not only a fascinating industry, but with the country's ever-changing economics, one I believe will continue to grow."

"I feel the same way, Gen. In fact, I've done quite a bit of research, too, going so far as to map out two acres of my property for six to eight homes."

"You're going to use the idea you pitched to me?"

"I didn't know you'd use it, but I felt it was too good a venture to pass up. Plus, it's a way for me to completely own and control a real estate venture, and to do something good for a community that's loved and supported me."

The more he and Genesis talked, the better they both felt. That they'd been thinking along the same lines about the same thing was confirmation that they worked well together.

Belonged together.

A thought Jaxson wisely didn't share.

"I want to show you something." He stood and headed toward the screened-in back porch that sometimes doubled as his office. He returned with a rolled-up architectural rendering.

"You want something to drink?"

"What do you have?"

"Beer for me. Wine for you."

"Sounds good."

He turned toward the kitchen.

"Jax?"

"Yes."

"Thanks for not making a big deal about how long it took for me to come around."

"You're here. That's all that matters. I've missed you."

"Me, too."

"One more thing."

"What's that?"

"Can I get a hug?"

That Sunday, Genesis met Jazz in a group setting at the McCormicks' church. An afternoon program that included a children's play. She arrived and sat with Jaxson, his sister Ruth, Mario and her other children, Susan, and about thirty other congregants. Granville worked as an usher. Hazel served refreshments. Jaxson didn't know who was happier, him having Genesis and Jazz meet each other, or Hazel because he'd finally accepted an invite and visited the house of the Lord.

Over the next couple of weeks their friendship returned as though not interrupted, centered around the tiny-house project. Genesis loved the overall direction. Even though getting resolution of the will being contested was taking longer than expected or desired, the dream had continued on paper. Jaxson's rendering of the potential village had been revised to include five acres of Genesis's property adjacent to Jaxson's two. At her suggestion, a playground and picnic area were added, with a place for outdoor exercise, which inspired Jaxson to mention a walking/biking trail around both properties and access to the pond. *Perfect!* The final drawings for the village had them both excited. Twenty initial plots with rectangular slabs of concrete for a variety of homes and sizes were mapped out. The slabs were sizable enough to accommodate wraparound patios for indoor/outdoor living, potted plants, patio furniture and grills. Each plot would come equipped with electric, water and sewer hookups. A small pavilion was added to the picnic area, along with a firepit. What started out as a plan had become a passion. Genesis and Jaxson looked forward to their vision coming to life.

Something else happened. The bricks rebuilt around Genesis's heart yet again fell away. Genesis's attention, at first focused almost exclusively on Jaxson the contractor and business partner, expanded to Jaxson the man. The fun, flirty, audacious woman who'd first caught his attention returned. Long talks focused on road access and tree lines turned into lunches and dinners together, and on this Friday night, to watching a movie.

They were at Jaxson's place. He'd initially invited her up to watch a video about a tiny-house village in Texas. Larger and more upscale than their current plans, this one featured a golf course, clubhouse and community pool. As they sat watching side by side, sexual energy sizzled between them. Innocent touches led to knowing looks. Jaxson slid an arm around her shoulders. The move was natural. The easy embrace, nice. Once the video ended, Jaxson suggested having a pizza delivered and watching a movie. Genesis agreed.

When the action flick was over, Jaxson further tested the waters by inviting Genesis to spend the night. Luckily for both of them, she agreed to that, too.

Twenty-One

Genesis turned and snuggled up against Jaxson, who was lightly snoring in his sleep. The temperatures must have dropped during the night. The room was cold but Jaxson's body felt warm. And hard. And amazing. She pulled his arm across her waist. He stirred, then squeezed her against him.

"Good morning, beautiful," he said in a voice groggy with sleep.

"I didn't mean to wake you."

"Less about waking me than waking this."

A gentle poke revealed that Jaxson's dick had risen from slumber. Genesis thought that after last night's shenanigans it would have overslept. Not that she was complaining. She couldn't see ever turning down a chance to make love with Jaxson. He was a master at the craft. No wonder he was so cocky in high school, a stud in college, a player in pro football, with friends who loved his benefit.

The feel of Jaxson's hand leisurely sliding from thigh to

breast interrupted her thoughts. She returned the favor. Within minutes they were in full heat, mingling legs and arms and morning breath with equal abandon. There wasn't a lot of foreplay. No pause for protection. Neither had slept with anyone else during their time apart.

A desirous look from Jaxson made Genesis wet. Add his tongue and a couple of fingers and it was off to the races. After sliding his middle digit down the crack and into her ass, he plunged himself deep inside her and began to stroke. She clenched her muscles around his girth, swirling her hips and her tongue, their kiss as deep as the tip touching her core. Over and over again. Seconds after her orgasm, Jax let go. The warmth of him exploding inside her was unexpected, but not unwelcome. He quietly slid out of bed, brought back a warm towel and lovingly removed his seed before returning to bed and pulling her against him.

Jaxson kissed Genesis's temple. "Good morning."

"Great morning." She added a quick kiss to his lips.

"What would you like to do this morning, besides more of what we've been doing?"

"Um, I don't know." She took a deep breath. "I can smell the pine trees."

"That's why I like real ones."

Genesis sat up, excited. "Know what I'd love to do?"

"What?"

"Get a tree for my house and decorate it."

"You got it. I wish Jazz was here to help us. Kids make the holidays so much fun."

She paused to adjust the sheet around her naked body. "I

was that kid. Decorating the Christmas tree was almost as exciting as opening presents. When reorganizing the shed, I ran across a box marked *Xmas*. Not sure if what's in there will cover a whole tree, but it's enough to get us started."

"All right." He gave her a quick kiss and hopped out of bed. "If you put on the coffee, I'll hop in the shower, then make pancakes while you get ready. After that we'll go chop down a tree."

Thirty minutes later, the sound of Christmas classics mingled with the smell of cinnamon, bananas and undeclared love. After a quick kitchen cleanup, they headed out to the pine grove and found the perfect tree. Jaxson loaded it on the back of his truck. Genesis retrieved the box from the shed. By the end of the morning, they'd strung every light and hung every bulb in the box. At the bottom were a smattering of old cards, used wrapping paper and miscellaneous junk. Genesis sifted through a few items and was just about to trash it when she felt a piece of cardboard. She moved the junk aside. A yellowed envelope of heavyweight paper had been taped to the bottom of the box.

She moved to the sofa, hoping to not find anything crazy, like a secret of some sort Cyrus had planned to take to the grave.

She pulled back the flap and peeked inside. Her jaw dropped. "Jax!"

Jaxson rushed from outside, where he'd gone to feed Nipsey.

"What's the matter?"

"Look!"

She handed Jax the envelope. He slid out the contents, a nice-sized stack of one-hundred-dollar bills.

"Well, I'll be damned."

"What do you think it is?"

"Um, this is called 'money,' Gen."

She swatted his arm. "I mean, why do you think it's here?"

"Probably because some people, especially the elders, don't trust banks. Cyrus was a hard worker, like my grandfather. No telling how many decades it took him to grow that stack."

The old box marked *Xmas* had held a present—$24,600.

"That'll take care of a lot of repairs around here," Jaxson suggested.

Genesis shook her head. "It's not my money to spend. I'm going to mail cashier's checks in equal amounts to Clarence and Cleo. Maybe they'll have a merry Christmas and in the New Year put the drama behind us."

Jaxson pulled Genesis into his arms. "That's big of you, sweetheart."

"It's the right thing to do."

Genesis sent the cashier's checks with Christmas cards and included a note. Two days later, she received an unexpected gift from her cousins. They dropped the lawsuit.

After the New Year, Jaxson's focus shifted to the tiny-house village. He didn't want to sit on such a great idea. He attended a city council meeting and met with the zoning committee. He brought on board Blake, who became the third partner. Contracts were drawn up. Everything aboveboard. Jaxson secured a sizable loan from his banker in Arizona to cover the initial investment for all of them. He didn't want Genesis to have any doubts! As for Blake, Jaxson considered it returning a favor. Blake had agreed to put a temporary halt to buying more properties until the village was done. Jaxson paid for an outside crew to continue work on the one flip outstanding, the Nashville apartments.

For the next three months, all focus and work went on the village. Foundations were poured. Roads and jogging trails were built. Utility and sewage lines were run. Trees were planted. The pond was expanded and docks were built. Blake's girlfriend, Pilar, worked in tech and gave Genesis the name of a master website builder. HolyMoundMinis.com was clean, interactive and easy to navigate. It took over two months to complete it, but once finished, the website was spectacular. The inviting colors. The enticing content from the writer hired. The beautifully natural surroundings photographed and used. Who wouldn't want to live there?

They launched the site but knew success would take more than crossing their fingers. Jaxson finally heard back from the South Carolina builders and flew out to visit their site. He came back with great ideas, and even greater enthusiasm. His excitement was contagious. Everyone felt good about what was being built. Genesis scoured the internet for communities, groups, anyone discussing tiny houses. Pilar pitched in, too. With a job that relied heavily on digital marketing, her expertise was invaluable. A couple of weeks after going live, and after placing an ad on a tiny-house community board, their site began to get views. Then page clicks. Then inquiries trickled in.

On a cold, windy day a week before spring, as Jax was in the back splitting wood, he heard a car pull into the driveway. He came around the side of the house. Genesis turned from the steps to the house she was about to mount and ran toward him, jumping up and down with a big smile on her face. She jumped in his arms.

"Whoa! What's going on here?"

"You'll never guess why I'm so happy!"

"Well, baby, I tend to have that kind of effect on people."

She squiggled off his embrace but couldn't help laughing. "I do enjoy your…effect…but that's not what brought me here." She sobered, took a breath and said, "We've got our first PLH!"

Jaxson's brow furrowed. "P-L-who?"

"PLH. Potential Lease Holder. This letter might be from our first village resident. Remember those ads Pilar suggested we run on several social media sites? They weren't in the budget, but she assured it would pay off, and it did. This isn't just an inquiry—it's pretty much an application!"

"Let's have a look." Jaxson reached for her hand and walked them up the steps and inside. They sat at the bar counter. "I love that you're excited, Gen, but an online application is a long way from a deposit."

"I know, but wait until you read her message." She pulled out her phone, scrolled to the website and leaned toward Jaxson so that he could see the screen.

Dear Holy Mound Minis:

Holy cow! (I couldn't resist.) I don't want to come off as crazy but you're an answer to a prayer. Mine is a long story but to make it short, my husband and I were forced to downsize last year. We have a three-year-old, a cat and a dog. A real family. Couldn't imagine giving any of them away (especially the kid ☺). It was rough. One day, my husband saw a tiny-home video. His dad has a background in construction. We decided to go for it. Took six months but they built it. Our home is just a tad over 400 feet and can be towed. Your village sounds PERFECT and we can move TODAY.

As you may know, finding a place to park a house isn't easy. For the last several months, we've been in my dad's basement, and once the house was finished, his backyard, which isn't zoned for this oversize addition. He loves us, and especially loves being around his grandchild, but no one would be happier to see us at Holy Mound Minis than him. Except my husband. And me! When I came across your website, I was in a bad place. At my wits' end. If we could set up some kind of video tour of the area, I'd be ready to plunk down a deposit. No kidding. This is not a joke. I look forward to hearing from you soon.

Hoping and praying...Chelsea

Genesis turned to Jaxson, eyes shining. "Well?"

"She definitely sounds serious," Jaxson said. "Damn near sent her life's story in the email."

"Which is why I feel so good about the message. Our

village is happening! We've got our first neighbor, Chelsea. And her family! And pets!"

Jaxson sat back, looked at Genesis and finally allowed a smile. "You're right, baby. This is happening. A village offering an affordable alternative to homeownership."

"It's crazy, Jax. One minute you're showing me a video, and the next..." She turned away.

"Hey, what's with the tears?"

"They're happy ones. For Uncle Cyrus, and you, and the people we'll help."

"I admit this feels amazing." Jaxson reached for his phone. "I'll check with our insurance company about adequate coverage for the playground and pond area. And with Blake to make sure everything is supersafe for the kids."

"That pond area might need its own fence."

"Definitely." He kissed her. "Now get back to business before you become a distraction. I've got work to do."

With a final hug to Jaxson, Genesis went back to her place. Since getting back together, they lived comfortably between each other's houses. She still preferred the office/dining room setup for her part-time customer service job. That night, however, Jaxson twisted her arm to return with the promise of his five-star chili. From the first bite, Genesis had quickly, honestly admitted that it was the best she'd ever tasted.

They ate, stacked the dishes in the dishwasher and were soon enjoying mugs of hot chocolate on an animal-print rug in front of a roaring fire.

"I can't believe this is actually happening," Genesis said, gazing into the dancing flames.

"And so quickly."

She nodded. "When you first presented the idea, I thought it was interesting but unlikely to work. Then you showed me that video..."

"And you started to believe."

"You were always so confident. How did you know?"

"Just a feeling. And then everything came together so smoothly. You. Blake. The builders. The loan. The zoning committee approving the project. The other neighbors in the valley welcoming the plan."

They sat with their backs against a square leather ottoman. Genesis shifted and lay down with her head in his lap.

"Do you always achieve your goals?" she asked, looking up at him.

He absently stroked her hair. "Not always. But mostly. Why do you ask?"

"Until recently, that was pretty much a foreign concept to me. I've discovered the pleasure of setting a goal and making it happen." She reached for his hand and kissed it. "Like how you and Blake take plans from 2D to 3D, turn drawings into houses. You were a type of role model to help me see how that's done."

Jaxson slowly eased Genesis into an upright position. He reached for the sweater she wore and pulled it over her head. "You know what I think?"

"What?"

He unsnapped her bra. Her breasts swayed like melons happy to be free. "I think I want to set another goal."

He scraped his teeth across her nipple and watched goose bumps spring up on her skin. He smiled, tweaked the other nipple with his fingers.

"How many orgasms have you had at one time?"

"Like in one…day?"

"More like one session."

"This is a weird conversation."

"To set a goal, baby, there's got to be perimeters." He got to his knees and removed her leggings and thong.

"In that case, I'll say one."

"Um." He aligned his mouth with her hot box, breathed in the scent. "You're making this too easy."

Lick.

The sweet invasion was unexpected. A hiss escaped Genesis's lips.

He shifted and made himself comfortable, his head between her legs.

"Open wide for me."

The authoritative command caused her Kegel muscle to clench. He slid his tongue between her folds and lapped up her dewy essence. Over and over and over again. His lips covered her nether ones, sucking and kissing. His tongue was a sword, piercing all control.

"Jax!" A guttural exclamation as her body began shaking.

He pressed his face into her bucking body, careful not to spill a drop.

That's one.

As Genesis lay recovering, Jaxson stripped off his clothes. He took Genesis's hands and pulled her up. She fell into his arms, her legs wobbly.

Jaxson didn't mind. In his arms was exactly where he wanted her to be. For a moment, he simply held her as the fire crackled around them, listening to Blake and Gwen saying they only wanted to love each other. Feeling Genesis's soft body swaying against his only made him harder. He picked her up. She naturally wrapped her legs around him. He slid her down on his waiting shaft.

"Ahhhh."

And the dance began.

Jaxson had been with enough women to know that the love he and Genesis made together didn't happen every day. She fit him perfectly—her ass in his hands, her head on his shoulder as he slid her juicy pussy up and down on his dick. Her nipples pebbled, inviting him to take a few more tastes. His fingers tickled her ass, one sliding inside.

"Oh, my God," Genesis panted.

"Yeah, baby." Jaxson placed her on the back of a couch that was the height of his hips. "This is all for you."

Her legs lifted and opened, as if to welcome him home. His thrusts were slow and measured, a little of him at a time. Teasing. Building up anticipation. Out to the tip. In to the hilt. Repeat. When Genesis's hips began to grind and swirl, he knew she was ready again. He picked up the pace and pounded her delicious flesh. She wrapped her arms around his neck and hung on for the ride.

"Yes! Yes! Yes!" she panted, before he slowed things down

again. He twisted his body to anoint her inner walls in the deepest places. To search for and then find that spot.

She screamed.

There it is. Two.

The fire burned down. The loving continued. He counted four orgasms before his mind lost that focus. Before thoroughly satisfying his woman became the only goal.

Twenty-Two

Genesis and Jaxson sat in a booth at Piquant, Holy Mound's new upscale restaurant. Across from them, Blake and Pilar enjoyed an easy banter. They all held flutes of bubbly. What was left chilled in a bucket at the center of the table.

Blake looked around, his smile wide, his blue eyes sparkling. "Who wants to do the toast?"

"I think Jax should do it," Genesis answered. "He's the one who saw the video that started this whole thing."

Pilar raised her glass slightly. "I agree. It's on you, Jax."

"That's right, buddy." Blake placed an arm around Pilar's shoulders. "It's on you."

Jaxson made a show of squaring his shoulders and clearing his throat. Genesis looked on in admiration at what a fine pair of shoulders they were and how perfectly they showcased the tan-colored pullover her man wore. One he'd paired with the same color brushed-cotton slacks and two-toned cowboy boots. Memories of what he'd done to her with the strong, thick fingers that grasped the delicate glass stem almost made her shiver. He looked at her and winked, as though he'd read her mind as well as he regularly played her body.

"This is a special moment," he began.

"A toast, not a speech," Blake mumbled.

Everyone laughed, including Jaxson. "Given what we've gone through in this process, I could probably deliver a sermon."

"I'll say amen to that," Genesis said, raising and waving her arm the way she'd seen the church ladies do when she'd finally attended an actual service.

"Seriously, though, I have to give props to you, Blake, for taking a chance on a man with no construction experience and making me your partner. I hadn't felt grounded since football, you know, part of something, part of a team. Flipping houses with you changed that. And making the smart decision to make Pilar a priority changed you. Pilar, you've made him a better man.

"And speaking of better." He turned to Genesis. "When I plucked your drenched ass out of the mud—"

"Jax!" Pilar exclaimed.

Blake guffawed.

Genesis play-punched his shoulder, then kissed his cheek.

"My bad. Let me say that another way. When I rescued you under very unique circumstances, I had no idea how much you'd change my life, too. I saw the video and thought about you, never thinking the idea would blossom and grow into what it's become. That you and I would become a team."

"Quarterback or safety?" Blake asked.

"Tight end." It was a reflexive comment said without thinking. Then he wriggled his eyebrows to show he saw nothing wrong with it.

Genesis smirked, half humored, half chagrined. "Okay, dude. That was strike two."

"What? Baby, you've got one of the best backsides in America. Nice and tight and—"

"Will this toast ever end?" Pilar emoted.

Like clockwork, the server delivered their appetizers.

"I appreciate all of you." Jaxson lifted his glass. "To Holy Mound Minis!"

"To amazing families!" Genesis added.

"To the timely appetizer delivery" was Blake's dry response.

Amid laughter, Pilar shouted, "Hear, hear!"

Genesis took a sip of champagne and continued. "She's not here but I personally want to thank Chelsea Skinner, Mike and their daughter, Tru, for being the first village residents. Currently, we have space for twenty homes. As of this morning, three of those spaces have homes parked, and half of the rest have been leased.

"Of course, I want to thank you, Jax. Like Blake said, it was your spark of an idea that lit this fire. I never would have thought of using the land to build a community. I also want to thank my great-uncle, the late, great Cyrus Perry, for knowing what I needed far better than I did."

"That was beautifully said, sweetheart." Jax leaned over and offered a quick kiss. "I love you."

She tried to play it off, but his declaration caught her off guard. He was probably more surprised than her.

The words felt good on his tongue. So much so Jaxson offered another kiss and said them again. "I love you, Genesis."

A pause and then she said to him, "I love you, too."

Both acted like what had just happened was no big deal. But what had happened was a Very. Big. Deal.

A few nights later they were chilling, spending a quiet evening at Genesis's house, when her cell phone dinged.

She reached for it. "Oh, wow. It's Mom."

Jaxson glanced over. "Everything okay?"

He watched her eyes go back and forth as she read. "I guess we'll soon find out."

"How's that?"

"You've been officially invited to meet the family. It's my mom's fiftieth birthday party, which means it's an invitation you can't turn down."

"I wouldn't think of it." He paused for a sec. "I guess Hank will be there."

"Of course."

"And he's okay with me coming?"

"I'm sure that had he not given his stamp of approval you would not have been included in this text."

On a Saturday night three weeks later, Genesis and Jaxson arrived at a club on the outskirts of Memphis. Genesis had told Jaxson the owner and her mother "went way back." Their mothers had been pregnant together. The children, now fifty, had known each other all their lives.

"Nervous?" Genesis asked Jaxson as they neared the entrance.

"Terrified" was his honest response. No one would have suspected this truth. When they entered the main room, eyes were drawn to him like a magnet. Men and women alike. He looked like someone who could control the room and everyone in it. But there was only one person he was concerned about. Genesis waved to someone across the room, reached for Jaxson's arm and pulled him in that direction.

They stopped in front of an attractive woman with Genesis's eyes and skin tone. Next to her was a nice-looking, well-dressed man in a suit covering a girth that suggested he didn't miss meals.

"Hello, Mom." Genesis leaned down and kissed her mother before placing a gift bag in front of her. "Happy birthday."

"What's this?" Lori asked. She reached for the bag, but her eyes were on Jaxson.

"That's part of your gift. This is Jaxson King. Jax, this is my mom, Lori, and my stepfather, Hank."

They exchanged pleasantries.

"Where's Hank and Habari?"

Lori nodded, indicating someone behind them. Jaxson turned to see Hank approaching with a nice-looking woman on his arm.

Hank stopped in front of Jaxson. He felt Genesis's eyes on him, along with the rest of the family. Wanting to defuse any tension right off the bat, Jaxson held out his hand.

"Hurricane Hank."

Hank paused. Looked at Jaxson's hand. Looked at Genesis. Looked at Jaxson, shook his hand. "What's up, Jax?"

Just like that, and with the soulful sounds of Muddy Waters grooving in the background, more than a decade of animosity dissipated. It seemed the room itself sighed in relief.

Hank leaned over and hugged Genesis. "You look happy, baby girl."

"I am."

"You've been chasing my sister since high school. I guess you finally caught her."

"Or the other way around."

"I don't have to tell you what'll happen if you hurt her."

"Nah, man. We don't have to have that conversation at all."

Muddy Waters gave way to James Brown telling everybody that he felt good. Jaxson pulled Genesis on the dance floor. Hank and his fiancée, Xenia, danced beside them. A mix of blues, soul and R & B kept the party jumping. When someone initiated the Electric Slide, partygoers packed the floor.

"Baby, I'm so happy!" Genesis exclaimed, Jaxson on one side and Hank on the other. "You being accepted by my family is more than I dreamed. Life can't get better than this!"

They stayed until the end, almost three in the morning. Halfway through the evening, Jaxson ditched the suit coat and rolled up his sleeves. Genesis danced out of her shoes. Everyone he met made him feel welcome. He and Hank reminisced about old times. Jaxson mentioned the tiny-house project and asked for his number to discuss something similar in Atlanta. The happiness in Genesis's eyes when she witnessed the exchange made subduing his pride and making the first move more than worth it. She didn't know it yet, but in Jaxson's mind, a plan was forming. One where, if he had his way, he'd be attending family functions with Genesis for a very long time.

Twenty-Three

One year later

A year had passed since Jax sat in a barber chair and became intrigued with tiny homes. All twenty lots were occupied. Expansion to accommodate more had begun. An unexpected boon had been their neighbors' reactions. Some were now considering having homes on their land, especially retirees who could appreciate extra income. A huge party was planned for the official one-year mark, the day Chelsea and her family turned into the gate and drove their bright yellow home down the nicely paved road. The entire valley had been invited, along with Holy Mound's mayor and several others who lived in and/or did business in town. There would be food and drink, fun and games and a flashy fireworks ending. The last a special request from Jazz, who'd be there acting up, along with the other village kids.

Tonight, however, belonged to Jaxson and Genesis. He'd

suggested they enjoy a private celebration of everything they'd gone through and survived to be successful business partners and a strong, loving couple. Past misunderstandings. Family feuds. The ghost of Paradise Valley. And finally…redemption. Jaxson sat idling in Genesis's driveway, waiting for the expression on her face when she stepped outside. Most women he knew would be impressed with a man who came to pick them up in a cherry-red Infiniti Q60, even one that was five years old. Genesis was not most women.

As she descended the steps, looking casually sleek in a pair of royal-blue-and-ivory-striped palazzo pants, a lightweight ivory sweater and heels, she eyed him with a slight smile and raised brow.

He exited the car to open her door. She smelled as good as she looked.

"Where's the truck? Please don't say you sold it."

"Okay, I won't say it."

"Jax! You didn't."

"No, I didn't. Leave it to you to prefer a Dodge Ram over a luxury ride."

"I have fond memories of that truck. It was the chariot that rescued me from a randy bull."

"No, darlin', I did that."

"I guess you did." Genesis gave him a quick kiss.

After making sure her seat belt was securely fastened, he bopped around to the driver's side and they were on their way. The ride in the car was as smooth as butter, the sound immaculate, the leather as soft as a baby's bottom.

Genesis ran her hand over the rich material. "Is this a rental?"

"It's mine. One of the few luxuries I kept from my baller days."

"You must have a storage space in Memphis."

Jaxson smiled a bit sheepishly. "I keep it in the barn."

"Ha! Good move. No one would ever imagine something like this being stored in something that looked like that."

"Hey, now! Watch yourself. My barn may need a little TLC but it's got good bones."

"If you say so."

The conversation flowed as easily as the ride, all the way to Memphis. Jaxson exited into the city, using his GPS to navigate the busy Saturday night streets.

"Where are we going?" Genesis asked. "And what's with this bougie celebration? I would have been happy at Holy Moly, or with a pizza burger from Tastee Freez."

"I think you're worth an upscale restaurant, don't you?"

Genesis shrugged. "I guess so."

"When I played ball, we had an assistant coach who was into all that metaphysical stuff—law of attraction, visualization, things like that. He'd listen to various spiritual teachers and then come into the locker room spouting stuff like, 'What you think about you bring about,' and 'Focus on what you want, not what you don't want.' Before games, some of us would meditate. We'd visualize certain outcomes. I've tried it off the field as well."

"Does it work?"

"It works if you work it. Like tonight. Imagine something amazing that you want to happen. Then use tonight's celebration as though what you imagine is real. That's sending a message to the Universe that we believe what is desired has already been achieved."

A beat passed. Then Genesis deadpanned, "Okay, Dalai Lama."

They cracked up.

They entered the Memphis city limits and arrived at a steak house that was one of Genesis's favorites. The next hour was filled with good vibes, great food and excellent conversation, much of it centered around Holy Mound Minis, though both had sworn to leave work at the door. When the dessert tray was wheeled around, neither could resist making a selection, even though they both were stuffed. Jaxson suggested they split a molten lava creation—chocolate on chocolate with more chocolate inside.

"What did you imagine?" he asked, once the server had set down the dessert and two plates. "What are we celebrating?"

Genesis rested her chin in her palm. "Let's see. We are celebrating the Holy Mound Minis blueprint becoming a franchise, with happy families enjoying debt-free home-ownership in all fifty states."

"Damn, girl. You catch on quick."

"Did I dream too big?"

He reached for her hands and squeezed them. "Not at all."

Genesis slid a plate in front of her and prepared to cut a slice of the cake. "Your turn. What are you celebrating?"

Jaxson didn't have to think; he didn't hesitate. "I'm celebrating you becoming Mrs. King."

Before she had time for the words to register, Jaxson pulled out a small, black velvet box and set it on the table. He reclaimed her hands.

"When I saw you across the room all those years ago, I said you'd be my wife."

Genesis gasped. "Really?"

"No, but that shit sounded good."

"Jax! You're a trip!"

"I couldn't resist. But seriously…even back then I felt that night was special. I didn't feel about you like I did about other girls. I was eighteen, too young to process those grown-up emotions. But I never forgot the feeling. Turns out, it never left.

"We've been through a lot together. We make an awesome team. We've made our business official on paper. I'd like to do the same thing with our love."

He opened the box to reveal a radiant diamond and slid to a knee.

"Genesis Hunter, will you do me the honor of becoming my—"

"Yes!"

He laughed, pulling them both up as the entire room full of patrons clapped and cheered. "Wait. I didn't finish the question."

"I'm using your method, already celebrating, so what we want will come true."

"I guess that means you're stuck with me."

"And thanks to Uncle Cyrus, stuck in the country."

Jaxson looked toward the ceiling. "Good looking out, neighbor."

All's well that ends well. *Yeehaw!*

★ ★ ★ ★ ★

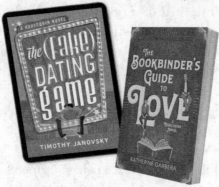